WALKABOUT DAWN

AUSTRALIAN SUPERNATURAL - BOOK FOUR

NICOLE R. TAYLOR

Walkabout Dawn (Australian Supernatural - Book Four) by Nicole R. Taylor

Copyright © 2020-21 by Nicole R. Taylor

All rights reserved.

This book is written in British/AU English.

No part of this book may be reproduced in any form or by any electronic or mechanical means, including information storage and retrieval systems, without written permission from the author, except for the use of brief quotations in a book review.

www.nicolertaylorwrites.com

Cover Design: Covers by Juan

Edited by: Silvia Curry

AUTHOR NOTE

The author would like to acknowledge the Traditional Custodians of country throughout Australia and their connections to land, sea and community. She pays her deepest respect to the elders past and present and extends that respect to all Aboriginal and Torres Strait Islander peoples today.

All representations of Indigenous Australians are used fictitiously and neither represent persons who live or have died.

For more information on Reconciliation in Australia, please visit:
https://www.reconciliation.org.au/what-is-reconciliation/

CHAPTER 1

Eloise Hart stepped out into the crisp morning air and breathed deeply.

The four main buildings that comprised the small Australian outback town of Solace glinted in the first rays of sunlight. The highway that cut through the middle stretched from north to south in a straight black line that faded in and out of the green and grey scrub. Rusty red earth lay like a blanket underneath, the bold colours as beautiful as they were harsh.

The days had been cooling ever so slightly, the harsh summer months fading into the promise of milder days and icy nights. Her lungs filled with crisp air, and when she breathed out, her breath billowed in plumes of white vapour.

The temperature in the outback could drop into the negatives once the sun went down, which seemed like a juxtaposition to Eloise. The landscape around Solace could be so arid, it was easy to forget that frost

—which always reminded her of microscopic quartz crystals—had a habit of clinging to the spiky stalks of the spinifex grass bunched along the roadsides and gather on eucalyptus leaves, only to melt once the sun began to creep its head over the flat horizon.

It had been a dry summer. Despite the storms brewing on the coasts, rain was scarce, but finally, the sky was showing signs of incoming cloud cover.

Kyne had told her about the storms that raced across the outback, though she hadn't witnessed one yet. In this part of the world, El Niño—a rather unfortunate weather event—hit hard, causing severe droughts across much of the country. Droughts which could last years on end. Then, when the rains finally came, the threat of flooding was an all too real danger.

The whole thing reminded Eloise of the sleeping menace that lay beneath Solace, and she shivered. *The heart of the ocean.*

The far horizon carried splotches of greyish-purple, the storm clouds bruising the otherwise blue expanse.

Behind her sat the opening to her new home, which she shared with fellow elemental and boyfriend, Kyne Brady. The dugout was buried into the ridge that reared up behind the town—the underground house not only an oddity, but a necessity. While the nights could be freezing, the summer months saw temperatures well above forty degrees Celsius—unbearable and nearly unlivable—

but underground, it was always a moderate twenty-four.

Donning her grey Akubra hat, she made her way down the hill towards town, relishing the cool, calm morning.

A flock of green budgerigars soared overhead, squawking as they flew across the sky, away from the clouds on the horizon. They settled momentarily in the enormous, old growth gum tree outside Blue's pub before shooting off again in search of a billabong.

Since arriving in Solace, Eloise had apprenticed at the local opal shop, learning how to cut and polish the precious stones that were mined out this way. It helped that she was an elemental—her supernatural powers guiding her hand towards the best cuts and the best gems. It was a job that had never crossed her mind, not until her motorhome had broken down five K's down the road and she needed some cash to pay for the repairs. But now she loved everything about it—cutting open potch to reveal the shards of colour within, buffing out the impurities to create something beautiful—and couldn't imagine doing anything else.

Jangling the keys to the opal workshop in her pocket, Eloise tried the handle and found it was already unlocked.

Inside, Hardy had his nose buried in a newspaper and didn't acknowledge her entrance, but she knew he'd already heard her. Frederick Marmaduke Hardy was a vampire, after all.

Taking off her hat, she ran her gaze over him. He seemed a great deal happier in recent weeks, even though Joseph Cheapside—his vampire BFF—had left town on a new quest. With their maker, Darius, gone, their centuries-long struggle with identity was at the beginning of a new chapter.

For Hardy, it was closure on his painful past and the promise of brighter things to come.

For Joseph, it was anyone's guess. He'd left soon after to figure it out.

Eloise could definitely see the change in Hardy. He was way less broody than before—his man-bun had returned to its usual artful messiness, and there was a sparkle in his immortal, frozen in time, twenty-something-year-old eyes.

"You're in early," the vampire said, looking up from the newspaper.

"You know, they have this thing called the *internet*," she told him. "That paper's at least three days old."

He grinned. "That's the drawback of living out in the middle of woop woop."

She chuckled and sat at the workbench.

Solace was over two hundred kilometres from the nearest regional centre—Lightning Ridge—which was at least one hundred and fifty from the next. In the outback, things took a long time to arrive, including the replacement parts for her motorhome.

Remembering the head gasket that had stranded her here almost a year ago, she smiled.

"What's that grin for?" Hardy asked.

"Nothing." She nodded towards the paper. "Anything exciting going on?"

He tapped the paper with his index finger, looking thoughtful. "Not much," he mused. "The usual human political squabbling. There's a cyclone brewing in the east, though."

She thought about the clouds she'd seen outside. "You mean, we might finally get some rain?"

The vampire shrugged. "Maybe."

Eloise let out a non-committal *humph* and turned towards the workbench.

"We're running out of opal," she said, checking the ziplock bag that contained the last of the precious black Kyne had brought in from his claim. That'd been months ago, before things had kicked off with the seal. "The other miners will be coming back soon, right?"

Hardy nodded. "In the next couple of weeks, I suppose. The weather's been good, and the forecast is decent."

Eloise leaned back in her chair, her brow creasing. Supernatural events were only going to increase, and after everything they'd been through, she didn't know how they could keep it from the seasonal workers who came into town for the annual opal mining season.

Hardy folded the newspaper and slapped it down onto the workbench. "What's that look for?"

"*Things* were easy to hide with just us," she replied. "How will we manage when the miners come back?"

"We've made do until now," the vampire told her. "And we'll make do when the time comes."

"How do you hide a magical tornado, a pack of dingo bikies, and a fae weapon of mass destruction? They're not exactly subtle."

"No, they're not."

"Was there a plan for this kind of thing before I came?" she asked.

"Honestly? No."

"No?"

"The miners who do have claims out here tend to live on them and only come into town when they need supplies or have opal to sell. They'll gather at the pub maybe once a week. Competition is fierce and theft is a real problem, especially if word gets out about a decent find. The guys who usually come out here stay put."

"*Ratters*," Eloise muttered, using the slang term for the thieves that plagued opal fields all over the country.

"If all else fails, I'll change their memories," Hardy went on. "And if it's worse than that, I'll compel them to stay away."

"I don't like it," she said, scowling. "I don't like it at all."

Hardy grimaced and wheeled his chair around until he sat beside her. "Eloise, everything will be all right."

"Will it?" She bit her bottom lip, her anxiety rising.

The threat of the Old Ones was a constant point of nausea ever since she'd found out about them.

"The mountain can't do anything unless it has you," he murmured.

Eloise let out a ragged sigh. "I know, but it still sucks."

"Of course, it does. Being the key to a prison holding back an ancient celestial tentacle monster would weigh heavily on anyone's mind."

Eloise snorted out a laugh and slapped her hand over her mouth.

"That's better," the vampire said. "No use worrying about what we can't control...*just yet.*" He eyed her for a moment. "Have you said anything?"

Eloise shook her head. She hadn't had the heart to. The Exiles had been through so much, so dropping another bomb into their laps felt too cruel to comprehend.

Hardy sighed. "You're going to have to tell the others about it sooner or later."

"Yeah, nah...not just yet."

"Eloise—"

"Have you heard from Joseph?"

Hardy shot her a disapproving look. "No. I don't expect to."

"Aren't you worried?"

"He's a five-hundred-year-old vampire, give or take a few decades," he replied. "Time has a different meaning to him."

Eloise frowned and sifted through the dregs of opal, trying to find a good piece to start cutting.

"Eloise, you have to tell them."

Her frown turned into a scowl. "I will."

But not just yet. Not until she figured out what it all meant.

Finn Oreah'anza stared into the flames of the campfire he'd built and rubbed his temples.

Ever since everything that'd happened in the pit with the vampires and the *ash'strad*—the fae weapon of mass destruction that'd almost torn him apart—he'd been feeling tired.

The darkness curled around the makeshift camp he called home like a cool blanket, the temperature dipping with the changing seasons. Clear skies and low temperatures meant frost, so he tossed another log onto the fire. Sparks twisted upwards in a spiral, merging with the stars pin-pricked on the bluish-black overhead.

This place was supposed to be forever, he thought. *It's not the same as home, but it's better than nothing.*

Twelve years ago, six fae had made the journey from Ireland to Australia on a whim and a hope, finally settling near Solace and the place of power that helped them survive in a non-magical world. That place power was the seal, of course.

Since Finn and the Exiles had discovered what lay underneath it, his uneasiness had only grown. The fae were feeding off the magic of a celestial being who was clamouring to be freed. No doubt it'd be angry at them if it ever did. No one liked to have the life sucked out of them, and he'd had first-hand experience to confirm it.

Casting aside the memory of the witch Vera, the Nightshade who'd possessed her, and his time spent locked up in the water tank in town, he sighed.

The camp had grown over the years, though the fae preferred to live alongside the land in tents and rudimentary shelters as opposed to the underground houses the Exiles favoured in Solace. The closer they could be to nature, the easier it was for them to remain fae.

The comforts of a house, a warm bed, life-giving magic in the air, and all the trappings of society were a distant memory. Finn preferred this life to his old one, but it'd taken a long time for him to realise it.

"Za'dreha."

Siora stood over him, her silver gaze fixed on his. She'd slicked her powder-blue- and turquoise-flecked hair back into a tight braid, making her angled features look more severe than usual. Tall, thin, and athletic, she was a classic picture of Unseelie beauty...but the cool air of superiority all *Shri'danann* fae seemed to possess was clearly present in her heart—the same airs Finn'd had in a past life.

"Really?" he asked, bristling at her rude greeting.

"We're really going there?"

She sat beside him, crossing her long legs before her. He knew she had something either prophetic or condescending to say, and he was going to hear it, even though he didn't want to.

Things had escalated around here for almost a year, and the fae had been on the receiving end of most of it. He was forgiving, but Siora...? She only knew the meaning of the word when it suited her, which wasn't often.

"It's time to leave, Finn," she told him without so much as a hello. "You know it as much as I do."

He shook his head. Whether it was stubbornness or something else, he didn't know. Leaving was the furthest thing from his mind.

"The *ash'strad* took a toll on all of us," Siora added. "We felt every explosion...but you know that."

Of course, he knew it. He'd stood at the base of the pit and tried to stop the final discharge of magic, but he hadn't been strong enough. If it wasn't for the druidess Andante, he and the fae would be nothing but red mist on the wind...but he wouldn't admit his weakness to Siora.

"It was the vampire Darius," Finn said. "It had nothing to do with the others."

"It's all linked. One cannot exist without the other. Do you think they would be here if it wasn't for the seal?"

"It would cause problems with or without us and

them being here," he said.

Siora narrowed her eyes and said nothing, but she had that look about her that he'd come to know meant trouble. She had a theory but wasn't willing to share it.

"Siora," he murmured. "What is it?"

Her gaze moved to his. "We've taken a vote."

"Without me?"

Her lips thinned. "We've chosen to leave."

Of course they had. "Where will you go?"

"I've heard talk about another place of power," Siora replied, making it clear she'd leave with or without his blessing. "We will go find it."

He snorted. "You've *heard*? You're leaving the one place that's keeping us alive on hearsay?"

"I have faith." She looked around and sighed. "Which is more than I can say for this place. I would rather risk everything out there than stay here. Finn... you have to come with us."

"I can't." His jaw tensed. "They're important to me."

Siora rolled her eyes. "Just say it, Finn."

"Say what?"

"Stop being so obstinate," she snapped.

"I'm not," he fired back. "You can't see that nothing has changed."

Siora shook her head, her lips thinning with displeasure. "We were your family once."

"*You still are.*"

"Have you forgotten so much that you would forsake the things you fought so fiercely for?"

Finn scowled, fighting his volatile personality. He wanted to lash out, to tell her he hadn't forgotten anything, but that was what she wanted.

"I haven't," he managed to say. "But it was a long time ago... Things have changed."

"*Yes...*" Her gaze raked over him, her silver eyes full of resentment. "Yes, they most certainly have." Reaching into her pocket, she took out the polished silver stone he remembered from their journey here—another artefact from their home world. "There's almost enough magic for us to travel. It will get us to our destination."

He narrowed his eyes. "And what if you don't find what you're looking for?"

"Don't worry about us, Finn," she said, standing. "Worry about yourself."

She began to walk away, leaving him alone by the fire. The other fae had gathered by her tent and watched their exchange with cool eyes. He'd find no sympathy with any of them.

"So that's it?" he demanded. He hated ultimatums, especially ones that challenged his authority...but he hadn't had any around here for months now. It was *her* they looked to.

Siora turned and stared down at him. "That's it."

Finn watched her walk away, making no move to follow. When had things changed around here? He scarcely knew...but what did he know?

Nothing, he thought. *Nothing at all.*

CHAPTER 2

Drew sat on the top of the ridge, looking down over the long shadows creeping across the outback.

The sunset had set the sky aflame, igniting the bruised clouds skidding inwards from the coast. A late summer cyclone was making landfall hundreds of kilometres away, but the very edges of the storm cell had reached all the way to Solace. Soon, it would rain for the first time in months.

Drew's dingo nose twitched as a fly settled on his snout. Lately, his animal shape felt more comfortable than his human one. He wasn't that bright—he'd missed out on a lot of schooling as a kid—but as a dingo, he understood a lot of things others couldn't, like the way the wind moved across the outback, the scents left behind by humans and animals, and the traces of magic that lay deep within everything.

He saw the auras around the supernatural Exiles

who called Solace home and knew their powers. Hardy the vampire, Kyne the earth elemental, Wally the werewolf, Vera the witch, and Eloise the elemental who could control the threads that bound their world to those beyond. Coen called it spirit, the rivers that flowed through the Dreaming.

Drew glanced at the Indigenous man sitting beside him and studied the flowing aura which surrounded him. There was no doubt that Coen was supernatural himself, but what he was and what he could do was as ambiguous as the words he said. The man was a riddle within a riddle, one that Drew had no hope of understanding. Maybe that's why he'd chosen the shifter for his mysterious lessons.

Coen was teaching Drew to 'see'.

Right now, he saw the changing seasons overhead, the parched earth below, and the simmering power stirring underneath the town. It lingered like an oil slick on water, undulating through various colours as it saw fit. Purple, red, orange, blue, green...it seemed to cycle through them all like a rainbow with no rhyme or reason. To Drew's eyes, the Old One seemed to be all things.

He thought about what Andante had told Eloise and decided it was no use trying to understand something that was part of the fabric of the universe. Maybe it'd made the whole thing by setting off the Big Bang.

Who was he to ask those questions, anyway? After all, he was just a dingo-shifter.

"I have to leave," Coen said, his voice breaking through the unsettled air.

Drew lifted his head. *"Leave? Where does he think he's going?"*

The indigenous man raised an eyebrow. "I have to follow the trails of those who came before. There are many paths through the Dreaming. Many have gone walkabout to discover."

The shifter hesitated. *"Did he just hear what I was thinking?"*

"Your mind is growing," Coen said with a chuckle. "Good."

Drew whined softly and shook his head. *"I'm telepathic now? How does that even work?"*

"Your thoughts are loud like thunder, but that's my name. You are meant to be the lightning."

"Lightning. Pfft, whatever that means."

"With thunder comes the rain, and lightning soon follows." Coen looked up at the cloud-streaked sky. "The rains are coming, see?" He pointed to the first stars of the night, peeking through the wisps. "The great emu has taken flight."

"Emus can't fly."

"But they have wings, anyway." The Indigenous man laughed. "In the Dreaming, up is down, the sky is the ground, and the flightless can walk in the sky."

"If you say so..."

"I don't say. The dark places between the stars do."

Drew snorted and rested his chin on his paws. *"Why do you have to leave?"*

"The Old One is restless again."

That was all he said, and it irritated Drew more than it should have. Sometimes he wished Coen would be straightforward about things, but he always went off on rambling tangents that confused him even more.

"What if someone else comes and tries to break open the seal?" he asked. *"What then?"*

"You will see for me."

"But I don't understand what you want me to see," he argued.

"You will when the time is right."

"But what if I'm too stupid?"

Coen didn't answer.

Drew lifted his head and blinked at the empty place where the Indigenous man had been sitting. He sniffed the air, but there was no trace of him, not even a lingering scent.

He stood and looked around, even though he knew he wasn't going to find anything, let alone 'see'.

Coen was gone, and Drew didn't know if he was coming back.

Vera Walsh stood in aisle two of her store, the *Outpost*, and angrily swatted her feather duster at the shelves.

Ever since trouble had kicked off with the seal, the whole town had been coated with a healthy layer of fine, red dust. Even magic had trouble getting rid of it, but she knew it had a touch of its own arcane energy, thanks to the celestial spirit trapped underneath the highway outside.

"*Bloody hell*," she cursed, swiping the duster across a stack of soup cans.

In the lull between all the supernatural chaos, her thoughts had firmly settled on a certain police officer, Sergeant Andrew Clarke.

Things hadn't been easy between them since Darius's arrival. Clarke had found out the truth about her and Solace the hard way—*again*—and it was a lot for him to take in.

He was a man of the law; he dealt with what was right before his eyes and magic...? Well, most of the time magic was an abstract concept. It wasn't all explosions and colourful sparkly fireballs, even though she could do some of that if she put her mind to it.

No, Clarke was a simple man, but that's what she liked about him. To him, a shovel was a just shovel, nothing more. Not like the things the Exiles had to deal with. Old Ones and illusions and who knew what else.

Clarke had left before the mess with Darius had come to a head, and he hadn't been back since. Vera couldn't deny she was hurt. He knew what they were up against, and he hadn't called or sent a text to see if she was still alive. Solace had almost been blown off the map by that fae bomb, and he couldn't pick up his stupid phone and call? He couldn't say, *Hey Siri, call Vera?*

A part of her couldn't blame him, but the other was livid. Absolutely, one hundred percent, murderously *livid.*

The flash of sunlight reflecting off glass caught her eye, and she looked out the window to the road beyond. Catching sight of a car pulling up out front, she wandered towards the till, swatting the feather duster as she went—not that it did anything worthwhile.

The door opened and Vera came to a grinding halt as she saw Clarke step inside. He was wearing his usual crisp blue police uniform, though his hat was askew and his boots had a layer of rust-coloured dirt across the toes.

Vera didn't know what to say, so she didn't say anything. She took a step back towards the aisle, her heart thrumming a wild beat in her chest.

Clarke took off his hat and set it on the counter, his gaze running over everything but her. He ran a fingertip along the shelf, leaving a clean streak in the ochre dust.

"It's..." she sighed, "it's full of magical static." Clarke didn't say anything, so she added, "It sticks like a magnet. I haven't been able to find a way to get rid of it yet. It was that stupid bomb—"

His gaze flew to hers. "Bomb?"

"Yeah," she said, his startled question smashing open the floodgates. "*A bomb*. A magical fae bomb that almost tore Finn and the other fae apart...and almost cracked open the seal. Not to mention, there's now a whole swathe of land on Walawala Station that no longer exists in our reality. Oh, and the bit where Darius almost killed us all." Her glare intensified. "If it wasn't for Hardy, Joseph, Eloise, and Finn, we'd all be dead. And by all, I mean the entire world would've been erased." Vera was really selling the finer points of continuing their relationship, but she was hurt. "We're all fine, by the way."

Clarke had turned pale while she let out her bottled-up anger. His skin had taken on a sickly grey sheen and his forehead prickled with sweat. He looked like he was about to keel over.

"I know we agreed that you should stay away," she went on, "but that was only until we'd dealt with Darius. *And that was weeks ago*."

"Vera, I—"

"You told me you loved me..." Frustrated tears filled her eyes. "But you can't love a witch, can you?"

"Vera, it's not about... It's..." He turned away, striding a few paces across the front of the shop.

"It's about what?" she demanded, waving the feather duster wildly. "I'm a freak of nature, is that it?"

"*No*." Clarke ran his hand over his face, then turned. He met her gaze, his complexion turning crimson. "I-I can't protect you...not against vampires and evil spirits. I—" He bit his lip. "I'm *human*."

Vera's anger melted away, along with the scowl on her face. She'd gotten it all wrong. *Badly*.

"Clarke, I..." She didn't know the right words. Not about this. The duster slipped out of her numb fingers and landed on the floor.

"Vera, it's got nothing to do with you being a witch," he told her. "Nothing at all." He spread his arms wide. "Look at me. I'm a cop, a sergeant. I'm supposed to protect you. I took an oath, but... A gun won't stop a vampire or a werewolf or...or a tentacle monster. I can't call in the bloody bomb squad for a magical device from another world."

He didn't feel like her equal, and while it didn't matter to her, it obviously mattered to him. Clarke wasn't just a cop; he was a *man*. An old-fashioned one it seemed, though it went both ways. She should be able to protect him, too.

"We're looking for a way to put an end to all of this," she managed to say. "It won't be like this forever."

The truth was painfully clear in Clarke's face. "But it might be."

She sighed, her heart heavy. "And there's the ultimatum."

A desolate rift opened between them, the silence sending her heart spiralling downwards.

"If you want to leave, then leave," she managed to

say. "I won't stop you. You're free to choose whatever you want...but you won't be able to come back."

Clarke shuffled from foot to foot. "You'll have Hardy erase my memories, won't you?"

Vera nodded. "I wish it were different, but—"

"The seal," he interrupted.

"The danger... It's bigger than all of us." She sighed, her throat burning as she tried to hold onto her tears. "Why does saving the world have to be so damn hard?"

Before she could take another breath, Clarke had her in his arms. "Stuff it," he declared. "Stuff it all to hell and back."

"What—" Her question was silenced by his kiss, and she melted against him, her heart on the verge of bursting.

He pulled away with a heavy breath and cupped her cheeks in his rough hands. "Love's worth the risk, right? No matter what crazy things life chucks at us, it's worth it."

"Y-you're not leaving?"

He shook his head. "But there can't be any more secrets between us, Vera. You have to be honest with me, no matter how crazy things get."

She clutched his shirt so tight, her knuckles had turned white, and she nodded. "You do realise things will keep happening, right?"

"I know."

"With the way things have been going around here, I wouldn't be surprised if it was this afternoon."

"Then let it," he whispered, moving to kiss her again.

As if on cue, the shop door was wrenched opened, and Drew strode in. The bell rang furiously as the shifter entered, but whatever he was worked up about seemed to dissolve the moment he laid eyes on Vera and Clarke.

"Oh, you've decided to come back, have you?" the dingo declared, narrowing his eyes at the sergeant. "And oh-so conveniently *after* that vampire blew up half the outback. *Suspicious*, hey?"

"Drew, leave it," Vera snapped. "It's none of your business."

"It's entirely my business." He looked Clarke over. "He's a cop, *and* he knows all about us. How long do we have until the government trucks arrive to take us for our alien autopsies?"

"Drew, calm down. I haven't told anyone," Clarke said, taking step towards the shifter. "And I haven't told anyone about what you did to Craig Roth, either."

Drew's face turned a deep shade of enraged as he turned his glare onto Vera. "*You told him about Roth?*"

"I had to tell him everything, Drew," Vera replied. "We owed Clarke the truth."

"*We* did?" he scoffed. "You didn't ask *my* permission."

Clarke stepped between her and the shifter. "I think you better turn around and walk away, Drew."

"*Never.*" He shoved Clarke, forcing the sergeant to

stumble back a few steps. "You keep breaking her heart, so I'll start breaking something of yours."

Seeing things were headed south, Vera lunged between the two men. Letting out an annoyed cry, she raised her hand and swung. Her palm connected with Drew's cheek with a piercing crack, the slap crackling with briny-coloured sparks.

The shifter yelped and held his face, falling silent. He stared at her in shock, his eyes wide.

"He's with us, whether you like it or not," she hissed. "Stop acting like a child."

Drew held up his hands in defence. He knew better than to rile up a witch like Vera unless he wanted to get zapped again.

"He's going to be sticking around, so you better get used to seeing him," she went on. When she heard Clarke mutter behind her, she turned and jabbed a finger at the sergeant. "That goes for the *both of you*."

"Yes, Vera." Drew scuffed the toe of his boot against the edge of the doormat, looking as sheepish as a schoolboy who'd been caught shooting slobbery spitballs across the classroom.

When Clarke didn't reply, she narrowed her eyes.

"I've got no problem with the dingo," he said. "But I *will* defend your honour."

Drew snorted. "*Honour?*"

"Why are you here, anyway?" She turned to Drew with a huff. "It's not because of Andy, so spit it out." *Boys. Can't live with them...*

"It's Coen," the shifter replied, narrowing his eyes at Clarke.

"What about him?"

"*He's gone.*"

Vera's scowl disappeared and she looked at Clarke. She knew they were going to be tested, just not so soon.

"You weren't joking about the whole 'this afternoon thing,' were you?" the sergeant muttered.

"I was," she replied. "I really was..."

CHAPTER 3

Blue wiped the back of his arm across his sweaty forehead and sighed. *This was impossible.*

Everything in the pub was coated with a fine layer of rust-coloured dirt and every time he swept, it tumbled back into place. He was convinced it had something to do with the iron ore deposit and the bomb Darius had set off, because iron was magnetic, but how it worked with magic was a mystery. Vera was having the same problem at the *Outpost*, and as far as he knew, she hadn't found a fix for it yet.

Sighing, Blue leaned the broom against the bar and pulled up a stool. If the bloke from the health and safety department came by right now, he'd lose his food safety accreditation. Luckily for him, Solace was hundreds of kilometres away from the nearest town... and at the bottom of any surprise inspection list.

The outside door opened, letting in a shaft of afternoon sunlight.

Blue expected to see one of the Exiles—usually it was his best mate Wally knocking off work early and coming in for a beer—but he blinked in surprise at the woman who'd wandered in.

She had on one of those flowing, patterned skirts with the little bells tied to the waist, strappy sandals, and a loose-fitting blue blouse. Her long grey hair was pulled into a tight braid, and though her face was lined with wrinkles, her stride had all the hallmarks of youth.

Blue smiled at her, her appearance reminding him of the hippy movement of his early twenties. He'd been more idealistic about the world then, less worn down by the way humans did things. It was all 'free love,' long days lounging by the beach, talking about politics, listening to his friend's terrible poetry, dreaming of a better world...and a lot of time spent getting high.

"G'day," he said, taking her in. "Sorry about the dusty floor. We had a big blow the other day. The stuff's impossible to get out once it's in."

The woman stared at him, then glanced around the pub.

Blue coughed nervously. "Can I get you a drink?" Even though he was used to the strangeness of the supernatural folk, not to mention the eccentric humans who ventured into the outback, there was something about the woman that felt a little off centre.

"I'm Andante," she said, ignoring his offer.

Blue raised his eyebrows. "Ah, so you're the druidess. I was wondering if you'd come and visit us."

"And you are...?"

"Oh, right." He slid off the stool and wiped his palms on his shirt before reaching a hand towards her. "I'm Blue."

Andante looked at his proffered hand and raised her eyebrows. "Blue?"

He nodded. "I used to have red hair before it all turned grey."

She snorted and looked him over. "Quite."

"Quite what?"

Andante ran a finger across the bar. "Quite the mess you have here."

Blue knew that's not what she meant, and if he went by what Eloise told him, it was best he let her do the talking. He knew the druidess was several hundred years old, had traveled several parallel worlds, and possessed an unknown power that could rip whole chunks of land out of their reality with a flick of her wrist.

"It settled after the business up north," he told her.

"Ah, the vampire."

"That's the one." Blue clicked his fingers. "Ever since, no amount of sweeping shifts the stuff."

"The earth is rich in iron and other minerals," she stated. "The silver orb turned everything upside down. Now it all sticks."

"You mean it stuffed up the magnetic field?"

Andante nodded. "Magically."

"Can it be, uh...magically unmagnetised?"

"Yes, it will fade with time, however..." She looked around the pub and gestured towards the floor. "May I?"

He nodded. "If you know how to fix it, by all means..."

Andante stepped into the middle of the room and held out her hands, palms facing down. Blue waited, trying to figure out what she was doing, but he didn't have any supernatural power so he couldn't sense or see anything—not until the purplish-blue light began to gather in her downturned hands.

Glowing, glittery threads grew outwards, reaching towards the floor, twisting and entwining into a mass that reminded him of tree roots growing outwards in search of water in parched earth.

He held his breath as the threads touched the gritty linoleum and began to snake across the floor, creating patterns that reminded him of the shapes inside a kaleidoscope—all triangles, hexagons, octagons, and points and angles.

The threads disconnected from Andante's hands and completed the shapes, then they began to settle into the floor, shimmering with blues, purples, and touches of green that reminded him of the ocean.

Blue's eyes widened as he stared at the fading, glittery magic. "Wow, that's really something."

"My people call it Colour," Andante told him. "We

weave the threads of reality into prisms...the sacred shapes that make up all things."

"Ah..." He didn't quite understand her meaning, but it looked impressive—like little bluish laser beams.

The druidess smiled at him. She knew everything she'd said had flown right over his old head but had the good manners not to tease him about it.

"Try your broom," she instructed.

Blue grabbed the handle and positioned himself, hoping for a miracle. He was well and truly sick of the stuff.

The bristles glided over the worn linoleum floor and the ochre dust cleared.

"*Strewth*." He swept again and chuckled. "Now *that's* magic."

Andante lowered her hands and glanced at the floor, not meeting his gaze.

"Did I say something wrong? I apologise." When she didn't reply, he rambled, "I'm just a human, you see, so every time I see something magical, I get a little silly. I'm just an old bloke in a pub in the middle of the outback. It doesn't take much to tickle my fancy." He felt his cheeks redden. "I didn't mean— I— *Oh, bloody hell*."

Finally, she met his gaze. "I've never had that reaction before."

"Oh, well, I suppose it's because I've never met a druid. I've met a witch, a vampire, a fae, a couple of elementals, a werewolf, a dingo-shifter...but none of them can do what you just did." He wrung his hands, feeling like a silly old coot. "It was real...*pretty*, what you just did."

Andante sighed and stepped towards the bar, selecting the stool next to Finn's usual place at the far end.

Blue set the broom against the wall. It seemed she'd settled for the time being. For how long, he didn't know, but he'd see to making her feel welcome—even if he felt like a damn teenager doing it.

Andante could help Solace, but she'd also been alone for a long time. Maybe she just needed to know there were people out there who wanted to know her... people who *cared*.

"Would you like to stay for dinner?" he asked. "Any special requests? I have a talent for cooking."

"I don't eat meat," Andante told him warily.

"That's fine, love." He waved a hand at the empty stool beside her. "Finn doesn't either, though I suspect you'd like more than just a bowl of hot chips, eh?"

"Hot chips?"

"You've never heard of hot chips?" He supposed she hadn't since she'd been living in a cave alongside the land. Deep fryers were hard to come by in the wilderness. "Leave it with me. I'll fix you up something special. Would you like a drink? Most drink beer out this way, being simple people, but I keep a couple of bottles of spirits for Hardy and wine for Finn. Opal mining's hard yakka, so beer's best. It's cold, cheap, and does the business."

Andante straightened and looked at him with her strange blue eyes. "You say a lot of words all at once."

Blue ran his fingers through his wiry moustache and chuckled. "I suppose I do."

A smile crept onto her face, and she glanced at the bottles behind the bar. "Wine," she said. "I'd like some wine."

***

Eloise wiped a stained cloth over her dirty workbench and bit back an equally filthy word.

Ochre dust still stuck to everything like little magnetic metal shavings. No matter what she or Hardy did, the stuff wouldn't budge. The *ash'strad* that almost blew Solace, the fae, *and* the seal was apparently the gift that kept on giving.

Hardy chuckled as he sensed her frustration.

"Oh, shut up," she bit.

"It's no use," he told her. "You're fighting a losing battle."

He'd been doing well since the whole mess with Darius. Eloise knew it had a lot to do with the closure he'd found with his early days as a vampire, not to mention the research Blue had done on his family.

Eloise sighed and lifted the piece of opal she was working on, looking past it to Hardy. Darius was dead and could no longer hold power over any of them, but the echoes of what happened up north at Walawala Station had stuck around. *Literally.*

Hardy raised an eyebrow. "All you're doing is working yourself up into a state, you know."

"But this dust is driving me *mad*," she complained.

"You and me both. It's messing with the belts on the machines."

"It's sticking to the opal. If I put it on the polisher, I'm just going to buff the imperfections back in." It was such a pretty piece, too—black with flecks of green and blue.

"Say a prayer," Hardy suggested.

"Dust begone!" she declared, then wiped her hand over the workbench, only this time the dust didn't roll back. "Hey, it's unstuck!"

Hardy let out a thoughtful hum. "Vera must have fixed it."

She laughed and grabbed the cloth. "So you mean it wasn't my magic spell?"

"Of course not," the vampire said. "You forgot to use your wand."

They were having a good chuckle when the shop door opened. The electronic buzzer chimed, but Hardy didn't get up.

"It's Drew," the vampire said a mere second before the shifter strode in. "He's in a *mood*."

Eloise raised her eyebrows as the dingo-shifter

flung himself into the spare chair beside her workstation, a cloud of ochre dust rising in his wake.

"Clarke's back," he growled.

Eloise sneezed and waved her hand in the air, trying to clear the grit. "And?"

"And..." Hardy quipped, "coming from Drew, Clarke's arrival is going to be bad news, no matter the outcome."

"Give it a rest, mate," the shifter complained.

Eloise smiled. "They're back together."

Drew glared at her. "How do you know?"

"I'm a woman," she waved her hand at him dismissively, "and I'm not clouded by alpha dingo or whatever you want to call it."

"Good for them." Hardy grinned and leaned back in his chair, the metal creaking. "It'll be handy having a cop around. We might need something cordoned off."

Drew's cheeks turned red and Eloise leaned forwards, placing her hand on his arm. The dingo blinked and she knew he felt her elemental power where her fingers lay.

"Leave her be," she told him. "She's happy. I know what you two have isn't romantic, but she's been on her own for a long time. Let her have this one."

"I see you've been learning things, too," he said. "Coen teach you that trick?"

Eloise shook her head. "I taught myself that one."

"He's gone," Drew said, his tone abrupt as he

pulled his arm away. "That's what I came here to tell you."

"Gone?" She glanced at Hardy, but he was so still, he seemed to have turned to stone. "Gone where?"

"We were up on the ridge this morning, and he told me he had to go." Drew rolled his eyes. "Said something about following paths left by others. That he had to."

"Is that all he said?" Hardy asked. "Did he say it just like that?"

The dingo shrugged. "You know what he's like."

And Eloise knew what Drew was like. Most of what Coen told him went straight over his head, but the Indigenous man was like that with most people. Plenty of things he'd said to her had the same effect, only revealing their meaning when the time was right.

"Yes," Hardy went on, "we know what he's like, but did he say anything else?"

"The same old things about me being the lightning and something about emus flying. He seemed to think the dark bits in the sky were talking to him."

"The dark places between the stars," Eloise corrected. "Most people look to the stars, the bright points, but Indigenous peoples look to the places between." She looked at Hardy as she began to piece together Drew's fumbling explanation. "He's gone *walkabout.*"

Hardy nodded. "Do you think he's gone to find answers to our Old One problem?"

She nodded. That was exactly what she thought he was doing. She'd seen the currents that made up the fabric of reality. They flowed like a mighty river, changing course here and there, with no rhyme or reason, like the way Coen described the Dreaming. It was all things and was always present. Time didn't matter, nor did direction. Everything existed all at once...and Eloise's elemental power was able to access it when the currents came close enough for her to reach.

If Coen had really gone walkabout along the currents, it made her wonder what kind of power he really had. Who—and *what*—was he?

"What gives me the shits is why bother teaching me stuff if he's just going to up and leave?" Drew complained. Clearly, he felt abandoned. "I don't know why he bothered, or why he thought I was a good choice. You'd be better, Eloise. You get this stuff."

"Drew, open your eyes," she told him. "Coen was teaching you because you can watch over Solace in a way none of us can. You can *see*." She poked him between the eyes, and he jerked backwards.

"*Ow*." He rubbed his forehead and scowled, though she knew it was more to do with his irritation at Clarke than anything she or Coen had done.

"Thunder and lightning go together," she added. "They come from the same place."

Drew's eyes widened as if he'd only just now made the connection. "Well, *anyway*." He stood with a sigh, attempting to pretend he'd known all along. "Coen said rain was coming, so I'm going to check my dugout roof for leaks."

"It could be metaphoric rain, you know," Hardy quipped.

"While I never got a proper education, I'm not totally stupid." The dingo pointed to the newspaper on the workbench. "I can read a weather report, *old man*."

Hardy chuckled as the shifter stalked out of the shop, the buzzer chiming as the front door opened and closed.

"He'll do fine without Coen," Eloise mused, thinking about the dingo's prickly anger. "He needs to trust himself...and us, too."

Hardy's chuckle turned into a full-bodied laugh.

"What? What did I say?"

"You might want to consider taking your own advice."

Eloise felt her cheeks warm and bit her bottom lip.

"When are you going to tell the others what happened at the pit?" Hardy asked.

She jutted out her chin in defiance. "I'm waiting for the right time."

"There never is a *right* time," the vampire told her. "The *time* is always right now."

He was right. When was it appropriate to tell your supernatural friends that an ancient tentacle monster was trying to turn you evil?

The more Eloise dwelt on it, the more she thought

the whole thing with the mountain corrupting Darius was a manipulation to get her to understand her role in the bigger picture...whatever that was.

Her power was the key to setting the Old One in the mountain free...and if it was set loose, it'd destroy their whole reality. Was that really all there was to it? There had to be more than simply undoing a magical lock.

Then there was the Old One under Solace. Did it want the same thing as the mountain? It was trapped too, so there was a good chance it would join with the mountain.

The more Eloise learned about them, the more she didn't understand. Who knew what emotionless, celestial beings wanted...if they wanted anything at all?

"I'll tell Kyne when he comes back from Black Hole mine," she told Hardy. "I promise."

"What about the others? Now that Coen is gone, it might be a good idea—"

"Let me tell Kyne first," she interrupted. "I don't want to worry anyone. Everyone's been through enough without this being dropped in their laps, too." *Especially Finn and the fae.*

"Do I have to give you a deadline?"

She shot him an angry scowl. "*Hardy, please.*"

"Fine," he conceded, turning back to his workbench, "but remember, this is Solace...and supernatural calamity is never far away."

CHAPTER 4

F inn looked up at the stars from his resting place beneath a twisted gum tree and sensed the gathering storm on the horizon. The air was tense with unspoken ferocity and his soul felt ragged around the edges.

Snorting, he twirled the *ash'strad* in his palm, watching the silver orb spin. He'd taken it from the pit before Andante had sealed away the iron ore. Why he didn't leave it there, he didn't know. It was a reminder of all he had lost, but his rising melancholy had little to do with the *ash'strad* and more to do with Siora.

The fae were restless and angry. Their old-world prejudices had not left them when they'd come to this reality. Earth was not their home, and it lacked the magic that kept them all alive. Sure, they were able to survive here in the Australian Outback, but it wasn't *living*.

All Finn knew was that things were going from bad to worse.

Sensing he was no longer alone, he secreted the *ash'strad* behind a simple illusion and let it settle at the base of the tree.

Siora emerged from the dark night, her ghostly figure reminding him of the first time he'd met her. It'd been on an evening like this, where the moon was low and the sky was shadowed.

But the scene could not be more different.

She came from a great Unseelie family, as did he. She was used to living in a beautiful mansion in the shadow of the north-western arm of the An Valran mountain ranges—otherwise known as the White Pinnacles in English—sleeping between silk sheets, being waited on by *De'ashlide* servants, and eating fine food off even finer plates.

She was not used to the heat, let alone the desolate and lonely outback, no matter how rich the flora and fauna was—and she was definitely not used to living in a tent and foraging for her supper.

How the mighty had fallen. They were all exiles and had to suffer their fate, even after all this time.

There was no going back.

"Even after I told you my truth, you still persist," he drawled. "Why torture yourself, Siora?"

"I would ask the same of you," she bit at him. "If there was a way to return to our world, would you go with us then?"

"Our people will not have forgotten," he told her. "Even though our enemies have all turned to dust, the memory of our actions remain. We can't go back. *Ever.*"

Siora scowled and sat beside him. "Why are you so against us, Finn? What have we done to displease you so?"

He'd once told Eloise Hart that the fae couldn't lie, but that was a lie in itself. Finn was certainly capable of lying, though he loathed to do it—it hurt his soul, even as his words hurt others. Some truths were more difficult to speak aloud than others, which was why he tried to remain silent at times like these, but Siora had a way of pushing him until he well and truly went flying over the edge.

"You hold onto the past when you should let it go," he snapped. "What we had is gone, Siora. It's gone, and it will never return. Stop fooling yourself, and stop fooling others." She flinched, taking his truth more personally than he'd intended. "Your stubborn pride will only lead to more misery."

"Look around you, Finn!" she exclaimed. "You are *miserable.* This place and those people have only made you suffer. They've used you and the seal will kill you. Don't you see?"

"I see plenty," he told her, his voice low. "I see more clearly than I have in a thousand years."

"Clearly?" Siora scoffed. "You are *deluded.*"

"I'm not convinced there's another place safe enough for us to go," Finn went on, ignoring her insult.

"The seal holds danger, but its magic never depletes. Can you say that for your new mysterious place of power? The place you have thrown your trust into on a whim and a rumour?"

"I *believe*," Siora said defiantly. "I have faith that our trials in this world have satisfied the conditions of our exile. Only good things can come of our journey...and only bad things will torment us if we remain."

A memory surfaced, of Siora when they'd first met in their own world. A young Unseelie, full of the fire of revolution. A proud warrior fighting for what she believed in, her passion intoxicating those around her until they too stood up and bore arms.

"You always had a way with words," he muttered, pushing away the unwanted recollection.

Siora took his hand, her magic attempting to bring forth his own. "Finn, this creature will devour you if you remain. You've felt its magic. How can you stay when you know what will happen if the seal breaks?"

Finn's jaw tensed as he fought his desire to bite back at her. His magic simmered—cold, dark, and terrible. If he answered her, then their path would become all too familiar.

Siora believed she'd paid the price demanded by the *Delei'an* for her past actions, and through her, so did the other fae. She'd convinced them with her silver tongue, distracting them from the truth and leading them into the same fire that had caused their downfall. There was no absolution, not for them.

Their souls were forever stained with blood and destruction, and the fact they hadn't been vaporised by the *ash'strad* was an ironic mercy. The best any of the exiled could hope for was peaceful misery.

"Perhaps," he murmured, looking away, "that's why I want to stay."

Siora jerked to her feet, her usually graceful movements stilted by anger. "This is the last time I will come to you," she said, glaring down at him. "This is the last moment you have to save what we once had, Finn."

He glared up at her, pushing his magic and rage away. "I don't respond well to ultimatums, Siora. I've made my choice."

"Is this your final decision?"

She'd come here for selfish reasons, to solidify her place of power over the other fae. This was her newest revolution, but more fool her. *He wasn't playing.*

"You knew I wouldn't change my mind," he told her. "Stay or go, I won't stop you."

He'd already let her go, but it was her who was holding on to a dark memory that she should have released years ago.

Siora turned her back on him, her slender form cold and rigid in the starlight. "I know you have lost your faith in me, Finn," she said, turning her head slightly so he could hear. "But I haven't forgotten what we once shared. You loved me once...and I never stopped." She breathed deeply. "I may be foolish, but I had to try."

Finn said nothing as she walked away and disappeared into the night. He said nothing, though his heart remembered and ached.

How it ached.

Was he wrong about her?

Looking up at the sky, his gaze was drawn to the darkness between the silver stars his people revered and he wondered what secrets lay in the shadows. The deepest places where ancient memory lived.

And then he began to doubt...

The sound of a jackhammer echoed down the shadowy drive and up and out of the shaft leading down into Black Hole Mine, where Kyne was hard at work chasing the rare black opal that ran through his claim.

The chisel rammed into the rock face, slicing away like a knife through melted butter thanks to his elemental magic.

It'd been a rough couple of days, but he was finally underground where his abilities shone their brightest. The opal seam he was chasing reverberated in the distance, less than a metre from where he was cutting. He was faring better than most, that was for sure.

The other opal miners were starting to return to

their claims around Solace, taking advantage of the good weather to clear up after the off season. Kyne had been out to see Trapper the day before, only to find him in the middle of packing up.

His mine had collapsed in several places during the off season, and the roof was unstable. A crack split through the main drive of his claim, and without a hell of a lot of props, the whole thing would come tumbling down.

Repairing the damage was going to cost too much —in both time and money. With no guarantees he was on a good thing, Trapper was cutting his losses and heading out towards Lightning Ridge. He knew another miner out there who was willing to split profits in exchange for an extra hand.

Kyne knew it had everything to do with Darius and the *ash'strad*, but he couldn't tell the poor bloke that a magical bomb brought to Earth from another reality was the cause of him losing his livelihood. He also couldn't tell him there *was* opal down there without sounding like a dodgy bastard. What could he do about it, anyway? He didn't have the cash to spend on getting it out, so Kyne said nothing. All he could do was shake Trapper's hand and wish the guy luck on his new partnership in the Ridge.

It was much the same story with the other regulars, Gunno and Nigel, who were weighing their options. Sell their claims to someone who had the cash to splash on repairs or cut their losses and head back east where there was more work...and more accessible opal.

Kyne was just as conflicted as they were. He knew there were opal seams running through their claims, and he could help them, but they all faced supernatural dangers by staying out here. The Dust Dogs, the Nightshade, Darius...they were all things humans would struggle facing—unbelievable things that could only be fought with magic. Besides, how could the Exiles keep all that and the seal a secret, all while keeping them safe?

Unless Hardy wanted to take up a full-time position wiping their memories, the best place for the miners was someplace else.

"Bloody hell," he cursed as the jackhammer slipped. It shaved off a slice of rock that tumbled to the floor, and nearly squashed his foot.

Setting the heavy tool down, he took off his hardhat and earmuffs, then wiped the back of his arm across his sweaty forehead. The worst of the summer heat was long gone, but it didn't stop it from getting stuffy underground.

"Kyne?"

Eloise's voice echoed off the rock, and the elemental turned towards the main shaft.

"I'm down here!" he shouted. "I'll be up in a sec!"

He made his way down the tunnel to the shaft where he saw her silhouette looking down at him from above.

The ladder rattled as he climbed the twelve metres to the surface—the level was deep here, the ancient coral reef taking a steep dive towards the Earth's core—and hauled himself out into the sunshine.

Eloise was waiting for him, the brim of her grey Akubra hat low across her brow.

"Look at you," she said, licking her thumb and wiping it across his cheek. "You're covered in dirt."

He leaned back and made a face. "Occupational hazard. I can shake if you like; share it around a bit."

"No!" She laughed and took a few steps backwards. "Don't you dare!"

Kyne chuckled and tossed his hardhat into the tray of his ute. "What brings you all the way out here?"

"A couple of things, actually."

It was always something. His shoulders sank and he rubbed the bridge of his nose. Just when he was staring to enjoy himself... But that was their reality, he supposed.

Eloise frowned. "You okay?"

"Yeah, just distracted."

"Wanna talk about it?" She laid a hand on his sweaty arm, her elemental magic fusing with his.

"I've been out to see the other miners," he told her.

Eloise looked as uneasy as he felt. "They're back already?"

Kyne nodded. "Trapper's mine is a compete write off. Collapses in three places, and a massive crack in the roof. He was packing up and heading back to Lightning Ridge."

Her cheeks reddened. "Oh no…"

"You can say it."

"Say what?"

He chuckled and flicked the brim of her hat. "You've got a good heart, Eloise. Better than I deserve."

She swatted him back. "Oh, shut up."

"Gunno and Nigel were both weighing the cost of repairs," he added.

"Is it worth it? I mean…is there opal down there?"

"They both think there is, but there's no way of knowing. There're seams running through both their claims, but there's always more guessing in opal mining than certainty."

"Unless you're an elemental," Eloise told him with a raised eyebrow.

"Nah, yeah," he said through a sigh. "I can't tell them either way, can I?"

"So…is there opal down there?"

He nodded. There was enough to make a pretty good season for all three men, if they knew where to dig. "I feel bad for them, but they can't stay."

Eloise understood—all the Exiles did—but it didn't make it any easier. These men had given up a lot to chase their dream of finding opal and to have all that business with the seal messing it up for them was a kick in the guts. And he couldn't even tell them *why*.

"I have an advantage they don't," Kyne murmured,

his thoughts running away on him. "And I've got money because of it."

"You want to buy them out?" Eloise had seemed to know where he was going with it before he did.

"Yeah. I was thinking about it." He'd have to enlist Hardy's help to blur the edges of the miner's memories, but it could be done, and then they wouldn't be out of pocket.

Eloise grinned and slid her arm around his waist. "And you say I have a good heart. You ought to look in the mirror, Kyne Brady."

"You said you had something to fill me in on?" he prompted, uncomfortable with the attention, kind though it was.

"Yeah, Coen's gone on a walkabout," Eloise told him. "He told Drew he had to follow paths left by others. There were a few other things, something about an emu and a storm, but you know what they're both like. I think Coen's gone to find answers for us from the Ancestors...or something like it."

"Gone?" Kyne mused. "For real this time? Well, now we know why he was spending all that time with Drew."

"There actually is a storm coming. Keep an eye out."

Kyne looked to the horizon, but it was blue as far as the eye could see. "I will."

"Oh, and Clarke's back. He made up with Vera."

He raised his eyebrows. "Really?"

"He's all, *Team Solace* now," she went on. "Drew's not pleased, but who's surprised?"

"*No one.*"

"There's one other thing..." Eloise began to tell him about what had happened between her and Hardy at the pit, the worlds tumbling out of her like an uncontrollable flood.

She told him how her true elemental magic had awakened, giving the vampire the power he needed to defeat Darius. However, her awakening had come with an understanding she hadn't had before.

Eloise had an affinity with the fifth element—spirit. Spirit meaning the threads that bound reality itself—time, space, and the place of all things within it.

"I didn't understand until I felt it," she explained. "That's why I see the black mountain. It knows who I am, it knows what I can do, and it's trying to get to me like it got to Darius." Her cheeks reddened. "There was never a key in that iron ore. It was all a trick—"

"To get you to awaken your power," Kyne murmured, taking her in his arms. "Bloody hell... *You* are the key."

"I don't know about being *the* key," she muttered, her voice wavering. "Maybe I'm just a magical lockpick. There's a coral key for the seal in Solace, so maybe there's one for the mountain, too."

Kyne held onto her, letting her ramble. It was good for her to let out her thoughts, and he was glad to hear them.

"Why didn't you say anything?" he asked once she fell silent.

"I didn't want to worry anyone," Eloise replied sheepishly. "Darius had just tried to blow everyone up, Hardy was going through all that stuff with his family, there was Andante, and just...*everything*. I didn't want to cause any more trouble."

Kyne sighed and ran his fingers down her cheek, tracing her jawline. "Never," he told her. "I want to know everything. We're family, and family helps one another, no matter what."

"I'm sorry."

"Don't be." He kissed her and walked her back into the shade of a gum tree. "You were trying to do what you felt was right, even though I wish you'd told me." And Coen was gone, though he hoped Drew had gotten it right, that the Indigenous man had gone to find answers to the million-dollar question—how to lock out the Old Ones from their world forever. "You should speak to Vera about it," Kyne added. "She knows more about magic than any of us. She might know a way to help block the Old One from trying to influence you."

She swallowed hard, and he wondered if that thought had occurred to her. It seemed clear to Kyne that the black mountain had been behind all the recent attacks on the seal. He believed both Old Ones were working together, though there was no concrete proof.

"I have to tell everyone about it." Eloise sighed and gazed up at him. "I just hope I haven't caused more problems by keeping it to myself."

"Do you want me to come with you?"

"Yeah, nah, I'l be fine. You've got work to do here and Vera will know what to do."

"She always does."

Eloise peeled herself out of his arms and fussed with the buttons on his shirt. "You need some help this arvo? I can stay the night and head back into town in the morning..."

Kyne chuckled and studied the flush in her face. "You can stay as long as you want."

The elemental smiled, biting her bottom lip. "I do love the stars..."

He threw his hands into the air. "The stars?" he scoffed. "Is that all?"

"Convince me otherwise," was her wicked response.

And he was more than glad for the opportunity.

CHAPTER 5

The *Outpost* was busy for a weekday morning.

The seasons had turned, bringing cooler weather and with it came tourists and miners, all seeking adventure...as well as groceries, water, and fuel. The cash register dinged cheerfully, filling Vera's business-oriented heart *and* bank balance.

She chatted with Gunno, one of the seasonal opal miners, while he shopped for some supplies. Apparently, he was thinking of selling his claim. The roof had come down during the off season, and fixing it was looking like a costly endeavour. Apparently, Trapper had already pulled up stumps and was taking his bat and ball back to Lightning Ridge.

Drew had given her a pointed look that said it had everything to do with a certain fae explosive. When Kyne came back from Black Hole Mine, she'd have a word with him about it.

The traffic lulled as lunchtime approached, and

Vera leaned against the counter and gazed out the window while Drew worked down the aisle, wrangling the last of the magnetic dust Andante had zapped the day before. The druidess had ventured into town to see Blue of all people.

Curious.

The door opened and Eloise came in, bringing a burst of hot air with her. The seasons had turned, but that only meant it was a few degrees south of boiling. The gauge had settled on simmering.

"Hey," the elemental said. "Have you got a minute? There's something I wanted to talk to you about."

Eloise looked a little uncomfortable, but she was like that. It hadn't even been a year since she'd arrived in Solace, and before that, the elemental had done everything in her power to avoid people for fear of accidentally messing with their minds. Her abilities were tricky and had caused her no end of trouble. Vera couldn't blame her for falling back into old habits, especially since they'd served her so well.

"Yeah," the witch replied. "You wanna go for a walk? Drew's out back."

"Sure." Eloise glanced down the aisle where the dingo was sweeping so furiously, it was a wonder he hadn't worn a hole in the floor.

"Drew!" Vera shouted, making the elemental jump.

"What?" The dingo-shifter's voice echoed from the back of the store. He was still angry with her for getting back together with Clarke, but it was too bad, so sad.

"I'm going out with Eloise for a bit," she fired back, rolling her eyes. "Watch the front."

No reply came—not that she was expecting one—and she nodded towards the door. "Let's get going while the going's good."

As they reached the end of the verandah, Vera saw the bruised horizon and raised her eyebrows. *Storm clouds.*

"Coen said something about rain," Eloise said, following her gaze.

"So did the weather forecast. There's a hurricane off the east coast. A big one, by the sounds of it."

"And the rain comes all the way out here? I thought we'd be too far inland, not to mention too far south."

She smiled and shook her head. "Not at all. Depending on how big the storm is and how fast it's moving, we could get a proper drenching. Lightning and rain racing across the outback is something to see. A black sky against all that...?" She gestured to the bold red and green that surrounded Solace. "I'd never seen colour quite like it until my first storm out here."

"So, are you and Drew are still fighting?"

"*Drew's* still fighting," Vera replied with a roll of her eyes. "We worked everything out between us months ago, but he still gets his hackles up."

"He wasn't in a good mood when he came to

Hardy's to tell us about Coen," Eloise said as they stepped down off the verandah.

"He and Clarke don't get along," Vera said, stating the obvious.

"He's just trying to protect you. Maybe he's a little too heavy-handed..."

"You can say that again." It wasn't that Vera was ungrateful that the shifter cared about her, but his intensity levels worried her sometimes. It wasn't good for him to be so angry all the time. "Drew has to remember that he's been supernatural all his life. Everything that goes on in Solace is normal to him, but it's not for Clarke. Of course, he's going to struggle with it. Keeping it a secret was bad enough—honestly, it was an outright lie—but he also had to come to terms with magic being a reality."

"I get it," Eloise said. "Love, lies, and the paranormal... It'd mess with anyone."

Vera was glad to have Clarke back in her life, but it'd also caused trouble of its own. Blue was the only other human to know the truth, and the more humans who did, the less control they had over it. It wasn't that she didn't trust Clarke—because she did—it was everyone else that worried her.

Shaking her head, she turned to the elemental. "Look at me, running off at the mouth again. You said there was something you wanted to talk about?"

"Yeah..." Eloise began to squirm, and Vera raised her eyebrows.

"Let's go sit in the shade by the boab," she said. "I don't do so well in direct sunlight, and I'm not even a vampire."

Eloise chuckled despite herself, and they wandered along the side of the highway to the bloated boab that guarded the entrance to the tunnel leading down to the seal.

They sat side-by-side on one of the twisted roots, listening to the sounds of the outback, which weren't many. The air felt charged by the looming storm—all tense and uneasy, like they were on the sharpest edge of something volatile. Vera's Brinewold magic reacted to the rain, even though it was still hundreds of kilometres away.

"What's eating you up?" the witch asked, pressing her palms against the boab.

"It's about what happened up at the iron ore with Hardy," Eloise began.

She frowned, even as the magic in the tree soothed her. "Go on..."

Vera listened to everything Eloise had to say—how her power had awakened, and how her understanding led her to believe she was the key to the mountain—all while making no comment other than to nod at all the appropriate moments.

"Curious..." she mused when the elemental was done. "Though, I'm not surprised."

"You're not?"

"No, not at all. It makes sense." The shade from the

boab cooled her skin as she mulled, shielding her fragile redheaded Irish pallor from the sun's burning rays. "You can manipulate ether—the stuff that binds everything together. It's just a fancy word for spirit or reality, which is time, space, and how it relates to everything else. Being an elemental makes you valuable to a trapped entity like the Old One. The seal is blocked tight with magic beyond anything I've ever known, but I reckon you might just be able to blow it apart given the right amount of *je ne sais quoi*."

Eloise's frown deepened. "I was thinking the same thing."

Vera sensed it wasn't all she'd been sought out for and decided her friend needed a little prod in the right direction. "There's something else on your mind?"

"I've been wondering why I haven't..." Eloise bit her bottom lip and gathered her thoughts. "Well, why I haven't been corrupted like everyone else. Like Darius and the Dust Dogs..."

"And me," Vera added.

"Well, I didn't want to say it... It wasn't your fault."

"I guess not," the witch said. "The Nightshade was a family curse, passed down from generation to generation. I was just unlucky, I suppose."

Eloise scuffed the toe of her boot in the dirt, drawing an arc in front of her. "If the black mountain is after me, then why doesn't it take control?"

"Maybe it's been trying?" Vera mused. "All those

dreams, you turning up in Solace, your true power awakening... Maybe it just hasn't found a way yet."

"That's reassuring." She didn't sound convinced.

"It's honest, is what it is," Vera told her. "Maybe you can't be corrupted?"

Eloise looked up, hopeful. "How do you figure?"

Vera had put a lot of thought into it over the last few months, ever since Kyne had told her about his shared vision with Eloise, and especially after everything Andante had revealed about the Old Ones. The more she'd tried to puzzle it out, the more she thought it had everything to do with Eloise's elemental magic.

So far, almost everyone had their turn wrestling with the magic bleeding from the seal—vampires, witches, shifters. The only supernaturals left were werewolves, the fae, and the elementals. Wally had been here for twenty years and had somehow resisted the Old Ones' magic. The fae...well, one eye was always on them, especially after the Nightshade had used Finn as a conduit, but Kyne and Eloise seemed impervious to it all, and not for lack of trying on the mountain's behalf.

"Kyne was the only elemental I'd ever met before you," Vera said after a moment's thought. "I didn't know there was such a thing in our world, but there he was, not knowing where he'd came from or why he was born. Half-human, half-something unknowable."

The elemental blinked. "Unknowable?"

"I've tried to understand how his power works over the years, but I've never quite reconciled it. You and him, your magic is different from mine, though we all manipulate the same things."

"Different, but the same..." Eloise frowned. "How so?"

"I was born with the ability to manipulate the elements," Vera told her. "But you and Kyne were born *of* them. Your connection is, and will always be, deeper than anyone else's." Seeing the confused knot her friend's expression had become, she laughed. "Magic is mysterious. The more you try to understand it, the foggier it gets."

Eloise snorted. *"I'll say."*

"I think the origin of your power has more to do with your ability to resist the Old Ones' advances than anything else."

The elemental's forehead creased. "Is there a way to block it entirely?"

"I can give it a crack, but I'm not sure my magic will help." She was still corruptible, even though the Old One had tried and failed. She didn't think it'd have another go, but she wasn't one to say never, especially when its options were starting to run out.

Eloise sighed, and Vera knew she understood.

As they sat enjoying the sunshine together, Vera's thoughts wandered as she attempted to piece together all she knew with what Eloise had revealed. She was the key to letting out the Old One in the black mountain. It wasn't a great surprise, considering what her friend could do, but it did make her wonder about the bigger picture.

What if Eloise's path led her to the elementals themselves? Did they have a part to play in all this? When Kyne had found them deep in the Pilbara, they'd cast him out—quite brutally—but would they do the same to Eloise?

"Do you think I'll have to go find them?" the elemental asked.

"Maybe," Vera replied, not at all surprised she'd come to the same conclusion. "But I think we should wait until Coen comes back. I don't think he would've left us like he has without good reason."

"I just wish I'd told him before he left."

"Don't worry about it," the witch said with a smile. "I think Coen knows more than any of us ever will."

Finn lingered in the solace of the outback, watching the storm clouds gathering on the horizon. Dark and menacing, they loomed in a growing purplish-black band between the green and red of the land and the brilliant blue of the sky.

He thought of Siora and what they'd shared when they were young. As the son and daughter of two great Unseelie houses, their relationship was welcomed as a rare love their parents didn't have to arrange. A union between them would have only solidified their hold over *An Valran* and the north, but that day had never come.

Instead, it'd been revolution, exile, and a thousand years of anguish.

Finn knew they could never go back...and not just to their home. It was only natural to doubt, but it wouldn't change what was true.

He turned his back on the brewing storm and made his way towards the camp, his thoughts settled for the first time in months. Solace was home now, and he didn't regret helping the Exiles protect it. Sacrifice was something he knew a great deal about.

When the camp came into view, he saw the colourful tents had been disassembled and packed into tight bundles and their belongings had been wound into large, human-made backpacks. The only structure that still stood, was Finn's.

Siora stood with the other fae, all six huddled close and talking amongst themselves. All bore the coloured hair of the Unseelie *Shri'danann*—shades of blue, green, and purple—their dependancy on the seal's magic the only thing keeping them from losing it all.

Finn knew these fae—some low born, others from great houses of their own, but all had played their part in the same rebellion that'd born Finn and Siora to Earth. They all understood the harsh reality of survival, and they'd all felt the effects of the *ash'strad*.

And they knew what it was like to follow a passionate leader into the terrible jaws of war.

As he closed in on the camp, Finn caught sight of the polished silver stone glinting in Siora's hand. He didn't have to see it to understand that they were leaving at that precise moment...with or without him.

He didn't know if his desperation was born of love past or present, or a long-forgotten memory of his time spent imprisoned and starved of magic, but he couldn't let them leave.

"Don't go," he said, striding up to Siora. "*Please.*"

She turned, her silver eyes flashing in the sunlight. The storm clouds billowed on the horizon, the bruised purple bringing out the same flecks in her powder-blue hair. Siora was stunning, a rare beauty amongst their kind, but her heart had hardened long ago. His doubts had blinded him, but he saw it now.

But still...he couldn't let her walk away. Not when it could lead to her becoming *craglorn*—a twisted, mindless monster, starved of magic.

Her eyes narrowed as the other fae assembled behind her. "How many times must we have this conversation?"

"As many as necessary." Finn stood alone, but his power didn't come from others—it never had.

"You're a shadow, Finn Oreah'anza," Siora spat. "I no longer recognise you. The fae I knew would never have let things get this bad. This world has *weakened* you."

It was true that they'd long lived in this world without purpose, but with the discovery of the seal, that purpose had been renewed—for Finn at least. They couldn't go home, so they had to make the most of this world, and the Old Ones threatened it.

"You stood for something once," she went on. "You had a fire inside you, but now…" her silver gaze raked over him, her disdain for him clear, "you're *nothing*."

Finn stared at her, his heart tearing in two. He looked to the other fae, but they all turned their backs on him, their faces hidden. They couldn't even look upon him, such was their shame.

"Siora, please," he managed to say. "You will all wither away if you leave Solace."

"*No.*" Her expression twisted. "We face certain death if we remain, which is what you have chosen. I will not lead these fae into the darkness of death, to suffer their afterlife cut off from the magic that is their birthright."

"That is our punishment," he snapped. "You can't save them from that."

"Perhaps," she turned away from him, "but at least I'm willing to try."

Finn grabbed Siora's arm and pulled her towards him, his magic rising. As her gaze met his, her power flared in kind…and she lashed out.

His insides burned and he fell to his knees with a shocked cry, then another blow collided with his chest and he was on his back.

Finn stared up at the sky, choking as he tried to draw air into his twisted lungs. Siora's shadow fell over him and he blinked furiously, trying to focus on her.

"*Ore di ah'anith an,*" she said, raising her hand. *This is the only way...*

When Finn opened his eyes, the sky had darkened. The sound of thunder rumbled in the distance, the threat of lightning charging the heavens with the unpredictable energy of nature itself. At least something around here didn't need magic to survive.

Finn breathed in the electrified air, his lungs burning with the aftereffects of Siora's magic, and he knew.

He was alone.

CHAPTER 6

Hardy leaned against the side of his opal shop and watched the horizon with his vampire eyes. The edge of the incoming cloud bank had finally reached the top of the ridge, though the dense thunderheads were still a long way from covering Solace.

Rain was definitely coming, but it wouldn't reach them for another day. Distance was distorted by the vast openness of the outback and a hundred kilometres could easily look like a few hundred meters. It was no wonder people often became lost—underestimating everything from fuel, water, distance, and weather. The land was as deceptive at it was beautiful. There was a metaphor in that, but his thoughts were too full of other things to puzzle it out.

Spotting Eloise and Vera wandering down the track behind the *Outpost*, he lifted a hand. They meandered across the side road, not bothering to look for oncoming traffic, and stood in the shade cast by the shop.

"Out for a stroll?" he asked, eyeing Eloise.

"I told her," the elemental said with a roll of her eyes. "And Kyne, just so you know."

Hardy looked to Vera. "And what do you think?"

The witch shrugged. "I think it's reasonable to assume the Old Ones have been interested in Eloise from the beginning, but with Coen gone walkabout, I think we just ought to keep our eyes and ears open until he gets back."

"I thought so," the vampire mused, nodding towards the ridge. "Coen was right about one thing already. Rain is coming."

"How can you tell?" Vera asked with a scowl. "You can't even see the clouds behind the ridge."

Hardy chuckled. "Occupational hazard."

"Like being a vampire is an occupation."

"It feels that way sometimes." His gaze returned to the horizon.

Sensing his uneasiness, Eloise pursed her lips. After all they'd been through in the past few months—paired with working together most days cutting and polishing opal—she'd picked up an uncanny habit of predicting his moods. She was quite good at it, too.

"What is it?" she asked when he didn't offer an explanation.

"Nothing," he replied with a grin. "Storms always send a tingle down my spine." Sensing movement across the highway, he nodded towards Wally, who was coming over to meet them. "Come to join the party, old wolf?"

"Who are you calling, old, hey?" Wally chuckled as he joined them in the shade. "Age is a state of mind."

"We were just talking about the storm," Eloise said. "What's your take?"

"My take?" He thought for a moment and shrugged. "The air smells heavy, which means it's going to be a real blower. Might want to make sure everything's tied down."

"Storms can get that bad out here?" the elemental asked, looking pale.

"Nah, yeah," Wally went on. "We can get some flooding in the old creeks and down in the abandoned mines. Hard rain on dry, flat land like this...? It doesn't seep into the ground right away. Things can get real muddy."

"I don't know what's worse," Vera said with a sigh. "Magnetic dust or sloppy mud."

"Magnetic dust," Hardy and Eloise declared at the same time.

They were laughing about it when Wally coughed loudly. He nodded towards the northern end of town and said, "I think we've got visitors."

Hardy stepped out of the shade and onto the highway as six fae walked towards them, spread out across the asphalt. Their colourful hair and billowing bohemian clothing was a sight to see against the backdrop of the Australian Outback, but he knew they weren't here for a cup of tea and a chat.

"Those are the other fae?" Eloise murmured as she stood by him on the road. She hadn't met them before, even though they'd helped search for her when she was lost.

"Siora is the woman in front." He gestured as the other Exiles joined them. "The others I know only in passing. They..." he trailed off, knowing Kyne had already explained their tense relationship.

The group stopped a few paces from the Exiles, mirroring the stance the Dust Dogs had taken all those months before. Hardy didn't like it one bit, preferring the omen of the storm clouds over a supernatural standoff any day.

"Siora," Hardy said with a courteous nod. "What brings you into Solace?"

"We've come to finish charging our artefact," the fae replied, holding up a polished silver stone. "Its magic will help us while we travel."

"You're leaving?" Hardy asked, looking amongst the gathered fae, noticing Finn wasn't with them.

She scoffed, "Don't look so surprised, vampire. You're a fool if you think it wouldn't come to this."

The storm clouds seemed to speed up as they crossed the tip of the ridge, and he glanced at Siora. *Was she using her magic? Why?* He wondered where they were going. Wherever it was, they didn't want to be followed, and the incoming storm was the perfect distraction for any Exile who dared to follow... including Finn.

Hardy's eyes narrowed. "You don't have to do that, Siora."

She smirked as the other fae murmured behind her, and Hardy knew something bad had gone down between her and Finn. He'd likely wanted to stay, despite what the trouble with the seal had cost them. Away from Solace, there was no guarantee of another place of power outside of Ireland. That much Hardy understood about their plight on Earth.

"So, was it your pride that kept you away all these years?" he asked, pulling no punches.

"Pride?" Her expression twisted as the storm clouds continued to billow. "Our situation is nothing to be proud about!"

"Your situation..." Hardy bit his tongue. Their situation was awful at best. The Unseelie were proud, magical people who'd been reduced to parasites in an unfamiliar alien world. He'd be pissed about it too, no matter the circumstances that brought them here. "Siora, we reached out to you for years, and you never wanted anything to do with us. Finn was the only—"

"And look where it got him," Siora spat. "Look where it got *us*."

"Where's Finn?" Eloise demanded. "What did you do to him?"

"Less than he deserves," the fae hissed. "Finn is nothing to us. Let him be a burden upon *you*."

"Burden?" the elemental exclaimed. "He's not—"

Hardy placed a hand on Eloise's shoulder. If they took one wrong step, it would come to blows and he wasn't sure they'd all come out of it alive. Fae magic was mostly unknown to him, despite having known Finn for many years. They could be capable of anything, and he wasn't willing to risk anyone's life over a misunderstanding.

"She's using magic." Vera tensed as her steely-blue power pooled in her hands. "The storm—"

"*Don't*," Wally warned.

"Finally, some sense," Siora said, glancing at the werewolf. "You don't want to try that, *witch*."

Vera jerked forwards with a snarl, but Eloise grabbed her hand and absorbed the Brinewold magic into herself.

"We don't want to fight you, Siora," Hardy said. "All we've ever wanted to do is help."

"Help?" the fae scoffed. "Is that what you call it?"

"We never intended to harm you."

"And yet, you did." She edged in front of the other fae. "We're the ones who have suffered the most because of your battle with forces beyond your control. You disregard our dependancy on magic for survival. You used us to save your precious elemental. You used Finn time and time again, and now he's turned his back on us! You never cared about our fate, only that of your insignificant town."

Hardy sighed, his heart heavy. He didn't want to

admit it, but she was right. Despite the Exile's best intentions, the fae had borne the brunt of everything that'd befallen Solace. Fighting over territory with the Dust Dogs, the Nightshade using Finn as a living battery pack, and the *ash'strad*...it'd almost turned them all into vapour.

Maybe they could've tried harder to reach out to the fae to join them in town. Maybe they should've cut Finn more slack with his Unseelie attitude. *Maybe...* It was too late now, but who was to say that anything they could've done would've changed the outcome?

It hurt knowing what the fae faced out there without contact with a place of power, but he had to let them leave. This was their choice, and forcing them to stay would only cause more suffering.

"I agree with you, Siora," Hardy managed to say. "I think it's best that you move on."

Her silver eyes narrowed and she pocketed the silver stone. Whatever magic she'd come here to siphon was now inside the artefact.

Eloise looked at him, her heart beating wildly. "But—"

"We've said all we can," he interrupted. "They want to leave, so we have to let them go. This is their choice. Let them make it."

Wally was the first to step aside. He moved to the verandah outside the *Outpost*, where Drew had finally cottoned on that something was going on outside. The dingo-shifter's nose was plastered against the window, but he had the sense to stay inside as Hardy, Eloise, and Vera left the highway and joined the werewolf in the shade.

Siora glared at the Exiles as the fae walked past, her silver eyes flashing coolly.

Where they were going or how they were going to get there, Hardy didn't know, but they'd managed to find Solace from the other side of the world. No doubt, they'd manage.

They stood in silence as the fae disappeared, their magic cloaking their progress as they reached the town limits...then, they were gone.

Hardy felt a heaviness settle in his heart and he rubbed the bridge of his nose. What was done, was done.

The bell on the door rang as it opened.

"Let's face it," Drew said, joining them on the verandah, "that was inevitable. They never wanted to be here."

"Perhaps," Hardy replied.

"We did what we could," Vera told him. "Wherever they're going, I hope they're happier."

"I'm going to find Finn," Eloise said as the illusion shimmered across the road. "Where is their camp?"

Hardy pointed to the northeast. "Finn has put illusions around the perimeter, so you won't see it straight away, but if he's there, he'll sense you."

"I hope so." The elemental grimaced and looked in the direction Siora and the fae had gone.

"Don't be out too long," Wally said. "You don't want to get caught in the rain."

Eloise hopped off the verandah. "I'll be back as soon as I can."

But Hardy wasn't paying attention. He was too busy watching the highway, his vampire eyes following the last traces left behind by the fae.

He hoped Vera was right...for all their sakes.

***

Eloise walked across the outback, weaving through the sparse trees and giving the spiky spinifex grass a wide berth.

She wasn't afraid of the wildness of this place anymore. Snakes barely registered when she saw them slithering in the sun, her memories of being lost had become distant, and the kadaitcha—the shadow spirits that lingered in the darkness—had long left Solace. After all that business with Rosheen and the Nightshade, the shadows had fled elsewhere.

Instead, Eloise's newly-awakened power guided her through every part of the world around her. She felt the currents of ether flowing just beyond her reach, but it wasn't the only thing. The earth, the trees, the sky, the air...it all glowed around her, showing the path forwards. Her eyes were opening and the truth of what the Old One had forced out of her was only now beginning to manifest.

Eloise was upon the camp before she realised. The illusion fluttered against her skin and her eyes adjusted as trees, rocks, and the remains of the settlement itself shimmered into existence.

Finn sat in the middle of the camp, the single tent looking rather lonely in the trampled remains of what used to be a thriving fae community. His shoulders were hunched, his back covered in rust-coloured dirt, and bits of fallen leaves were stuck in his midnight-blue dreadlocks.

Eloise took a step towards him. "Finn?"

The fae looked up, his silver eyes shining in the eerie pre-storm light. He didn't seem surprised to see her, but then again, he looked rather numb.

"Are you alright?" she asked.

Saying nothing, he picked up a stick and began breaking off bits. The wood cracked, the sound echoing through the stillness.

Eloise bit her bottom lip and approached the fire pit. Sitting beside him, she studied the blackened coals.

"They came through Solace," she told him after a moment. "It was...tense."

Finn snorted and threw the pieces of stick into the empty fire pit. "They brought old prejudices into a new world," he murmured as if he was speaking himself. "They serve no purpose here. None at all."

Eloise studied him, trying to work out if it was

regret the fae was feeling. "Did you want to go with them?"

"I wanted to stay here."

She was relieved to hear it, but now he was alone. Siora and the other fae had gone and with them, they'd taken his last connection to his home world.

"Siora was selfish," Finn went on. "She wanted to live here as we did in Lor'Iyslar, but it could never be like that. We can never go back, so this must become our home, no matter the cost." He looked at her, his silver eyes dull. "We have nowhere else, but...they never wanted to fight for this world, so perhaps it's best they left."

"Will they be okay?"

Finn shrugged. "I don't know. They put all their hopes on a rumour that there's another place of power strong enough for all of them."

"And that stone will help them get there before they lose their magic?" she asked, but her question went unheard.

"She was right. I'm no better than her," Finn muttered. "I lost faith. I deserve everything I get and more besides."

"I know you, Finn. I don't believe it."

"I was bad, Eloise. As bad as they come." He shook his head, his eyes filling with frustration and awful memories. "I fought for all the wrong things and lost. *Badly*. I lied, stole, tortured, and *killed*. I knew all about the *ash'strad* because I've used one before." He threw the last piece of stick into the cold fire pit. "Exile and damnation... That's what I deserve and even then, it will never be enough."

Murder? Eloise didn't know what to say. She knew Finn had been sent to Earth for crimes committed in his past, but she couldn't reconcile those deeds with the fae who sat before her.

"Damnation?" she whispered instead.

"We believe that if we die here, away from our true world, that our souls will float in darkness, forever starved of the magic that is our birthright."

Now she understood. That was their true punishment. Exile in a world starved of magic was bad enough, but in death, they could never taste it again.

Purgatory, Eloise thought. *Eternal darkness alone, starving.*

"For all her faults, Siora wanted to save the others from their fate. She and I..."

It was then that Eloise realised there was more to their relationship than mere circumstance. They'd known each other from before. They'd fought together and perhaps even loved on another, but she felt like it wasn't her place to ask.

"Revolution?" she asked instead.

Finn nodded. "A pathetic grab for power. Evil overthrowing good."

Eloise couldn't find the words to heal what hurt him inside. She wanted to fix his broken heart, to help him see that he'd changed, that he'd paid the price for his past crimes... But maybe there wasn't a way. Maybe this was his story alone.

"The storm's almost here," she said, watching the clouds creep closer. "I'd feel better if you came back into Solace until it passes."

"It's not the first storm I've weathered out here," Finn told her. "I'll be fine."

It wasn't about him being out here. It was about him being alone with his turmoil.

"You can stay in my van," she offered. "It's undercover and has a nice bed, a shower, and a toilet. There's even a little kitchen. You can use it for as long as you like."

Finn stared at her, surprise in his eyes. "Even after knowing what I did, you'd still offer me your home?"

The elemental shrugged. "Yeah. Of course. You are talking about something that happened a thousand years ago. That's a long time to work on character development."

He didn't look convinced—thoroughly depressed and in the midst of a personal crisis was a more apt description.

Eloise scowled, her dislike of Siora only growing. She'd left Finn with terrible doubts and a shattered heart. It didn't seem right.

"Finn, I know you've been through a lot, but—"

"I've been harsh and unkind to everyone in Solace," he argued. "I drove away Siora. I fight with Drew. I insult Vera. I use Blue for potatoes. *Potatoes.* I don't even have money to pay him. I've made Kyne's life one long problem after another. And Hardy—"

"*Finn.*"

He scowled. "*What?*"

"I know who you are *now,* and I'll probably never truly understand what being Unseelie means, but to me, you're *good*. To all of us, you're a good man." She wrapped her arm around his waist and rested her head on his shoulder. "And above all, you're family, and this is what family does for one another, through thick and thin."

It was a long moment before he relaxed, but as she felt the tension leave him, she smiled.

Together, they watched the approaching storm clouds, the darkening sky ominous with thunder and lightning. Eloise hoped it wasn't an omen and that they wouldn't need sandbags, because it was a truly beautiful sight. The raw power of nature was something to behold.

"Okay," Finn said, resting a hand on her knee. "I'll come. But just until the rain stops."

CHAPTER 7

The wind was already picking up as the Exiles split up.

Eloise took off into the scrub in search of Finn while Hardy went back to the opal shop to close up. Wally did the same, returning to the garage with his hand holding his grease-stained hat on his head.

Drew dragged the *Outpost's* signs in off the side of the highway, leaving them stacked just inside the front door. The benches were nailed to the verandah, so the signs were the only thing they had to worry about being taken by the wind.

Finally, they sought refuge inside before the wind kicked up all the red dust they'd just purged from the shop and blew it back in with them. The linoleum floor was already stained to the point it was far from the off-white eggshell it was when new.

Drew secured the door and turned to Vera, who had already retrieved the broom.

"What did Eloise want?" In all the drama with the fae, he'd almost forgotten Vera had gone off with her.

The witch opened her mouth to reply but closed it.

The dingo scowled. "Is it secret women stuff?"

"You know, you're getting real angry lately. Something on your mind?"

Drew sighed and shook his head. "Do you want me to check the generator?" If the power went out, they'd need to turn on backup power so the refrigerated and frozen foods wouldn't spoil.

"Drew, you can talk to me about it," Vera went on. "After everything we've been through—"

"I know," he interrupted. "With Coen gone, he's kind of left me with a lot, and..." He let his thoughts dissolve, not wanting to acknowledge them himself.

But Vera wasn't about to let it go. "And what?"

"Nothing."

Thankfully, she let it go. "Eloise has some stuff going on with..." Her shoulders sagged. "Well, when she was up at that iron ore pit, her powers sort of awakened."

Drew raised his eyebrows. He understood what that felt like, especially now that he realised he could talk to Coen while he was in his dingo form...at least a little. Why he hadn't mentioned it to Vera, he wasn't sure. Maybe it had to do with Clarke coming back. Was he still jealous of the cop? *Maybe.*

"She thinks the black mountain has been trying to

get to her like it did Darius," she continued. "But so far, it hasn't been able to corrupt her like it did him."

"And it won't," Drew said fiercely.

"You say that like you know something." Her eyes narrowed as she waited for him to elaborate.

Drew shrugged, not wanting to commit to a solid answer. "Coen likes her, and when Coen likes someone, it means something."

"He likes you, too."

"We're talking about Eloise."

"So...her power is just the thing the Old One needs to let it out of its prison."

The dingo tensed and turned his gaze onto Vera. "Why didn't she say anything?"

"I don't think she wanted to worry us."

Even as she answered, Drew knew it was something Eloise would do. The elemental had a big heart and never wanted to be a bother to anyone. He knew it had a lot to do with her upbringing and how her powers had first manifested. She'd accidentally touched people and turned their minds against her—a reflection of how she felt about herself. Drew had his own turbulent childhood, so he understood.

He opened his mouth to reply but turned to the window as a car pulled up outside. Seeing the white and blue police 4WD, he screwed up his nose. *Clarke.*

"What's *he* doing here? A little out of his way, isn't it?"

"Please, try to be nice," Vera said, following his gaze.

"I'm just thinking of all the fossil fuel he's burning, not to mention the kilometres he's putting on government property."

"*Drew*."

"Okay, okay." He crossed his fingers behind his back as Clarke got out of his 4WD. "I'll be good."

Sergeant Andrew Clarke strode into the *Outpost*, fully uniformed, followed by a gust of hot wind that carried the musky scent of rain.

Storms in the outback often gave off a distinct smell from the heat and dry earth, paired with the boldness of eucalyptus and other plants. It always reminded Drew of something wild beyond his grasp, like a blanket lay over the world they knew. Considering he could turn into a dingo that could *see*, it was saying something.

"Clarke!" Vera exclaimed. "What are you doing here? I thought you were working today?"

"The storm was moving in fast." He gave her a swift kiss on the lips and set his hat on the counter. "I wanted to make sure you were okay. Forecast says it's gunna be a rough one."

"You came out all this way? Why didn't you ring?"

Clarke raised his eyebrows. "Have you checked your phone lately? The tower in the Ridge was hit by lightning this morning. Whole town's lost service. The repeater will be down here because of it."

Vera clucked her tongue and gestured to Drew. She barely used her mobile phone, opting to keep it stashed underneath the front counter on the days she was at the *Outpost*.

Drew picked it up, the charging cable dangling from one end. It said 'No Service' in the top corner, so he checked the EFTPOS machine and saw it was offline, too.

"No service," he told them. "Landline's cut, too."

Vera let out an exasperated sigh. "I knew I should've renewed my satellite service."

Drew glanced at the sergeant. He had to make an effort to at least get along with the bloke for Vera's sake. The cop didn't have to come all the way out here from Lightning Ridge—a two-hundred-plus kilometre round trip—but here he was...all because he couldn't get Vera on the phone.

"What's the flooding situation like out here?" Clarke went on. "The dugouts flood at all?"

"There's enough elevation on the ridge that any water will run away from them," Drew told him. "Kyne built most of the dugouts up there, and he made sure to do them right."

"No doubt," Clarke said with a nod. "I saw the job you and he did on that place up top. Looked solid."

"*It is.*"

"What about the seal?" the sergeant added. "Didn't you say it was underground?"

"There's nothing we can do about it if it floods,"

Drew answered. "Anyway, where the entrance is, I reckon it'll be fine."

"He's right," Vera said. "In all the years I've been out here, it's always stayed dry. It must have something to do with the magic keeping it closed, because all the mines around here can get a bit damp during the wet."

"One less thing to worry about at least," Clarke mused. At least he was trying to understand all the crazy magic out here.

"All right," Vera said to the men. "The seal is cared for, but the *Outpost* isn't steeped in ancient magical juju. Let's start locking things up. That wind has got some epic bite in it."

Drew grunted and gave Clarke one last glare before striding down aisle three. He knew something else that had an epic bite...and it wasn't the wind.

Eloise and Finn walked back to Solace in silence. Everything that could be said, *for now*, had been spoken back at the camp.

She felt the storm creeping up behind them as they followed the track, the air charging with the electricity brought by unyielding lightning strikes. Every now and then, she was sure she saw the faint flashes that confirmed the tingling sensation zinging down her spine.

There was a lot of truth in the saying 'the calm

before the storm,' though she thought it ought to be amended to 'the *anticipation* before the storm.'

Eloise glanced at Finn. "Do you get storms like this in your world?"

"Yes," he replied with a nod. "This world shares many of the same things as mine."

"What's the biggest difference? You know, besides the whole magic thing."

"The colours. The sky is bluer, water and ice reflect like crystal, though the earth is brown and beige as it is here. Many of the plants share the same hue, though there are many colours there that don't touch Earth. Grass is green, but there are many places where it fades to purple and blue. The animals..." He smiled as if he were looking at a magical vista shimmering with an iridescence Eloise couldn't see. "Magic changes things in ways not many could imagine."

Eloise tried to imagine it, but even though she saw purple trees and glowing flowers, her mind's eye couldn't conjure an accurate image of the fae world. It must be beautiful, mysterious, and something right out of a fairy tale. To think Finn hadn't seen it in a thousand years drew a tear to her eye.

"I'd like to hear all about it sometime." She smiled at him as Solace came into view. "If you want to tell me, that is."

Finn said nothing as they reached the highway. Maybe it was too soon.

The wind was picking up and it tugged at the brim

of her hat. Fixing the chin strap, she caught sight of Clarke's police 4WD outside the *Outpost*. Inside, he was talking with Vera as Drew glowered in the background.

Farther down the road, Hardy was helping Wally pull down the roller doors at the garage. The vampire made short work of it, securing the latches while the old werewolf locked the nozzles into the fuel pumps. The metal sign by the road, that advertised the current per litre price of diesel, fell over with a clatter and began to skid, but the vampire was on it in a flash, returning it to the garage before it became airborne.

"I don't like this wind," Eloise said as she and Finn headed towards the pub.

The fae sniffed the air, his silver eyes appearing to shimmer in the odd storm-light.

Eloise hesitated. "Is something wrong?"

"No," he replied. "No, I don't think so."

"The news said something about a cyclone on the east coast," she mused. "Apparently, it's a pretty bad one. Category five."

Finn shrugged. "Maybe that's it."

Blue was behind the bar when they went inside the pub.

Eloise peered around the publican into the kitchen, but it was empty. "Kyne isn't back yet?"

"No. He should be along soon," Blue told her as they sat at their usual table. "He won't stay out longer than needed, not with the wind blowing like it is."

Unless he's underground chasing opal, Eloise thought uneasily.

She knew how he could get when he was following a seam because she'd felt the same rush. The shine of potch in the wall was a lure too strong to fight, even for an elemental who knew what was at the centre of it. She could only imagine the desperate hope a human miner felt seeing the same thing.

"You want something to eat?" Blue asked, looking at Finn.

The fae scowled and shook his head. "I need to start washing dishes to clear my tab."

He looked bewildered for a moment. "What tab?"

"I'll have some," Eloise said quickly. "I think we're going to be here a while. Snacks will be needed."

"Righty-o." Blue frowned at Finn, then headed for the kitchen.

The door opened as soon as he disappeared. A sharp gust of wind billowed into the pub as Hardy and Wally appeared. The vampire shut out the weather and shook the dust from his hair.

"That wind is blowing something fierce," he quipped as his gaze settled on Finn. He made no mention of the standoff with Siora and the others as he sat at the table with them.

"All locked up?" Blue asked, returning to the table.

"Best we can," Wally told him. "Damn near lost the sign out on the highway."

"There'll be a few branches down tomorrow," the publican mused.

"Well, since we've got time to kill, maybe Eloise can tell us a story," Hardy said with a chuckle.

"Joseph really rubbed off on you, didn't he?" she asked, screwing up her nose.

"Closure is really quite freeing," the vampire mused.

"What story?" Wally straightened up, suddenly more interested in her than his beer, which was saying something.

So Eloise told them about her powers awakening up at the *EarthBore* site, then about the mountain and its creepy manipulation, without which she would never have tapped into the deeper magic she apparently needed to let out the Old One from its mountain prison.

Finn listened intently, but said nothing, his continued silence worrying her the longer it went on. She'd really like to know what he thought, sarcasm and all.

"What would be nice," Wally said when she was done, "is to know who plugged up those holes to begin with."

"Bloody oath," Blue echoed.

Eloise caught Hardy's gaze and the vampire chuckled. After all her agonising, she'd been worried for nothing. No one seemed fazed. In fact, they seemed like they'd been expecting it.

"I've got a story for you too, Eloise," the publican added. "Andante stopped by."

Everyone fell silent, but Hardy laughed again. "So that's how the dust became unstuck."

Blue nodded, looking a little red in the cheeks. "She's quite the woman, isn't she?"

Eloise caught Hardy's eye and it was her turn to chuckle. It looked like someone had a crush on a certain druidess.

There's never a dull moment in Solace, she thought. *Never a dull moment at all.*

Drew had just finished securing the bins out the back of the *Outpost* when he smelt the first drops of rain. The sky was turning faster than he'd ever seen, midday fading to twilight in a matter of half an hour.

Hurrying back inside, he locked the back door and returned to the front counter where Vera and Clarke were watching the darkening highway.

"It's creepy," the witch murmured, rubbing her palms up and down her bare arms, her silver rings clacking together. "I feel a little numb."

"We should go to the pub," the shifter said, his own balance a little askew. "Everyone will be there. If the power goes out, I can come back and get the generator going."

A rumble of thunder boomed overhead, the vibration rattling the windows.

Vera clapped her hands over her ears and swallowed a cry. "*Bloody hell.* That was a loud one!"

Another deafening crack split the air and a flash lit up the windows as a bolt of lightning struck the windmill across the road. Red hot sparks flew in all directions as Vera shrieked, flying into Clarke's arms.

"*Shit a brick,*" the sergeant exclaimed. "Did any of those embers catch?" A grass fire out here would be devastating after the summer they'd had, and it wasn't like the local fire brigade would be out to help any time soon.

"Doesn't look like it." Drew sniffed the air as the afterimage of the lighting strike flared bright in his vision. It smelt a little magic-y to him.

"Drew?" Vera put a hand on his arm. "What is it?"

He sniffed again as another rumble of thunder sounded outside. The storm shouldn't have arrived for at least another day, and after all that business with the fae earlier, it was more than enough evidence for him.

"That blue-haired shiela," he hissed. "She sped up the storm. I can smell it."

Vera gasped. "*I knew it.*"

As the three stood there, the first drops of rain began to fall. Big, fat, blobs hit the roof, pinging against the corrugated iron like ricocheting bullets.

Clarke unclipped the police radio from his belt and turned it on. It crackled with static, not changing as he flipped through each channel. He obviously expected to hear a little chatter because he frowned when nothing came through.

"Lightning Ridge, this is Sergeant Clarke, over." Static. "Lightning Ridge, this is Sergeant Clarke, *over*." He shook his head.

"No one there?" Vera asked.

"They're there..." he replied. "We monitor chatter from the truckies as well as police bands, but they're silent, too. There's just too much interference."

Drew snorted. He thought it had more to do with that blue-haired fae and her meddling with the storm than anything natural. From the look on Vera's face, she suspected it too, but there was nothing they could do but wait until the storm had blown itself out. Once the rain had gone, things would even out again. They always did.

"Looks like I'm here for the duration," Clarke said, glancing briefly at Drew. "Wanna make a run for the pub before it really starts to belt down?"

Vera nodded. "Drew?"

"I'm right behind you." He scooped up the keys to the *Outpost* from behind the counter. Turning, he saw Vera and Clarke had threaded their fingers together and scowled. "I could do with a beer. *A big one.*"

CHAPTER 8

Kyne didn't know how long he'd been down his new cut at Black Hole Mine, but time always faded away when he was chasing opal.

The chiselled tip of the small handheld jackhammer cut into the rock face above the seam, chipping away the soft sandstone in clumps. The vibrations rattled up his arms, the noise dampened by his heavy-duty earmuffs.

People called it opal fever—when the pull of a stone so beautiful, rare, and valuable was so strong, the miner chasing it lost all sense of the world around them. Time, hunger, relationships—they all fell to the wayside when a big strike could just be around the corner...and it was ten times worse when the first signs of an opal seam appeared in the wall. Glossy potch threading through the russet- and tan-coloured sandstone layer of the ancient coral reefs.

For an elemental whose talents lay firmly in the earth end of the spectrum, it was easy for Kyne to fall victim to the siren song. He could feel the opal in the ground, calling him towards it.

All he had to do was dig.

Eloise had left that morning. He'd thought over all she'd told him about the black mountain and the expansion of her powers, and he knew there was nothing they could do about it, not directly anyway. With Coen off on another walkabout in search of answers, Kyne thought it was best to wait until the Indigenous man got back, and until then, life was returning to its usual state of cautiousness.

The jackhammer carved through a soft pocket of sandstone, his power helping melt it away from the seam like butter. Switching the machine off, he ran his hand over the rough edges of the raw potch and felt the familiar pull of the good stuff—black opal.

Taking off his hardhat and earmuffs, he tilted his head towards the ceiling.

What was that sound?

A low rumble and hiss echoed from above, and farther down the drive the *tink, tink, tink* of something dripping on metal echoed off the rock face.

Leaving his tools behind, he ventured down the tunnel, the electric lights flickering. His boots crunched on loose rock and dirt as another rumble vibrated overhead. The shaft came into view just as the halogen bulbs popped, then cut out completely, plunging the mine into total darkness behind him.

Kyne approached the shaft and looked up at the circle of dull light above. Checking his watch, he saw it was just on noon, but there was no blue to be seen.

The storm, he thought as a drop of water splashed against the cracked face of his digital watch.

For a moment, he wondered if he'd left it too late, but he shook his head as another rumble of thunder echoed down the hole. No, it was early... The storm had picked up steam while he was busy chasing opal. *Sneaky bastard.*

Rain began to fall the moment Kyne began to climb the ladder. It came into the shaft at an angle, hitting the side of the wall with so much force, it dislodged dirt and pebbles, sending them tumbling downwards. He hightailed it the rest of the way, hauling himself out of the mine and into the weather.

The sky was so black, it felt like the sun had set and night had descended on the claim. It was eerie and his skin tingled as the wind blew the stinging rain against his cheeks.

Kyne made short work of securing the claim as lightning flickered in the distance, flinging the hatch over the shaft so more water wouldn't pour in, then grabbing the portable generator before it fried completely. As the wind picked up steam, his camp was next, his sodden sleeping bag slapping into the tray of his ute. His other bits and pieces got flung in higgledy-piggledy—the cast iron pot, cooking utensils, his Tupperware container of tea, the camp chair all clattered noisily as they joined the generator and sleeping bag.

Finally, he secured the tarp over the tray, but by the time he climbed into the driver's seat, the rain was falling in heavy sheets, slamming into the side of the ute with enough force to rock the cab.

Kyne shoved the key into the ignition and hit the accelerator, the ute tearing out of the claim and onto the track towards Solace. There wasn't any time to waste. He'd get stuck out in the open if he wasn't careful. Rain was a miracle in the driest parts of the country, but it was just another thing that could turn deadly in a matter of moments. Floods were all too common in the wet season, and the amount of dry creek beds out here was staggering. Not many people realised how quickly they could fill with raging torrents of water.

Kyne cursed as the ute rocked and rolled down the uneven track, which had turned to mud in a matter of minutes. Rivulets of water flowed across the ochre dust like intricate veins, spreading as the storm raged overhead.

The front wheel crashed into a hole, rocking the whole car, then bumped up and out, but when the back hit, the ute lurched to a stop. He pressed his foot on the accelerator, revving the engine, and the wheels spun. Checking the 4WD gearbox was engaged to 4L, he tried again.

The ute coasted to the side as the tyres slipped in the mud and with nothing for them to grip, they began to sink.

"*Shit*," Kyne cursed, wrenching the gearbox into neutral. Looking over his shoulder, all he could see was the thick sheets of rain slicing across the track behind him. He'd have to get out and push.

Thank bloody hell I'm an earth elemental, he thought as he killed the engine. *But I could do with a little help with water right now.*

Rain stung his cheeks as he got out, thunder rumbling in the distance as lightning shot across the horizon. Slipping and sliding, he rushed the best he could to the back of the ute.

Kyne anchored his shoulder against the tray and dug his boots into the squelching mud. Then he let go of his power, letting it flow through him and into the ground beneath the ute. If he could just get the mud to flow in the right direction, he could solidify it enough to get going again.

He felt his magic flare, but the ute wouldn't budge. He tried again, but this time, his link to the elements flickered, then went out entirely.

Stunned, he blinked furiously as water flowed down his face and into his eyes. He'd lost contact with his powers before—back when he'd returned from the Pilbara. The elementals had kicked him out, not wanting anything to do with him, and from the moment he'd left, he couldn't feel his connection with the earth anymore. He still didn't understand why, even in the wake of getting them back, but maybe it was just something as simple as emotional trauma—a *human* response. Now, as he tried to move his ute, it felt the same, yet slightly different.

This wasn't him.

Something or *someone* was screwing with his powers.

Another flash lit up the sky, the crack so loud and furious, it shook the ground. His boots scrambled in the mud, and he fell as a deafening explosion ripped apart a towering gum beside the track.

The next bit happened in slow motion. Sparks and embers flew into the air, spitting in the rain as the bolt of lightning impacted with the tree. It split down the middle and began to fall, half backwards and the other half towards him.

Kyne's heels scrambled in the thick mud, but the ground was so slick, all he could do was slip and slide.

The tree crashed towards him, and he flung his arms over his face. It was all he could do.

Finn sat at the table in the pub, staring at the bowl of hot chips before him, but he wasn't really listening to the conversation. Even if he was paying attention, he wouldn't hear much. The rain made a deafening clanging on the corrugated iron roof and the windows rattled as the heavy clouds clashed overhead.

The electric lights flickered every so often, but they struggled on, remaining lit as they waited out the storm.

It'd already been a long day, and Finn was so drained he'd become numb. He couldn't see a way forwards anymore, and he saw no connection to why he was here at all. *One blow after another…*

Eloise paced in front of the windows looking out over Solace. Beyond was the yard outside the pub, then the highway, and Wally's garage. Finn couldn't see any of those things due to the rain, just the ancient gum tree that grew out front. The branches whipped back and forth, the violent gusts ripping twigs and leaves, hurtling them through the air. It was a wonder the thing hadn't split in two.

Everyone was here, even Sergeant Clarke. But there was one notable absence.

"Kyne should've been back by now," Eloise murmured, peering out the window. "Something's wrong."

She wrung her hands, her anxiety so potent, it began rubbing Finn the wrong way. He couldn't blame her, though. The storm sent a shiver down *his* spine.

"I'll head out and look for him," Hardy said. "He's likely stuck on the track or waiting it out at his claim."

"I can't ask you to go out there," Eloise said, her

shoulders sagging. "I know you like to think you're indestructible, but have you seen that wind?"

"Yes," the vampire replied. "I'm looking at it right now."

"It's like a scene out of that movie, *Twister*," Vera stated. "I don't think even a vampire can resist that kind of wind gust."

"I'd call it in, but I can't get my radio to work," Clarke added, nodding at the black, plastic contraption he'd sat on the table. "It's just static."

"It'd be the lightning," Hardy mused, tapping a long, pale finger on the radio. "I haven't seen so much since...well, *ever*."

Clarke nodded. "There isn't much the SES or the police can do until the weather clears, and I reckon they'd be tied up with reports coming out of the Ridge. They're just human, after all."

Finn scowled at the sergeant's tone. *Just human.* Magic was great and all, but it made them no better than the *De'ashlide*—the fae name for non-powered people—of this world. Sometimes he wished he wasn't so magical.

"I could scry for him," Vera said to Eloise, "but I can feel the static in the air. It doesn't feel... Well, it kinda feels magical."

There was that word again.

'I know you think you always get the rough end of the stick, but you've always been part of our family.' Kyne's words came back to him, and he blinked. They'd been

standing in the bottom of the iron ore pit, the *ash'strad* spinning between them, and he'd—

"I'll go," Finn said, looking up. The Exiles stared as if they'd just noticed him sitting there.

"This isn't an ordinary storm, is it?" Eloise's cheeks drained of colour. "Siora did more than speed it up, didn't she?"

"Her parting gift," he murmured. She was always a little too vindictive for her own good. It was just another way of saying she embodied the cliché of the evil Unseelie.

"This is fae magic?" Vera asked, her eyes wide. "I thought it felt strange."

"It's unusually strong," Finn added. "The seal helped amplify her powers. I can pass easily with a little...*finesse*."

Eloise strode towards him. "Finn—"

He held up his hand to stop her. He'd taken all the hugs and kind words he could for the day. She'd given him more benefit of the doubt than he deserved. Siora was wrong about them using him. This was how he paid back his debt to Lor'Iyslar while being worthy of the Exiles calling him *family*. He had the power to find Kyne, so that's what he'd do.

"*A'ladrei*," Eloise said, her accent a little off. She grimaced as if she realised. "Did I say it right?"

"Yes." Finn nodded. "Just about."

Without another word, he turned and opened the door, heading out into the storm.

As he crossed the yard, the wind howled as if it were full of the tortured souls of the damned.

Since awakening, Finn had done little more than cast illusions and tame the smallest of beasts—snakes, lizards, and the odd bird of prey. Nothing significant and nothing to counteract the magic of his own people, but now it was time, whether he liked it or not.

His body felt strange as he called on his deeper magic…his birthright. As it filled his being, he sensed the ever-present seal and the Old One beneath, just beyond his grasp, yet fuelling his entire existence.

Finn's magic was as natural to him as breathing, yet it carried a staleness—the same smell that'd lingered in his home after months of being away from it. Cold familiarity.

His magic surged as he pushed it outwards, parting the wind and rain, creating a little bubble around himself. It cast away most of the weather, though he was still buffeted by the wind as he crossed the highway and was soaked with rain as he turned onto the track.

Mud squelched underfoot and his heels flicked the brownish-red clay up the backs of his legs, but he was past caring about his looks anymore. He'd lost almost everything the moment Siora left, but he wasn't about to lose the last thing he cared about—his Exiled family.

"You could've had this, too, Siora," he told the wind. "You and the others. But I wasn't enough, was I?"

The wind didn't answer, even though he felt her all around.

"*Ore di ah'anith an,*" he said, echoing her last words. "*E'shrilae.*"

Goodbye.

CHAPTER 9

When Finn Oreah'anza found the spent *ash'strad* in the courtyard of his ancestral home, he knew it was over.

He'd found the silver orb laying askew on the cobblestones, shining despite the lack of magic it contained. A shaft of unseasonable sunlight fell upon it, beckoning him closer...but he didn't need to clearly see the *ash'strad* to understand what it meant.

His family, his friends, his people...they were all gone.

He'd find no bodies, no traces that they'd ever been here. No one would carve their stories into *lor'ashlar*, he'd bury no ashes underneath, and his family wouldn't ascend to the next life.

It was brutal retaliation for the crimes he'd committed against the Seelie, a final, destructive blow designed to end a bloody rebellion.

He'd stopped one single step through the

portcullis, his silver eyes trained on the *ash'strad*, unresponsive as a dozen *Shr'lei de Delei'an*—Blades of the Queen—surrounded him.

Twelve swords at his throat. Twelve of the mightiest Seelie *Shri'danann* binding his magic. Twelve assassins. Twelve divine harbingers of justice.

It was a wonder they hadn't sent more.

Ultimately, that's how he found himself laying in the mud at the base of an unknown tree, in a cold world starved of magic.

Banished.

Exiled.

Condemned.

Alone.

How many souls had he damned in the name of power? *Countless.*

At first, the flow of magic from Lor'Iyslar was enough to sustain him—enough for him to keep his mind and remember what he'd done.

The people of this world were strange to him. They saw his coloured hair and silver eyes and called him a demon—an evil creature they feared would steal their souls. After that, he had used illusions to hide the truth of what he was.

The humans, as they were called, had no magic of their own. Only a select few seemed to be more. They had their own name for that, too—*witch*. Finn found them distrusting, closed-off, and elitist. He often found those qualities in the Unseelie, but it was a poor comparison.

Occasionally Finn would see another fae amongst the drab peoples of the green and grey land called Ireland. Silver eyes would shimmer through thick illusions, but the fae behind them never approached. *Were they other exiles? Had they come through the portals willingly?* Those questions always went unanswered and if they recognised him for the things he had done, he never knew that, either.

His existence was reduced to scavenging for scraps of magic on the edges of human society, deceiving feeble minds for gritty bread and lodging under the eaves of ruined outhouses.

How the mighty Finn Oreah'anza had fallen.

Trying to find the way towards redemption, he wandered the rolling hills and the craggy cliffs of Ireland for a decade, but the path never revealed itself. Always alone, the shadow of night reminded him of the desolation he'd caused in his home world. Crumbing, smoking ruins filled his dreams, the screams of innocents echoing in his magical blood, travelling through the open portals guarded by the witch's sacred hawthorn trees.

During the first few years, Finn called for his family during the small hours of the morning, but they never replied. And he called for Siora, never knowing if she'd been executed or sent to Ireland.

And that was how Finn lived, wandering alone until the day the portals slammed shut.

As the last scraps of fae magic drained from the Earth, he felt the witches shine like beacons in the darkness. Bright sparks of life his desperate heart desired to consume above all else, but he knew taking the light into himself meant their deaths. To live, he needed their magic. To live, he needed to kill.

But hadn't he taken enough lives? Whole cities had fallen to his command...and his own hand.

This was his punishment.

Starvation. Desolation. Eternal damnation.

Without magic, he would devolve, his mind twisting and his body withering.

Until that moment, he'd been pushing away the word for the thing he'd been struggling with. For ten years, he'd felt it deep in his heart, haunting his dreams, drowning him in his sleep.

Remorse.

He felt it now—every inch—and that's why he sealed himself away in cold darkness, deep underneath Ireland where he would suffer his torment alone. Where the witches would be safe.

Unable to die, he'd devolve into a twisted creature, his mind lost and his sanity gone.

And there he would stay for all time.

It was only fair.

"Finn."

His eyes opened and he saw her in the darkness, her silver eyes shining as her blue hair fell about her face.

Siora.

"Finn, it's time to wake."

He'd searched for her amongst the drabness of this world for a decade, but she was gone. She was a dream.

"Finn, it's me... Siora."

He didn't feel the connection to his magic until she laid her hands on him.

"Siora?" he croaked. "Is this a dream?"

"*No,*" she whispered. "It is real."

He was awake? If he was returning to himself, then the portals must have reopened.

He felt strong as he rose—though his clothes were reduced to ash and his midnight blue hair had matted together—and Siora's hands gave warmth to his long dormant bones.

"I've been searching for you for a long time," she murmured, helping him stand. "The world awaits, *da val'ash.* Come."

Siora led him out of the dank darkness towards the light, her hand warm in his. Her magic fed into his starved body, coaxing his foggy mind to awaken, even as the air filled his lungs.

Then he saw the sky and ocean. They were still there, just as he'd left them.

They stood together at the mouth of the cave,

watching the waves crash against the cliff below. The water raged as the caps foamed white, the pure, unrestrained power of the ocean sucking the saltwater back down into the deep.

"Breathe," Siora said, her voice familiar yet alien to his ears.

Finn filled his lungs several times and blinked as the wind rushed around him. The world had regained its focus, and when he felt steady on his feet, they made their way down the cliff to the beach.

He stood in the ocean and closed his eyes, the waves crashing around his waist and the sand dragging out from under his feet. The smell of salt and rotting kelp filled his nose—the raw scent of life—but he still felt numb. It had nothing to do with the icy temperature of the water, and as intoxicating as the wind felt on his bare skin, Finn still carried the same feeling he had when he closed himself in that cave.

Remorse.

He was alive again and his magic was returning, but at what cost? What had this world suffered so he might live again?

Finally, Finn turned and waded back to shore where Siora dutifully waited on the sand.

Threads of her purplish-blue hair had worked themselves out of their tight braid and trailed across her face, but she didn't lift a hand to tuck them behind her ear.

Finn picked up the clothes she'd brought for him

and began to dress, the seawater soaking into the unfamiliar material.

"How long has it been?" he asked, his toes digging into the damp sand. "How long since the portals closed?"

Siora glanced away, her expression troubled. "A thousand years."

He felt his heart drop. *A thousand years?*

"You're taking it far better than I had anticipated."

"As opposed to what?"

"The Finn I remember would have shouted his disbelief at the wind," she murmured.

The Finn Siora knew had died the moment he stood in the courtyard of his ancestral home and saw the *ash'strad* that had killed his entire family. But he didn't have the heart to tell her that. She seemed unchanged, the fire for rebellion still firmly lit in her heart.

"Come," she said, breaking the tension between them. "I've made a camp out of the wind behind the bluff. It'll be warmer there."

She led him away from the cliff and onto a trail leading between a mass of ragged grey rocks. Within the shelter of the wild land, she'd made a camp with a fire pit and had even assembled a tent made out of a strange, colourful fabric.

Finn knelt by the fire and lit it; his hands numb as he struck the flint. After a dozen attempts, Siora took it from him with a sigh, then proceeded to make short work of stoking a fire.

"Sit," she commanded, speaking in fae, which sounded unfamiliar. "Let me see if I can do something with that hair." When he sat, she ran her fingers over his head and sighed. "What a mess... I think it's best we cut it all off."

"No," Finn said, pulling away.

"Still vain, I see."

"Everything else may be gone, but the hair still grows on my head. I want to keep it."

She shrugged. "Suit yourself."

The fire crackled and shone with threads of blueish-green as the flames consumed the saltiness in the burning driftwood. Finn stared into the glow as Siora worked with the matted mess on his head. She used a pair of shiny silver scissors to cut and a black comb to pull, sending sharp tugs of pain through his scalp, though he didn't complain.

"This world has changed in so many unbelievable ways," she said as she worked. "I will guide you once you're strong enough. You will see the machines the humans have created. Things that move and fly without magic."

"Machines?" He raised his head, earning himself another painful tug on his hair.

"Devices made from metal and plastic. Machines to take people places—cars, aeroplanes, trains. Machines to do work in gardens and farms. Machines to send and gather information called computers. They use a thing called science to power their world."

"Not magic..." This new world sounded more alien to him than the Ireland of the past, which made him wonder aloud, "Where did you go when you first came here?"

"When they sent me here, I must have arrived at a different portal to you. I was alone and no one else followed. Soon after, I found some other exiled Unseelies, and we lived together for a time, trying to assimilate with the humans—the Irish. The witches knew what were were, of course, but the humans did not. Magic was hidden here, as you know, and still is. We are the outsiders here." Not like the *De'ashlide*—the non-magical fae—of their world. Everything was reversed. "I tried to live the best I could, all while searching for a way back through the portals." She hadn't found a way back, that much he knew. She set down the scissors. "There. I think that will do for now."

Finn ran his wrinkled hand through his hair, his fingers probing the knotted lengths of hair Siora had fashioned for him. "What are they?"

"They're called dreadlocks."

"Do they look good?"

"Yes," she told him, her voice filled with the smile she no doubt wore. "You make everything look good, Finn."

He lowered his hands and massaged his wrinkled skin, feeling like an old man, but it was only a matter of time before his body returned to what it was before. "Do you know why the witches cut us off from Lor'Iyslar?"

"There was some trouble with a witch who wanted to steal all our magic," Siora explained. "There was a terrible war with the covens over it. She was syphoning their magic so she could destroy the hawthorn trees and break into our world. That's why the portals closed. It was the only way they could stop her."

"One witch?" Finn scoffed. "And it took a thousand years to resolve?"

Siora sighed. "Their problem created the craglorn."

His brow creased. "Craglorn?"

"That's what they call us in their language, the creatures we became. The lost...and the lonely."

He snorted and threw another stick into the fire, sending a gust of sparks spiralling towards the sky.

"In our crazed states, we hunted them. Whole covens were destroyed, and families were torn apart. Witches went into hiding, and magic was almost lost for good."

"Sounds like it was a problem of their own making," he said darkly, his words striking his heart where it hurt the most. "Are they all open now? The portals?"

Siora's brow creased. "Only one. It's in a place in the north, in a village called Derrydun. It's occupied by the Crescents."

Finn had heard that name before. They were a coven of witches, and powerful ones at that.

"Forget about it," he scoffed. "They'd never let us near it."

"They might...but it's under Seelie control," Siora went on. "They have some kind of treaty."

"Then we can *really* forget about it."

She frowned, her eyes glinting in the firelight. "One day we'll go back. You'll see."

"After what we did?" Finn shook his head, scowling so hard his temples throbbed. "The Seelie still rule after a thousand years, Siora. They'll never forgive the past...nor should they."

"Perhaps, but until then, we still have our lives and I intend to live mine."

Live her life? In this place? It was a wonder they hadn't perished at the hands of the witches, and now that they'd returned to their true forms, their presence would be even more unwelcome. He couldn't see how anything about their circumstances had changed.

"I heard about a place far from here where we can survive," Siora went on, the words tumbling forth in a rush. "In a land the humans call Australia."

"Australia?" The word sounded foreign on Finn's tongue and very far away. *Impossibly* far.

"Yes," Siora said, her eyes lighting up.

He saw her hope, bright and warm—two things he thought he'd never feel again—and he wondered about this mysterious land. Did it hold magic of its own? Was there a hidden path back to Lor'Iyslar there?

"It's a long journey," Siora continued, "across land and many oceans. In the south of this world—farther than any explorer has been in our own—we will find it." She reached into her pocket and retrieved a shining silver stone, then held it out to him. "There is magic at its heart."

Finn stared at the artefact from their home world and wondered how she'd found it. The stone hummed with potent magic that warmed his bones and he began to hope that this mysterious Australia really existed. It could be a new start for the both of them.

"How do you know?" he asked, looking up at her.

"I have faith, Finn." Siora snatched her hand back, taking his tentativeness as skepticism. "There is nothing left for us here; there is no path home. We must look for hope elsewhere."

Finn sighed. He'd only just awoken, but Siora had risked a great deal to find him. He should at least pretend to have hope. "What do you know of this place? This...*Australia*."

Her eyes lit up. "The humans call it a sunburnt land with a beating red heart. There are mountains and rainforests, beaches with white sand and clear blue water. There are strange animals—animals that are found nowhere else—that hop about on two legs, and others climb in trees. The people who lived there first have called that land home for tens of thousands of years. There is magic there, Finn. Lots of it. They found it and nurtured it, and we can live there, too." Her smile widened until even Finn felt her excitement. "Does that not sound beautiful?"

"Yes," he whispered, his resolve cracking. "It does."

"Will you come?" Siora took his hands in hers and pulled him towards her. "*Please*."

"I..." He rubbed his eyes. "I have to think..."

"Forgive me," Siora said, her body tensing. "You've only just awoken, and I've put a heavy burden on you too soon."

"It's fine." He shifted so his body sat flush with hers. "After so long...you're excited. The last time I saw you..." She was in chains, her eyes filled with terror, and he was being hauled towards an open portal. "Perhaps when my magic strengthens."

Siora said nothing, allowing him some time to gather his thoughts. They simply sat together by the fire, watching the unfamiliar stars overhead, the bluff sheltering them from the bitter wind roaring up over the cliffs.

"I searched for you in the beginning," she murmured. "But your illusions were always better than mine."

"I did, too..." He did not know how to tell her how the remorse over their actions had eaten him from the inside out. She was always the most passionate about their reckless cause, and he didn't know if she'd understand. Perhaps in time, she might. They'd loved each other once, but a thousand years and a million spent lives had passed since then. They would have to start over again in this new world.

They could be happy once more, and he could atone. Couldn't he?

And for the first time since he'd come to Earth, Finn felt a glimmer of hope bloom in his twisted heart.

"Yes," he told her. "I'll go to Australia with you."

CHAPTER 10

Kyne lay in the mud, the stinging rain relentless as it beat down on him.

The gum tree had pinned his legs to the ground when it'd fallen, and no matter how hard he tried, he couldn't budge it. His elemental powers were still firmly out of reach.

His left leg felt numb, and he knew something wasn't right.

Another crack of lightning lit up the bruised sky and he swore, his heart beating double-time.

He was contemplating the highs and lows of his life, and how his obsession over opal had led him to becoming stuck underneath a gum tree in the middle of nowhere, when a face appeared above him.

"*E'dreha.*"

"Finn?" Kyne stared up at the fae.

His silver eyes shone in the dreary glow of the storm. "You've got yourself into a pickle, haven't you?"

"Pickle? I wouldn't have chosen that word, but *sure*."

Finn snorted and slid his hands underneath the tree. He heaved, his face turning red and his muscles straining, but the gum didn't move. He said something in his native language that sounded a lot like a string of foul words, then tried again.

"Stop," Kyne said. "It's too heavy."

"Your magic?"

He shook his head. "I can't reach it. There's something about this storm—"

"Of course," Finn declared, throwing his hands in the air. "*The gift that keeps on giving.* Take some of this!"

Kyne blinked the water from his eyes as the wind and rain eased, and he looked up at the fae. "Did you...?"

"Try now."

Relieved to find his connection to his magic restored, Kyne placed his palms on the trunk of the gum. Instead of lifting the tree, he funnelled his abilities to where they were strongest—the earth—and melted away the hard rock beneath the mud and sand. His legs sank as the pressure eased, and the moment he was loose, he felt a rush of hot blood, followed by a sharp, stinging pain.

Letting out a hiss, he held his breath and gritted his teeth, then hauled himself out from under the tree.

Finn grabbed Kyne's arm and pulled him the rest of the way, helping him to his feet. The elemental hopped as pain shot up his leg and clapped a hand on Finn's shoulder to steady himself.

The fae glanced downward but said nothing about it. "What do we do about that monstrosity?" he asked, pointing to the ute.

It hadn't budged, but the rear tyres were stuck in mud up to the rims. The usual beautifully hued ochre dirt of the outback had turned into a thick, clay-like sludge that stuck to everything like superglue. Getting the ute out of it would take a miracle.

Kyne shifted his weight onto his right leg, not wanting to look at the damage the tree had done on the other. He felt it well enough and would worry about it once they got back to Solace. At least it didn't feel broken.

"We have to dig out the wheels and make a stable surface under the tyres. They need grip to get out of the mud."

Finn's nose curled. "Dig?"

"*Yeah*. Unless you've got another magic trick up your fancy fae sleeve you're not telling me about."

The fae narrowed his eyes and looked down at Kyne's leg. "I'm not carrying you all the way back."

"Then we dig."

Fortunately, Kyne had a shovel in the tray. They took turns at digging, Finn more than Kyne.

The rain and wind raged around them in a thick squall, but Finn's magic kept the worst of it at bay. They still got soaked through, but at least they weren't knocked sideways as they shoved broken branches and bits of rock under each of the ute's tyres.

Kyne had never needed recovery tracks the whole time he'd been mining out here—he don't have to, considering his elemental powers—but now he was regretting not having a set. The first thing he'd do when the storm was over was go online and order some...and get Wally to help him install a winch on the front bull bar.

"Get in and try it now," Finn said.

"I don't think I can." Kyne leaned against the side the ute and shook his head. "That tree got my leg pretty good."

"Do I have to do everything around here?" Finn clucked his tongue and got into the driver's seat.

Kyne followed, sitting in the passenger seat, glad to be out of the rain. His clothes were soaked and muddy, but ruining the upholstery was the last thing on his mind.

Eying Finn as the fae studied the dashboard, he asked, "Can you drive?"

"How hard can it be?" Finn looked at the gear stick, then at the steering wheel, then turned on the left indicator. Clicking filled the cab as he grinned at the elemental. "See?"

Kyne coughed. "Let me rephrase that... Can you drive a manual?"

"A manual what?"

A tense crash-course on the clutch, gears, and

accelerator followed as the storm continued to howl around the ute. Afterwards, Kyne said a silent prayer that he, and the transmission, would make it back to Solace intact.

Finn stalled the engine three times before he got the hang of the clutch, but when the ute finally gained traction, they shot up and out of the mud like a rocket. Kyne winced as the gearbox crunched as the fae shifted into second, and they were on the move.

They bumped along the track, Finn's magic keeping the worst of the storm out of their way, but his driving was terrible. It felt like he was aiming for every pothole, each jerk of the ute sending a stab of pain up Kyne's leg.

"Thanks for coming to find me," the miner said.

"I couldn't leave you out here. Eloise wouldn't have forgiven me."

Kyne's heart twisted at the mention of Eloise. *She must be out of her mind.*

"Don't worry about our little desert pea," Finn added. "She's tucked up, all safe and sound at Blue's with the others."

Kyne heaved a sigh of relief. "I've never seen you use your magic like that," he said. "Only your illusion at the camp and when you charm your pets."

Finn sat huddled over the steering wheel like a little old lady, watching the track. He didn't reply, which was a standard Finn response, but still, something felt a little off.

"You need to change up a gear," Kyne said, grimacing at the distressingly high revs in the engine.

"Oh, right." The gearbox crunched and whirred.

"Is everything all right?"

Finn sighed and glanced at him out the corner of his eye. Something was definitely up.

"The storm?"

"Siora's parting gift." He rolled his eyes as they bounced over another hole. "They didn't want to be followed."

The fae had left? This was news to Kyne, but he'd been out at Black Hole Mine for a week. "When did this happen?"

"This morning. I tried to talk them out of it, but as you can see, it didn't end well. Which is why I'm out here ruining a perfectly good shirt instead of the vampire."

Kyne raised his eyebrows, but could he really be *that* surprised? After all they'd been through, it seemed like an inevitability. "Why didn't you go with them?"

Finn snorted. "Have you already forgotten what you said to me in that pit? *Typical.*"

Kyne could never forget standing at the bottom of that hole in the iron ore, the silver *ash'strad* spinning impossibly fast, the magical charge building. He'd felt the destructive power vibrate in his bones and rattle the fillings in his teeth. But Finn'd had the worst of it and still put everything on the line to save Solace, the Exiles, and the fae. Despite his surly disposition, Finn had done a lot for them, and even if he'd never done any of those things, he'd still be a part of their supernatural family, no questions.

No, Kyne would never forget that moment. He couldn't.

"No," he snapped, "I haven't. I meant every word, but they're your people, Finn." His last connection to the world he'd been exiled from, his ancestral home.

"Siora's proud," Finn said after a moment. "She's Unseelie to the bone."

Kyne braced himself in the passenger seat as the ute bumped along the track. He understood. She'd made Finn choose—his people or the Exiles—even though she knew what was at stake. The threat of the Old Ones bore down on them all, but Siora was doing what she believed was right for her people. It didn't matter if Kyne or anyone else thought it was wrong.

"Do you think they're going back to Ireland?" he wondered. "They need magic, right?"

"I doubt it," Finn replied. "The fae have a long memory. Siora wouldn't risk it."

What had Finn done to get sent to Earth? What crime was so bad that he'd been exiled to another world where he would be starved of magic? Kyne didn't know, but did it really matter? The Finn he knew now was the one he cared about. They all had pasts, but they also had their present, where actions mattered more.

"Then another place of power," the miner murmured. "I wonder where?"

Finn's hands tightened around the steering wheel. "Who cares? Siora made her choice and the others bought into it. I tried to stop them, but..." He glared out the windscreen at the storm beyond. The wipers flicked back and forth, the rubber blades squeaking across the glass.

"What will happen to them if they don't find another source of magic?" Kyne almost didn't want to ask, but he felt he had a duty.

"In this world, when a fae reaches their limits, our magic is the first thing to go."

"Then what happens?"

"We...*devolve*."

For a moment, the pain in Kyne's leg dulled in comparison to the thoughts that flashed through his head. "Devolve into what?"

"Mindless monsters with black, leathery hides, clawed talons, and a hunger for magic. Demons. *Nightmares*. The Irish witches call them the craglorn."

"Craglorn?"

"It's an old word derived from their language, Irish Gaelic." Finn tightened his grip on the steering wheel. "It means the lost and the lonely."

Kyne looked out the passenger side window to hide his frown. He knew Finn feared for Siora and the fae. They'd taken a magical artefact with them, but they also ran the risk of turning into one of those craglorn creatures if it wasn't enough. And who knew what chaos they could cause in the human world if they did.

"You can't fix everything," Finn muttered.

"How do you know what I was thinking?"

"I don't have to. It's the kind of person you are—you lead and you fix. That's why you went to the elementals, wasn't it?"

Kyne tensed.

"You went because you thought you were broken," Finn went on. "That's why you lost your magic when you came back."

"What's your point? I thought we were talking about *you*?"

"It's easier to talk about *you*. You were never broken, Kyne...you were insecure."

Somehow, the miner thought Finn was talking about his own problems. He was just using Kyne as a way to mask it.

"*You're* not broken, Finn," he said as the track smoothed out.

The lights of Solace shimmered through the heavy rain as Finn wrenched the wheel to the right, turning the ute onto the highway so sharply, it was a wonder they didn't go up onto two wheels.

That was his answer, the miner supposed.

As Finn parked at an odd angle outside the pub, Kyne pulled the handbrake.

Better safe than sorry.

Eloise stood by the window in the pub, her anxious gaze glued to the chaotic scene outside.

The storm hadn't eased since Finn had left. Rain lashed the highway so fiercely, she could hardly see the garage that sat a mere forty metres away. The wind blew the dense droplets in all directions—sideways, horizontal, and even back up again.

Her thoughts darkened with every passing squall. Kyne was out there somewhere. Her head was stuffed to the brim with visions of him trapped down in the Black Hole Mine as it flooded with raging water, bogged in his ute, struck by lightning, or blown into the sky Mary Poppins style. She even had visions of him being washed away in a torrent of muddy flood water that gushed down one of the many deceptively dry creek beds around Solace.

And now Finn was out there, too. *If he got hurt...* The fae was having one hell of a day.

"I've never seen a storm like it," Blue murmured, joining her by the window.

"There's going to be one hell of a mess that'll need cleaning up after this," Wally mused. "I reckon I'll have to pump water out of more than a few holes around here."

"We'll make sure your mine is dry by the next full moon," Hardy said.

"At least the power hasn't cut out," Clarke offered, trying to make his presence useful.

Eloise barely registered the conversation. She wrung her hands and shifted her weight from foot to foot. If they weren't back in the next five minutes, she was going out there. She was an elemental after all, and she had experience with both spirit and earth elements. How hard could it be to wrangle a little water and air?

Just as she was about to wrench herself away from the window, a pair of yellow headlights broke through the gloom, and Kyne's ute pulled into the yard at an odd angle.

"They're back!" she cried as Finn got out the driver's side and went around to help Kyne out of the other door.

In the blink of an eye, Hardy flew out the pub and was beside them, helping the fae bring the miner inside. Their sodden boots squeaked on the linoleum floor as they trailed water and mud behind them.

Eloise sobbed as she flung her arms around Kyne, not caring that he was soaked to the bone and caked with a layer of ochre clay.

"I'm okay," the miner murmured. "I'm okay."

"I was so worried," she wailed. When he flinched, she realised he was hurt. His jeans were torn and bloodied, and her heart twisted. *Your leg!*

"It's just a scratch. Promise."

"Liar."

"Nothing a bit of vampire intervention can't fix," he whispered in her ear.

"He got himself stuck under a tree in the mud," Finn declared, sitting at the table. "Has anyone got a towel? I need to dry my hair before it goes mouldy."

"Your dreadlocks can go mouldy?" Drew asked, earning himself a swift kick from Vera. "*Ow!*"

"Now is not the time," the witch hissed.

Hardy grasped Kyne underneath the arms and helped the elemental hop over to a chair.

"Here." Clarke pulled over another chair and eased Kyne's leg up. "Keep it elevated."

Eloise sat beside Kyne as Hardy tore away the damp leg of the miner's jeans.

Vera was already beside him, her gaze studying the wound. "We've got to clean out the dirt," the witch said, clucking her tongue. "What were you doing? Wallowing around in the mud? You're lucky you didn't sever an artery."

Eloise swallowed hard as she saw how bad it really was. The tree had torn a fifteen-centimetre gash across Kyne's thigh, leaving behind a puncture that still looked fresh—definitely not just a *scratch*. It looked like the worst of the bleeding had slowed, but her stomach rolled at the sight of it. Either Kyne was in shock, or he had one hell of a strong disposition.

Blue rushed into the kitchen and came back with a plastic tub, a bucket, and some towels, one of which he tossed to Finn. "Here."

"I was down in the mine on the jackhammer," Kyne explained as Blue positioned the tub underneath the miner's leg. Eloise noted Kyne was doing everything in his power to not look down. "The storm was on me before I knew it was even happening. By the time I'd secured the site and got onto the trail, it was a muddy mess. The ute got bogged well and good, but when I got out to get it unstuck, I realised my powers were out of reach."

"You couldn't use your magic?" Eloise asked, raising her eyebrows as the publican dumped the bucket of warm water over his torn-up leg.

He shook his head, hissing as the water washed the grit out of his wound. "That's when lightning struck the tree. Came right down on top of me." He looked over at the fae. "If it wasn't for Finn, I'd still be out there." He nodded once in that stoic, sharp way men did when they didn't want to show their feelings. "Thanks, mate."

Finn shrugged and picked up Clarke's beer and drank the whole thing. Considering he hated the stuff, it was a miracle it all went down and stayed down.

"That should do it," Blue said, putting the bucket down. "Clean as a whistle."

Hardy shifted his chair closer, the legs scraping across the lino. "Allow me."

Eloise looked away as Hardy bit his wrist. She trusted the vampire with her life—and vice versa—but she didn't like how his eyes turned all black when he tasted blood. It creeped her out to see him in his predatory state.

"Christ, that stings," Kyne hissed as the vampire went about healing his leg.

Eloise grasped his hand and finally lowered her gaze. Hardy's blood had definitely coated the gash, but nothing was happening. "Shouldn't it be doing something by now?"

"It isn't working," Hardy said, frowning. "That's never happened before."

"What a raging bitch," Finn declared, rolling his eyes as he patted his dreadlocks dry with Blue's towel. Some of his usual Unseelie abrasiveness was beginning to shine through his melancholy, which Eloise took as a *good* sign.

"I take it you mean Siora," Vera said with a sigh.

"She knew I was out there?" Kyne asked. "This is her magic?"

Finn shrugged. "I doubt she thought she'd get that lucky."

"I don't think I'll ever understand fae," Drew muttered.

"Me neither," Wally said in agreement.

Clarke coughed nervously. "I'm not sure I understand any of it, but at this point, I'm just going with it."

Eloise watched the exchange as a worried pang thrummed in her heart. She couldn't believe that Finn actually meant what he was saying. It was clear he cared deeply for Siora—maybe not recently, but in the past there had undoubtedly been something between them.

"The storm is still screwing with our magic, isn't it?" Kyne asked.

"Inside, outside," Finn drawled, "it's all the same. You don't have to get wet to go for a swim."

"Then we'll try again after it passes," Hardy said.

Drew held up his hand. "I don't think that will help." He sniffed the air. "You smell like blood, but it has the sickly tang of fairy about it."

"Sickly?" Finn asked incredulously. "We smell like rose petals, *thank you very much*."

"He's right," Vera interjected before they could kick off into one of their trademark sarcastic arguments. "Supernatural loophole." She pointed to the storm outside. "You got that wound from a tree that was struck by lightning generated by Siora's magic, then it was soaked in charged-up rain and mud. I'm afraid it's going to have to heal the old-fashioned way."

Kyne groaned and tightened his grip on Eloise's hand. "*Perfect.* I've got a whole load of opal out there just waiting to be cut."

"*Kyne Brady!*" Eloise practically shrieked. "Your leg is torn apart, and you're worried about bloody *opal*?"

"Don't worry," Vera said. "I've got all kinds of poultices that'll help, but it'll need stitching first."

"It won't help my opal," he grumbled, looking a

little green. The colour must have been triggered by the word 'stitching.'

"Forget the opal," Wally said, trying to defuse the situation. "No one will be getting out there any time soon. The track will be washed out *and* a ruddy mess for at least a week, if not longer. That's if the weather holds."

"I think you're rich enough, mate," Drew drawled. "We could do with some help sweeping up tomorrow."

Clarke raised his eyebrows. "Rich?"

"Kyne owns three quarters of the town," Vera said to Clarke. "He comes with an inbuilt opal detector, and it's one hundred percent accurate."

"That's right…" the sergeant said. "Earth elemental."

"Oh, screw the opal," Eloise exclaimed. "It isn't any good to you or anyone else if you kill yourself digging for it."

"Never a truer word spoken," Clarke murmured with a nod. He'd know; he policed Lightning Ridge— the next closest opal fields to Solace.

"I think the weather's easing," Blue declared, breaking the deteriorating conversation. "I can see across the highway now."

"I think you're right, Blue," Vera said loudly, holding up her hand where a small drop of steely-blue magic began to gather in her palm. "I feel less numb than before."

"Someone will have to go check on the other

miners," Kyne added. "They should've all cleared out, but I want to make sure."

"I can get some officers to do welfare checks when the radios come back online," Clarke offered.

"Or Hardy can just run to every claim and back in thirty minutes," Drew said with a roll of his eyes. "*Amateur.*"

The sergeant scowled at the dingo. "Can I do *anything* around here?"

"You look pretty," Finn declared. "Do that."

Eloise let out a sharp sigh and Kyne squeezed her hand. Things were bad enough with the storm and the constant attacks from the black mountain; rivalries between the Exiles was the last thing she wanted to deal with.

She hadn't told everyone the truth yet, but from the way Drew had been looking at her, she suspected Vera had already spilled the beans to the dingo. That meant everyone knew, yet they were still arguing about opal, money, and testosterone levels.

At that moment, Eloise wished Coen was here.

"After all these years, this is the first time I've seen any of the fae use magic like this," Hardy said. "Why don't you?"

Thankfully the conversation had taken a turn, but Eloise still wasn't sure if it was a *good* turn.

"It's different here," Finn replied with a shrug. "Magic from our world is best, that's why it was a risk to leave Ireland. The open portal was our link to

Lor'Iyslar. The magic here is from elsewhere, so not as good, but good enough."

Eloise realised the fae's powers will never be as strong as they were in their own world. And for Finn, the memory of the things he'd done in his past was stopping him from using them beyond small necessities, like the illusion around the camp and his pet snakes. Maybe it was like that for the other fae, or in Siora's case, perhaps it was simply pride.

"So," she began, glancing at Kyne, "her magic blocked all of ours?"

"Yeah," the miner murmured. "That's why I couldn't get out from under that tree."

Suddenly, Eloise was glad she didn't head out into the storm.

"Hey," Clarke said. "I think the rain has stopped."

Eloise rushed to the window, followed by Vera, Drew, and Hardy.

Outside, the weather had eased. She could see the garage across the highway, glistening against the black sky. The wind and rain had died down, leaving muddy puddles and broken bits of gum tree strewn across the yard.

Just like it'd started, the storm had finally blown itself out.

CHAPTER 11

The boab tree was about the only thing that'd fared well during the storm.

Eloise and Drew stood in the shadow of its robust trunk, the eerie blue sky glowing overhead—a stark contrast to the sodden ground the storm had left behind.

Red clay streaked across the highway, puddles gathered in every dip and divot, cracks formed in flaky surfaces as the sun dried out the topmost layers of earth, and many of the shrubs and gums had been stripped of their leaves. The spinifex grass seemed untouched—the plant's spiky barbs still as vicious as ever.

Eloise thought about Finn and Kyne out in that weather—the savage wind, biting rain, and the unpredictable lightning—and frowned.

Finn had risked himself *again* for the Exiles, and now he was alone. Well, not exactly alone, *alone*; he was currently up at her and Kyne's dugout. The miner was helping the fae set up her little motorhome where he reluctantly agreed to stay for a few days while they cleaned up after the storm. Whether he was going to stay in town or not was a discussion for another day.

As for Kyne, he was annoyed that he couldn't help her and Drew with the seal. Vera had stitched up his leg and slathered it in stinky goop, then ordered him to rest. Eloise quickly learned that rest wasn't a word that inhabited Kyne's vocabulary. He already had a pair of crutches and was clacking around town trying to be useful...which he was not.

Eloise looked down at the trapdoor hidden at the base of the boab, hoping the seal had come through the deluge without a scratch. Siora had used her magic to dissuade the Exiles from stopping the fae from leaving, but had she intended the chaos that'd followed? It was difficult to say, what with the tentacle monster manipulation going on.

"Here goes nothing," Drew said, wrapping his hands around the handle.

Metal groaned as the dingo-shifter hauled the trapdoor open, sticky clay shifting as the hatch rose.

"Christ!" He waved a hand in front of his face. "Get a whiff of *that*."

Eloise wrinkled her nose. "Is it good or bad?"

"Smells..." he sniffed again, "damp."

"*Great*."

Drew stuck a leg into the black hole, feeling for the

ladder with his boot. "Wait here a sec." He scurried down into the darkness, then a splash echoed up and out of the shaft. "Um..." his voice followed, "I think a bit of water got it after all."

"How much is a bit?"

"Uh...you're going to need to put your boots out to dry after this. And your socks...and your jeans."

Eloise was on her third pair of steel-capped boots since she'd arrived in Solace. What was a fourth, other than another eighty bucks out of her bank account? More business for Vera, that's what.

Shoving the torch she'd brought into the waistband of her jeans, she climbed down the ladder. She let out a startled cry once she landed in the knee-deep water. "Bloody oath, that's cold!"

Drew's eyes shone in the semi-darkness, and he chuckled. "Don't worry, your feet will go numb in a minute, then you won't feel a thing."

"Your logic astounds me, Drew," Eloise said as she retrieved the torch from her jeans. "It really does." She raised the torch and shone it down the tunnel, trying not to let her teeth chatter as coldness seeped into her legs.

"I'll lead." Drew held out his hand and laughed as she swatted it away. "Suit yourself."

The water was already starting to stagnate as the musty smell of damp earth filled her nose as they sloshed down the tunnel. She stumbled a few times, glad the shifter was there to grab her before she fell face-first into the sludge.

Eloise knew something had changed the moment they left the manmade passage and entered the cave underneath the highway—and it wasn't just the water level, which had risen to their waists.

She pressed the heel of her palm over her stomach and grimaced. "Do you feel that?"

"Like I'm going to chuck up half my stomach lining?" the dingo asked wryly. "*Yep*."

"I need some antacid." The water dragged at her legs as she took a step towards the seal, shining the torch into the depths. It was too murky to see much of anything, but she could make out a hint of bluestone. "Can you see anything?"

"Yeah." Drew grabbed her arm. "I wouldn't go any closer."

Water sloshed around her, and she looked up at him. "Why not?"

Her heart twisted at his troubled expression.

"Something's leaking into the water," he told her. "Looks like...oil. All coloured and swirling."

Eloise followed his gaze but saw nothing except the same murky, brownish-red water they'd been wading in since they climbed into the mine. "Where? I feel plenty nauseous, but I don't see anything."

"I think this is why Coen was teaching me how to *see*," Drew said, his voice echoing off the rock. "I'm going under. Pull me out if something tries to drag me down, okay?"

"Are you sure you want to do that?" Her nose wrinkled. "I'm not sure getting that in your eyes is a good idea."

He shrugged and turned to the seal. Heaving in a gigantic breath, he ducked underneath the surface, bubbles rising in his wake. Water ripped out across the surface, the slosh echoing eerily in the cave.

A pang of nausea threatened her breakfast and she held her breath. *Please don't puke. Please don't puke...*

Drew was only under a few seconds before he surfaced again. Running a hand through his damp hair, the dingo-shifter retched.

"Drew?" She tugged on his damp sleeve. "What is it?"

"I think we better get out of this water."

He didn't have to tell her twice.

Outside, they sat in the sun, with their boots and socks sitting side by side, and let the warmth dry off the dampness. Now that they were out of the water, her stomach felt settled and the nausea was almost gone.

"The seal is cracked," Drew stated, still looking a little green. "Magic is leaking out of it...or at least, I think it's magic."

Eloise leaned her chin on her arms and stared at the side of the *Outpost*. The brickwork was all cracked, the concrete rendering long flaked away under the power of the sun.

Was it the magic of the Old One, or the Old One itself?

"That's what you could see in the water," she said. There was no use vocalising her other fears—Drew understood them as well as she did.

"We should get the water out as soon as we can," he added. "I'll check with Wally to see if he's got a spare pump. Otherwise..."

"Otherwise, what?"

"I'll have to ask *Clarke* to bring in one from the Ridge." He said Clarke's name like it tasted rotten.

"Give the guy a break," Eloise drawled.

"*Sure.*"

Eloise rolled her eyes. "Are you feeling okay? You still look a little rough around the edges."

He shrugged. "I'll be fine."

"I only stood in the water, and I felt like I had a bad bout of gastro. You went under. Maybe you should take a shower first."

"I'll get Wally to hose me down with the pressure washer." He chuckled and ran his hand through his dusty blond hair.

"*Ouch.*" That thing was industrial strength.

"Who needs their top layer of skin, huh?" The shifter stood and picked up his socks and boots. "I better get on it." He held out his hand, but Eloise shook her head.

"I'm going to sit for a moment."

He shrugged. "Suit yourself."

She watched as Drew crossed the road barefoot, trying to focus on how he could walk around the outback without getting third-degree burns on the soles of his feet, rather than the poison leaking out of the magical rock underneath the town.

Looking up at the boab, Eloise wished Coen was with them. He'd know what to do about the cracks.

Coen? Coen, are you there? she called with her mind, reaching out with her magic.

But he didn't answer.

<hr>

"It could've been much worse," Vera said, looking up at the hole in the *Outpost's* roof.

One of the large gums at the back of the building had lost a limb, the end of which was laying on the corrugated iron roof, leaving an impressive dent underneath. There was a hole where the metal had twisted away, resulting in a leak inside the storeroom, but everything else seemed to be intact.

Clarke picked at the damp shelving, peeking into the sodden cardboard boxes. "Have you lost any stock?"

"Those are spare bits for the shelving units," Vera said. "I might have to toss a few boxes, but that's neither here nor there. At least the power didn't cut out. Cleaning out spoiled food is the worst."

"So, no stuffing our faces with melting ice cream?"

"No." She laughed and shook her head. "You look so disappointed."

"As long as there's sprinkles, I'm down for it."

Her grin widened. "I didn't take you for a sprinkles kind of guy."

"I'm full of surprises." He stepped over the puddle on the concrete floor. "Have you got a tarp? I'll get that branch down and cover that hole until you can get someone out here to fix the roof."

Vera waved her hand dismissively. "Oh, don't worry about that. I'll get Hardy up there later. He'll toss that branch down in two seconds flat."

Clarke said nothing, but she caught his frown a split-second before he turned towards the back door.

"Let's go see how the rest of the town fared," she said. "I want to see how much damage that lightning strike did to the windmill. I bet it's cooked."

"Sure."

They emerged into the sunshine; the blue sky eerie after such a turbulent storm the day before. The usually bone-dry, reddish dust felt more like damp sand underfoot and there were actual puddles on the side of the bitumen road.

Resisting the urge to run and jump in each one, Vera held Clarke's arm as her head swam.

"It's muggy out here today," she said, tightening her grip. "Don't you think?"

"A little." He glanced down at her. "Are you all right? You look a little pale."

"Yeah, it's just the weather. I wonder how many mils of rain we got."

"At least a few inches above average, I reckon," Clarke replied.

Across the highway, Vera could already see the ancient windmill had lost two blades and looked a little charred. But the moment she set her right foot onto the white line in the centre of the road, she doubled over and retched. Sharp, stabbing nausea ripped through her stomach, and her head spun.

"Vera?" Clarke wrapped his arm around her waist and used his free hand to brush her wild, curly red hair away from her face. "What is it? What's wrong?"

"It's the seal..." she managed to rasp. "It's right under our feet."

Clarke gasped and looked down at the asphalt, turning a little pale himself. "This isn't normal, is it?"

"No... The storm... It must have..." Vera retched again and jerked out of Clarke's grasp.

She sucked in a deep breath and stumbled towards the *Outpost*. Clarke rushed to her side and helped her up onto the verandah, where she collapsed onto the bench.

"I think I need a bucket," she moaned.

Clarke smoothed her hair away from her face. "That Siora sheila... Her magic was strong enough to do this?"

"Looks like it." If the fae was strong enough to screw with the seal, then maybe it was a good thing they left before the Old One had worked out how to corrupt them. The realisation was a little harsh, but it *was* the fate of the entire world they were trying to secure.

Footsteps crunching on gravel pulled her attention, and she saw Eloise appear around the side of the *Outpost*.

The elemental took one look at her and leapt up onto the verandah. "What's wrong?"

Vera limply waved her hand and pinched the bridge of her nose.

"Something's making her sick," Clarke said. "It hit her the moment we reached the middle of the highway." He cast a dirty look at the road. "That's where the seal is, right?"

"It is," Eloise replied. "Drew and I were just down there."

"The seal?" Vera asked, squinting up at the elemental. She felt a migraine threatening the edges of her brain and pushed at it with her magic. The throb lessened, and she was able to focus on her friend.

"That's what I wanted to talk to you about."

Vera groaned and wrapped her arms around her middle. "The storm messed it up, didn't it?"

"There's a load of water down there," Eloise told them. "The whole thing is submerged. Whatever Siora did to the storm has seeped into the water. It must be reacting to something the seal emanates because I felt like throwing up, too."

Of course, Vera thought. Just like Hardy couldn't heal Kyne's leg, the contaminated storm water was messing with anything magical it came into contact with, including the seal.

"Are you all right now?" Clarke asked.

"I feel fine now I'm out of there," the elemental replied. "But Drew went under to check the seal."

"He felt it, too?"

Eloise nodded. "Yeah, but he was fine once we came out. I told him to take a shower just in case, but he didn't seem fussed."

"Typical bloke," Vera muttered.

"Then why is Vera sick?" Clarke set a protective hand on the witch's shoulder.

"It must be because of the Nightshade." Vera sighed and screwed up her nose. "My susceptibility to the Old One's influence must still be a thing."

"Drew's gone to find Wally. He thinks pumping out the water will help." Eloise looked at Clarke. "We might need your help getting hold of some equipment from Lightning Ridge. I reckon pumps'll be hot property after the rain we've had."

"I reckon I can wrangle something," he told her. "I know the blokes at the hire place."

The radio clipped to his belt began to crackle, then a voice came through. *"Sergeant Clarke, come in. Sergeant Clarke?"*

Eloise sat beside Vera on the verandah as Clarke took a few steps away. The elemental looked as if she wanted to say something, but she paused to listen in on Clarke's conversation.

"I've been waiting it out in Solace," he said. "The storm came down here so fast, it was too dangerous to move. The radios were out, and the phone tower must have gone down."

"It's lucky you didn't try," the cop on the other end replied. "The water rose over the highway. We had road trains and B-doubles lined up for half a kilometre. It was a right mess."

"Any fatalities?"

"None reported; three rescues, though. That weather came out of nowhere. Caught a lot of folks unawares. Lightning hit the *Telstra* tower in town. Cooked it."

Clarke nodded, even though the officer couldn't see him. "How's the traffic situation now?"

"The road is clear enough for traffic to resume, and the backlog is finally clearing. Ford dispatched Gabe and Henderson to monitor."

"All right. I'll be back at the station as soon as I can."

"Understood."

The radio let out a little trill as Clarke clipped it to his belt again. He sounded so official and commanding when he put his police voice on, and it gave Vera a little thrill to know a man like that was her boyfriend.

No one said anything for a long moment. Vera knew Clarke had to go back to the Ridge. It was his duty as a police officer, and what could he do here other than hold a damp face washer against her forehead? He wanted to care for her in the way a man did a woman, but Vera had always been independent—and that wasn't even taking her magic into consideration.

"I'll get you some cold water," Eloise said taking the cue before she disappeared into the *Outpost*.

Clarke sighed, clearly torn. "Vera, you look like death warmed up. I can't—"

"What a thing to say to a woman," she interrupted. "You're supposed to say fever makes my skin glow with youthful radiance."

"*Vera—*"

"Andy, it's okay," she told him. "There's nothing you can do here. There's people out there who need your help more than I do." The expression that passed over Clarke's face hit her where it hurt. "I..." She knew there wasn't anything she could say to make the truth sound any better.

"I know," he said after a moment. "I hate not being able to do anything about this stuff." He knelt before her. "I don't want to leave knowing that thing under the town is making you sick."

"As much as I'd love to play doctor with you, there're innocent people out there who were put in danger by Siora's storm, and you're the sergeant." Vera cupped his face in her hand. "They need you, and I'll be fine. Eloise is here, then Kyne'll have to come back and get his bandages changed, and Blue's just down the street."

"And when Drew hears you're sick, he'll be all over you like a rash."

Vera leaned away and scowled. "*Seriously?*"

"Yeah, that was a cheap shot." He ran his hand over his face and sighed. "I'm sorry. I'm just…"

"I know." She attempted her best smile, even though she felt like vomiting *Exorcist*-style. "I'm feeling better already. I just have to stay away from the road until the water gets pumped out, that's all."

"All right…" Clarke didn't look entirely convinced, but he seemed to accept her explanation. "If you need that pump, let me know."

"I will." She kissed him on the lips, lingering as long as her fragile stomach would allow.

Eloise emerged as the muddy police 4WD pulled out onto the highway and roared off towards Lightning Ridge.

"You're not feeling any better, are you?" she asked, handing a bottle of icy water to the witch.

"Nope." Vera's hand tightened around the plastic, and it made a crinkling sound that echoed in the stillness.

"Then I ought to tell you the bit I left out…"

"You don't have to," Vera said, twisting the cap off the bottle. The tabs clicked as the seal broke like an oddly relevant metaphor. "I already know."

CHAPTER 12

Kyne leaned against the door of Eloise's van, watching as Finn poked about inside.

The fae opened and closed every drawer, looked in the shower cubicle, opened the toilet seat cover, and even sat on the driver's seat.

"Our little desert pea used to drive this monster?" he asked, grasping the steering wheel.

"Yep. All over the country."

"Hm..." Finn looked over the controls and studied the automatic transmission, which was different from the manual in the ute. "She need a special licence?"

"No, it's an auto." The miner chuckled. "Much easier to drive than the ute."

"Interesting..."

"It has everything you need," Kyne went on, seeing the cogs in Finn's head turning in a dangerous direction. "I'll put solar panels out so you'll have power. You won't get any from the panels on the roof under here."

"What do I need power for?"

"You'll need it to work the water pump and the lights, for starters."

His brow knitted together. "Sounds complicated."

"It's not, really. You're just not used to it, that's all."

Scowling, Finn climbed out of the driver's seat and sat on the step with his legs dangling out of the side door.

Kyne took the fae's sour look to mean he didn't like Eloise's van. "You won't hurt her feelings if you don't like it, you know."

"It's a...*nice* van," he muttered. "I'm just not used to...all that. It's been a long time since I slept inside anything other than a tent or a cave. The cave lasted the longest, and it didn't even have a mattress."

Kyne raised his eyebrows, wondering for the first time what the fae's life had been like before he'd settled in Solace. He'd never asked, getting the distinct impression he wouldn't get a straight answer if he did. Finn's business had always been his own and no one else's, that is, until Eloise had arrived, but she had that effect on all the Exiles.

Finn sat up a little straighter and his scowl faded. "She's coming."

Kyne turned but couldn't see anyone. "Who? Eloise?"

The fae nodded. "Can smell her coming a mile off. Isn't that an elemental thing?"

"Uh...no?"

"*Awkward*," Finn drawled as Eloise came into view on the path below. "Must be my imagination."

"Is that why you call her desert pea?"

"I don't know what you mean." He smirked, his silver eyes sparkling with Unseelie sarcasm as Eloise came into earshot.

"Hey," she said, joining them in the shade of the carport. "How's the van?"

Finn coughed, then tried to deflect. "There's a problem, isn't there?"

Eloise glanced at Kyne, then back at the fae. "How do you know?"

"Isn't there always another plot twist around here?"

"True," Kyne agreed with a nod.

Eloise sighed. "It's the seal."

"Told you so," Finn muttered.

"The cave is filled with water," she explained. "Drew said he could see something leaking out of the seal, like oil. I couldn't see it, but it made us both sick."

Kyne frowned. "Sick? How do you mean?"

"Like I wanted to throw up my stomach lining and sit on the toilet for a week."

"*TMI*," Finn declared.

"Vera's got it worse," the elemental went on, "and she didn't even go down into the cave. She can feel it above ground."

"Well, it did turn her crazy," Finn declared, stating the obvious. "There's bound to be side effects."

Kyne ignored the fae. "Where is she now?"

"Home working on a spell to try to contain the leak. Drew's gone to find Wally so they can drain the water out, but that's not the half of it..."

"*Here we go*," Finn declared, rolling his eyes.

"The bluestone..." her gaze shifted uncomfortably, "is cracked."

Kyne leaned against the side of the van, taking his weight off his aching leg. It had to happen eventually, right? Eloise's arrival had been the herald of something more than just another Exile joining their ranks. They all knew it. The Old Ones knew it. Coen knew it. They just didn't say it out loud.

Sooner rather than later, they'd have to do something about the seal and the apocalyptic tentacle monster underneath...*permanently*.

"First things first," Kyne said, taking the lead, "we get the water out. *Then,* we assess the damage."

"Spoken like a true miner," Finn declared.

Eloise laughed despite the trouble they all seemed to be in. "I wanted to check on Andante, too. I'm worried the storm might've got through her magic and messed with her. You'll need your bandages changed soon, so I thought you could go stay with Vera?"

"You stay with Vera," Kyne said, knowing she had a gentler hand than he did. "I'll go check on Andante. I know the way."

"But your leg—"

"The bandage doesn't need changing until tonight."

Eloise clucked her tongue. "That's not what I meant."

"I know, but my leg will be fine."

"Take Blue," Finn told them. "He's got a crush on the druidess, and I bet he could carry Kyne in a pinch. I've seen him pick up one of those giant goannas by the tail and throw it across the yard outside the pub."

Kyne and Eloise stared at the fae for a moment, stunned.

"What?" Finn asked, blinking back at them.

"Okay, so I'll go down and check on Vera," Eloise said, acquiescing. "But if you tear those stitches, you'll be in trouble."

Kyne chuckled and waved her off. "Blue will give me a piggyback long before I tear anything."

"Okay, just be back before dinner. You too, Finn." She kissed Kyne on the lips and took off down the path towards Solace.

Finn waited until she was gone and stood. "Speaking of going to check on things... I'm going to see what's left at the camp."

Kyne looked him over and nodded towards the path where Eloise was already out of view. "You heard her, be back by dinner."

"That's not a very specific time."

The miner raised an eyebrow. "It's six."

Finn shrugged and nodded towards the crutches leaning against the van. "Don't worry about me. Worry about yourself."

Kyne sighed and closed the van, the side door whizzing across the runners and driving home with a bang. With all the things to worry about around here, his leg was the least their concern.

Finn looked at what was left of his home away from home and grimaced.

Sodden earth squelched underfoot, the sun doing nothing to dry the mess left behind by the storm. Apart from the torn shreds of his tent, the wind and rain had erased all traces that the fae had ever lived here. Twelve years were just...gone.

Picking through the remains of his belongings, Finn amassed a pile of things that were worth saving, which wasn't amounting to much—a stainless-steel pot, a handful of candles, and some cutlery. The others had taken everything that was worthwhile with them.

He picked up a book, the bloated pages curling the spine. Sighing, he tossed it aside. There was little worth saving, though he already knew that.

Why did you come?

A sharp burst of rage filled his heart, and he kicked the pot as hard as he could, letting out a strangled cry as his foot connected. The pot clattered across the rocky ground, tumbling across the outback pathetically. His magic flared as he grabbed the torn edges of his tent and began wrenching at it, the pegs ripping from the ground. He stumbled as the fabric came loose and his fingers slipped. His boots slid in the mud, and he fell to his knees, his chest heaving.

His vision blurred as Finn fought back the frustrated tears he'd been holding in since Siora and the others had left. The sun dimmed as a cloud raced across its face, and that's when he caught sight of something silver tangled in the mess of this tent.

The spent *ash'strad* lay amongst the tattered fabric, shining ominously, but he chose to focus on the object beside it.

Finn picked up the knife, took it out of its leather sheath, and balanced it on his palm. It lay flat, the eight-inch blade counterbalancing perfectly with the hilt. It was the only thing he'd kept with him from those first days in Ireland. Made of hardened steel and seal bone, it was a fine example of Viking craftsmanship of the time.

Things were tumultuous back then with Viking settlements encroaching on the eastern cost, and the later invasion of the Normans. Kings fought for crowns, and the people suffered all the more for the noble families' lust for ultimate power. It was a correlation to his story that was an unwelcome reminder of his fate.

Closing his fingers around the hilt, Finn slipped the knife back into its sheath.

He couldn't stay here.

He knew that now, but his path wasn't the same as Siora's. A thousand years stuck in darkness had led him towards redemption, but the others had chosen differently. They still blamed the witches—even though the covens that'd closed the portals were long dead—along with the Seelie, who'd used their own brutal tactics against them to end the civil war.

Twelve years had passed since the portal to Lor'Iyslar had reopened, and nothing had changed Siora's beliefs and erased her need for vengeance. Not even the arduous journey to the other side of the world had shifted sentiments amongst the other fae they'd collected along the way. Perhaps all that'd happened since had simply solidified them.

They sure know how to hold a grudge.

It wasn't just his past that prompted him to look elsewhere. Now that the seal had begun to crack, he knew his dependance on its magic would only make things worse for the Exiles, maybe even force the cracks to spread faster than they could be repaired...if they could even be resealed. Then, there was the threat of becoming corrupted by the Old One—he'd felt the entity's true power when the Nightshade had used him as a glorified battery—and it was a thought too terrifying to comprehend. If it got to him, it would wield a power too terrible for this world to bear. The storm Siora conjured was only a taste and look at the damage it'd wrought.

But if he left, his magic would deplete.

That's the whole point, he thought. All those long years ago, he'd dedicated himself to the wrong cause, but now it was time to do the right thing. When he'd been sent to Ireland, he'd only been playing at redemption, swatting around the edges and avoiding the true pain of his past. Now it was time for the real thing, and he was ready.

Looking at the soggy, bloated paperback, he thought about Coen. He wasn't sure what brought the Indigenous man to mind, but perhaps it was all part of the grand design. Who was pulling the strings remained a mystery, but Finn understood he wasn't meant to know everything. No mortal creature was, even those made of magic.

Perhaps he'd find the answers out there amongst the realm Coen called the Dreaming. Answers that'd eluded him for over a thousand years.

Finn picked up a shred of fabric and wrapped the *ash'strad* inside, then slid the knife into the waistband of his trousers. He stood and turned towards the vast emptiness of the Australian Outback—the magical land Siora had described with so much hope twelve years ago on that beach in Ireland—and took his first step.

Finn was going on a walkabout.

The rock sailed into the darkness and landed below with a loud *plop*.

"Can't say I'm surprised," Wally muttered, scowling at the mineshaft.

"It was a storm designed to keep us busy," Hardy replied, his vampire eyes seeing farther into the darkness than Wally's werewolf senses.

They stood at the top of the mine the old mechanic used on full moons, assessing the damage left behind by what the news was calling 'the storm of the century.' If only they knew...

"I've been thinking," Wally said, taking off his hat and wiping his brow. "What if the fae don't find what they're looking for out there? What if they're forced to come back?"

Hardy shoved his hands into his pockets, keeping his expression unchanged. He'd been puzzling over the exact same thing. Siora had made sure to burn all bridges leading back to Solace. She'd destroyed them so thoroughly, there was no way they could come back...even if they wanted to.

"I don't think they will," he said after a moment. "I don't think Siora's pride will allow her to."

"Yeah, well, desperation does strange things to people." Wally snorted and fixed his grease-stained hat back atop his greying head. "If they do show their mugs around here, they won't be handing out daisy chains and singing *Kumbaya*."

"Yes, well, I didn't want to say it out loud." Magic was essential to the fae's survival. If they didn't find their rumoured place of power, they could return to Solace and try to take control of the town by force.

The Exiles had managed to stand against some fairly tough odds up until now, but after witnessing Siora's power, Hardy knew they wouldn't stand a chance against her...and there were eleven more fae who hadn't even lifted a finger to help her. He didn't even think Finn could tip the balance enough to make a difference.

No, if they came back, they wouldn't stand a chance meeting them head-on. They'd have to get dirty. *Real dirty.*

"If they do come back, then we'll just have to do what we've always done," Hardy added. "There's no other option."

Wally didn't have anything to say to that. He knew the odds just as well as anyone.

"First things first," the mechanic said. "I don't want to be running loose on the next full moon—we all remember how that went last time—so we better head back into the garage and get some stuff to sort out this water. The sooner it's out, the sooner I can get down there and check the structural integrity."

Hardy nodded. The whole area was made up of soft

rocks left over from the ancient coral reefs, and that much water could crumble the roof and walls. It didn't matter how many supports Kyne had hammered in down there after the last breach, the whole thing could sink in on itself and bury Wally alive if they weren't careful.

They had a lot of work ahead of them without taking the damage in town into consideration. The list was getting longer than both their arms combined.

"Drew," Hardy said, catching the shifter's scent before he'd even turned around. "How goes our favourite tentacle monster?"

"Not so good," the dingo said, standing by the mineshaft. He peered over the lip and into the darkness, his nose wrinkling. "Filled with water just like your hole, old wolf, but with a few added extras."

"I'm guessing it's not a bonus set of steak knives for the first fifty callers," Hardy drawled.

"If only," he replied. "It's a more generous offer—cracks, leaking magic, and sickness for all."

"I guess you'll be needing my pump, eh?" Wally grumbled.

"Sorry, mate." Drew clapped him on the shoulder. "Tentacle monster trumps werewolf."

CHAPTER 13

Blue walked beside Kyne, the vastness of the outback surrounding Solace opening before them.

"So, we just walk east?" he asked as the miner's crutches made an annoying *clacking* sound every time he took a step.

"Yeah, but don't leave my side."

"Why not?"

"You need my elemental magic to guide you, otherwise, you might get lost."

Blue swallowed hard. "Lost?"

"Last time Eloise and I came out here, the Min Min guided us, but they seem to be a little shy today." Seeing the look on Blue's face, he added, "Don't worry, I remember the way."

"Thank goodness for that." He rolled his eyes. "How do we know we've found her?"

"When we pass through the illusion, you'll know."

"Illusion?" he wondered out loud. He knew about the illusions the fae used around their camp to hide it, and briefly wondered if it was the same kind of thing. "Like a forcefield?"

"Yeah, I suppose that's one way of putting it, but you can go through this one."

They kept walking, the sun beating down on their shoulders like there hadn't been rain and wind in apocalyptic levels the day before. *Just another day in Solace.*

As he skirted a particularly large clump of spinifex, Blue wished Kyne had given him more notice they were going to visit Andante. He'd really liked to have brought a freshly-cooked vegetarian lasagna. She seemed to enjoy it the other day and it made him proud when others liked his cooking. Maybe he was old-fashioned, but his mother always said it was good manners to take a plate of food when going to visit someone.

When Blue was finally clear of the spiky grass, he looked up and had to do a double-take.

"*Strewth,*" he murmured, gobsmacked at the sight before them.

Enormous beehive-shaped towers shimmered through what he assumed was the illusion and rose into the sapphire sky. Each were made of banded stone in yellows, oranges, and browns that stood out bold and bright against the blue. They were quite the sight, and just as unexpected.

"Quartz sandstone," Kyne told him with a chuckle. "As far as rocks go, they're pretty cool."

"I've lived in Solace for more than twenty years... I never knew there were karsts like this here."

"I reckon no one does, thanks to Andante. If the humans knew, it'd be a tourist attraction by tomorrow."

Blue grunted, his mind's eye filling with fevered visions of campsites with shiny white caravans as far as the eye could see...and the mounds of rubbish that came with them. *If only people picked up after themselves,* he thought. *Left no trace.*

"Maybe it's a good thing," he said after a moment.

"Yeah," Kyne said with a sigh. "Especially with the seal."

Blue nodded, even though it'd never crossed his mind. He *was* only human.

They walked a bit farther, the *clack* of Kyne's crutches echoing through the open air. The ground appeared dry and there were no signs of wind or rain damage to any of trees or plants.

"I don't think the storm came through here," Blue said, scratching his head.

"It's probably Andante's magic," the elemental replied. "She's got this place sealed away in a pocket of reality."

"Oh..." He had no idea what that meant, or how someone could have the power to do such a thing, but sure. He'd seen stranger things.

They approached the closest karst. Kyne was out in

front, but as far as Blue could see, there were no signs that anyone lived out here.

They didn't realise Andante had found them until, sensing someone was watching them, they both looked up.

The druidess stood on the path, gazing at them with raised eyebrows. She clearly found their visit unexpected and slightly irritating.

"Hi," Blue said, waving.

Seeing Kyne's crutches, the druidess nodded to the opening in the rock behind her. "Come."

The temperature was cooler inside the cave.

Blue looked around, taking in every inch of the rudimentary home Andante had made for herself. A bed made of leaves and woven blankets lay on a stone shelf, and a fire pit sat in the middle. It wasn't much, and certainly didn't appear comfortable—*or modern*—but she seemed to like it.

Deciding to use his manners, Blue didn't look closer, but couldn't help noticing the walls were full of carvings. They reminded him of old Norse runes, but he didn't know the other, more complex sigils. He *did* know they were probably full of magic, and he should never mess with things like that, so he kept away from them.

Andante screwed up her nose. "What is that awful smell?"

"Uh, that's probably Vera's poultice," Kyne said. "For my leg."

Andante stared at him.

"A tree fell on me during the storm," he explained, squirming. "According to Finn, Hardy couldn't heal it because of the magic in the rain, so I have to let it heal the old-fashioned way. Stitches and...*goop*."

Andante narrowed her eyes at him and looked down at his leg. "Drop your trousers."

The miner blinked. "Huh?"

"That's why we're here," Blue blurted. "About the storm, not his leg. We wanted to make sure you were okay."

"The fae's magic doesn't worry me," she said, her tone softening. "There is something *incompatible* between our people."

"So, you're okay?"

She nodded. "Are you?"

Kyne choked, earning himself another glare from the druidess.

"As well as can be expected," the publican replied. "We've got a bit of a mess on our hands, but nothing we can't clean up with a bit of elbow grease. Though there's a little problem with the seal."

"I wouldn't call it 'little,'" Kyne stated. "The seal is cracked and leaking Old One magic all over the place. Vera is sick, and the rest of us don't feel so hot, either."

Andante raised her eyebrows. "Drop your trousers," she commanded again, making it clear she wasn't in the mood to discuss their problems—at least, not with Kyne.

Blue chuckled. "You better do what she says, boy."

Kyne let out a sigh, set his crutches against the stone wall, and promptly dropped his trousers. Now that his bandaged leg was free of his jeans, the stench from the poultice wafted out into the close air of the cave, giving Blue a nose full.

"Bloody hell, that pongs," the publican exclaimed as Kyne sat on a rock. "It smells like—" He quickly shut his mouth, remembering they were in the presence of a lady.

"Don't look at me like that," the elemental complained. "This is all Vera."

Andante knelt before Kyne and unwrapped his leg, then used the bandages to smear the greenish-brown goop from the wound. She clicked her tongue, inspecting the stitches, then held her hands out, her palms facing downward.

Blue watched in fascination as the same purplish-blue threads she'd shown him at the pub began to leave her hands and trail downwards. They merged into Kyne's leg, filling the gash with a glowing light that reminded him of holographic contact paper—the kind kids used to cover their schoolbooks.

"That kind of tickles," Kyne said, squirming.

"Stay still," Andante snapped.

Blue shrugged and they let the druidess complete her work. When she was done, and the light from her magic had faded, both men leaned over and inspected the gash.

Vera's carefully placed stitches had dissolved, but the wound was much improved. It was still red and a little tender looking, but Blue reckoned it wouldn't split back open any time soon.

"That's the best I can do," Andante told them. "The fae's magic interferes."

"Like the dust?" Blue wondered.

"You seem to know a lot about other kinds of magic," Kyne said as he stood and hiked his jeans back up. "Do you know anything we could do about the magic leaking from the seal?"

Andante shrugged. "What do you do when a crack needs sealing?"

"*I should've known.*" The miner's expression turned sour, like he'd had the run around from her before. "Why are you always so evasive?"

"Druids are not known for our...directness," she told them. "We believe in the journey, not the destination."

Kyne sighed. "Yeah, that's important, but—"

Blue slapped the youngster on the shoulder. "But she means they prefer not to give out all the answers when it's clearly more beneficial for us to find them ourselves."

"So, you won't help us with the seal?"

Andante sighed. "There's not much I can do."

"Why?" Kyne demanded. "If there's any time to dish out all the answers, now would be the perfect opportunity."

"My people—*Merlin*—made a pact with the Old Ones long ago," she snapped. "If I were to go against them now, it would mean disaster. Not just for you, but for all my people."

"Merlin?" The publican frowned. "As in, King Arthur and Merlin the magician?"

"Yes. They all live, though perhaps not in this reality."

"So, Merlin was a Druid like you?"

"Merlin is the greatest of my people...if he still lives. He made the pact with the Old Ones on his own, without consulting anyone but himself," Andante hissed and rolled her eyes. "He forced many things on the Druids—many things they did not want but were made to suffer, regardless."

"Sounds like quite the story," Blue said, hardly understanding what she was saying. He could handle vampires, witches, and werewolves, but anything more than that, he tended to just smile and nod. Fae, elementals, Coen, and now Druids came under the latter. "What is this pact?"

"Long ago, my people became the hunted. A dark power rose in another reality, and they desired our magic above all else. Our numbers dwindled and we were but a few, until Merlin knelt before the Old Ones." Andante's eyes seemed to darken as she explained the story as simply as she could. "To protect our homeland, the Old Ones agreed to create a barrier around it called the Darklands—a whole reality designed to allow the Druids to pass and keep all others out...but only the worthy make it to Thríbhís Mhór." She glanced at Kyne, but he made no comment. "That is the Old Ones' price. They collect souls of the unworthy to fill their void so the Druids can live in peace."

"Hardly seems like a fair trade," Blue stated. "Who are these slimy Old Ones to decide if some poor bugger is worthy? What does that even mean?"

"Like I told Eloise, the Old Ones have no emotions. They will not empathise with you or this world. They are higher beings who see the universe differently."

"They're not human," Kyne drawled. "That's what you mean. We're nothing but single-celled organisms slopping around in what they consider primordial soup."

"Perhaps not that low," Andante replied blandly. "But the fact still remains... I cannot help you with your seal."

Before Kyne could snap back a reply, Blue said, "Not to worry. Coen will be back soon with answers and until then, Vera will cook up one of her spells."

Andante's eyes narrowed at the mention of Coen, but she said nothing about him. Instead, the druidess said, "Let me show you something." She glared at Kyne, then turned back to Blue with a smile.

Kyne sighed and picked up his crutches. "I think I'll go wait outside." Apparently, the invitation was only for Blue.

As the miner went back the way they'd arrived, Blue followed Andante down a tunnel that wound in the opposite direction. Ahead, sunlight streamed in from another opening, and he wondered where she was taking him.

Leaving the tunnel, they stepped out onto a stone platform into the day. Blue had to blink a thousand times a second as his eyes adjusted, but when they did, the publican was rendered speechless.

Banded karsts seemed to stretch for kilometres, the enormous rock formations bubbling up out of the flat expanse like nothing he'd ever seen before. There were several natural wonders like this across the outback—Purnululu, Karlu Karlu, and Uluru just to name a few—but even they seemed to pale in comparison to the place Andante had hidden behind her illusions. Even he, a mere human, could feel the magic in this place.

"Why did you come here?"

Andante's sudden question took him aback, breaking the spell the land had cast over him. "Eloise was worried, but she's helping with Vera and the seal, so she asked Kyne to come check on you."

"Listen to the question again, Blue," she murmured. "Why did you come here?"

"I wanted to see you again," he blurted, the words tumbling out of him like they were brought forth by magic.

She smiled as if she knew more than even he did.

"Druids live long lives and I have already seen most of mine."

Her statement spoke to the things he was wondering about her, and even things he hadn't thought about yet. It also seemed to be designed to skip over a lot of conversation she must have thought was pointless. It seemed a little direct for a Druid, but maybe that was the point.

I thought women were confusing... he thought, *but Druids take the cake.*

"Then live whatever you have left to the fullest," he told her. "You still have time. You can still go out there and see more. *Do more.*"

"I already did more than I ought to," Andante snapped. "I helped the fae stop the vampire's explosion."

"I didn't mean it like *that*," Blue said, feeling his cheeks redden. "I meant you should live for yourself. Forget your magic and see the world. Enjoy yourself."

It was her turn to look embarrassed. She pursed her lips and turned her face away.

She must have quite the past to jump straight to the worst conclusion, Blue thought. How many others had tried to exploit her powers to travel through different realities? Perhaps the trauma was caused by those bad guys who'd hunted her people to the brink of extinction...the ones who'd forced Merlin to make the pact that stopped her from helping the Exiles with the seal.

"Maybe you could go home?" he offered.

"I can't go home," she whispered.

Blue saw red and clenched his shaking hands into tight fists. "Because you think you're not worthy?"

"It's not what I believe. It's the Old Ones' judgement."

"Stuff the Old Ones," he said, the words exploding out of him. "I might just be a silly old bugger, and a plain old human to boot, but they won't stop me from living my life. Not even all the magic in the world could, and I certainly won't let some creature thing I don't even understand stand in my way. And neither should you. I've seen what you can do, and it's... It's... *It's beautiful.*"

Andante blinked, her face flushing deep crimson.

Blue ran his hand over his face and coughed. "Erm... I'm sorry. I didn't mean... I got a bit carried away with myself." He laughed to cover up his nervousness, but he only ended up sounding half-crazy.

Get a grip, you flaming galah, he thought. *How old are you?*

"Oh, Blue..." Andante sighed, the sound echoing long and sad into the open air. "There's so much you don't understand."

He grunted. "It's a recurring theme around this joint. I'm just a simple bloke, after all."

"It will never be easy for you living amongst supernaturals."

"And it was never easy for them living amongst humans," Blue told her. "Life isn't easy for anyone, magic or no magic."

They stood together, gazing across the earthy-coloured karsts and to the outback beyond. Blue could see why she liked it out here. He could imagine the beating red heart of Australia reached into infinity, and if there was something beyond that, it would touch there, too. It was a place where nature thrived, animals lived in peace, and the troubles of human existence never worried.

Unspoilt. That was the word. It was a concept he wasn't sure he could comprehend as a human being.

Just as he was beginning to understand his depressing part in the universe, Andante spoke.

"There are many higher beings," she mused, looking across the outback. "The Old Ones were merely present at the beginning of all things. I would not be surprised to find a few more lingering around the edges of this little place." She lowered her gaze and wrung her gnarled fingers. "Your elementals..."

"Kyne and Eloise?" Blue tensed. "What about them?"

Andante smiled and looked towards Solace, or at least where Blue imagined it was. "You have created a welcoming energy in your pub, Blue. Perhaps you have a kind of magic of your own." She pointed to a path in the rock. "Follow, and you will find the elemental."

She'd signalled their talk was over, leaving him

with a scrap of Druidic wisdom to puzzle over. He followed her pointing finger and took a step towards the path, but hesitated.

"Andante?" Blue asked, but when he looked back, she was already gone.

Knowing she wasn't coming back, he followed the path that cut around the curve of the karst where Andante's cave was hidden. Naturally formed stairs led the way downwards and soon, he was back on solid ground. Another turn led him to Kyne, who was sitting on an outcropping of rock, waiting.

Hearing him approach, the elemental looked up. "Get lucky?"

"Get stuffed," he replied, his brow creasing. "She doesn't like you much."

"Yeah, nah," Kyne said. "I was mean to her when we first met. I guess all supernaturals have long memories."

Blue shook his head and looked up at the karst. *Just how long was Andante's memory?*

"We better head back," he said after a moment. "There's a lot of clean-up still left to do."

Kyne frowned and looked the publican over. "What did she say to you?"

Blue held out his hand and helped the miner to his feet. "Nothing I didn't already know."

The rumbling drone of Wally's water pump radiated across Solace as Eloise sat on a camp chair underneath the fluro green-and-gold beach umbrella Hardy had set up for her and Vera.

Watching the water flow out of the thick hose dangling down into the mine, she felt her stomach gurgle like it had when she'd gone down there with Drew. She pressed her palm over her abdomen and glanced at Vera, who was lounging beside her. The witch was sipping on a straw that fed into a bottle of bright orange Gatorade.

Wally was a knot of anxiety, hovering over the mine and checking the hose a thousand times per second. Watching him fuss gave Eloise heartburn.

The next full moon was six days away, so they had time to spare—not that it didn't make the old wolf any less anxious. He still carried regrets over getting loose all those months ago, even though that'd been the Dust Dogs' fault.

Still, she understood where he was coming from. Kyne's generator had fried during the trip back from Black Hole Mine, so they'd had to prioritise draining the mine under Solace due to the cracks in the seal. Even Clarke was having a hell of a time tracking down another pump. Seemed even the police sergeant didn't have enough sway to commandeer equipment from the local opal miners. They sure were a passionate lot.

As Wally paced, Drew was looking down the shaft, scratching his head and pretending he knew what he was doing. The water flowed down the highway, feeding off to the north. Thankfully, the land tilted that way, sending the tainted stuff away from town. So far, whatever magical goop was in it didn't seem to have any noticeable effects on the plant life.

Hardy joined them in the shade, pulling up another chair under the brim of the neon umbrella. "Are you feeling any better?"

"I guess," Vera replied. "I'm just waiting for the water to drain away so I can get down there and get my barrier spell up and running."

"Do you have to go down there?" Eloise asked, fretting. "If you feel unwell up here, then down there—"

"Proximity matters in times like these." The witch waved her hand absently. "It'll be fine."

"I'll go down with you," Hardy offered. "I don't seem to be feeling it as much as everyone else."

Eloise straightened up. "You're not?"

The vampire shook his head. "No. I don't think my undead status is quite compatible with whatever gunk the Old One is leaking out."

"*Gross.*" She screwed up her nose.

Vera laughed and Eloise hoped the Gatorade was helping, but it was more likely the spell the witch had used to fend off the strange magic, though it was only a temporary fix. The barrier spell was supposed to be a little stronger...for the time being.

Gravel crunched as Wally and Drew wandered over from the boab.

"It's going to take a few hours yet," the werewolf said, adjusting his hat. "There's a lot of water down there."

Eloise bit her bottom lip and began to worry it with her front teeth. Getting the water out was only step one. If they only knew who'd put the seal there in the first place, it might give them a clue as to how to fix the damage done by Siora's storm.

"Don't do that," Vera said, swatting the elemental's arm. "You'll split your lip."

"What are we going to do about the cracks?" she asked. "I'm not sure we can wait for Coen. What if he doesn't come back?"

"Coen always comes back," Wally said.

"Until he doesn't," Drew muttered.

"Maybe there's something in that rock?" Hardy offered, shooting a disapproving look at the dingo-shifter. "We can send Kyne down there to have a look when he and Blue get back."

"Maybe..." Vera mused. "It's worth a try at least."

"At this point, anything's worth a try," Eloise said with a frustrated moan.

"We could always *Sikaflex* it," Drew said with a shrug. *Sikaflex* was an industrial-strength sealant they'd used when he and Kyne had built the dugouts.

"Somehow, I don't think the stuff's rated for magical leakages," Wally said, shaking his head.

The Exiles fell silent and watched the water gush out of the hose, then flowed down the edge of the highway, and finally disappeared off into the scrub.

Eloise shifted in the camp chair, her senses tingling. Was it from the tainted water, or was it something else? They'd set up the bright beach umbrella and the chairs like they were having a summer picnic by the seaside, but it felt wrong somehow. Like a piece was missing.

Hardy leaned towards her, picking up on her uneasiness. They'd worked together so closely over the last few months that they seemed to be in tune with each other. A vampire and an elemental, who would've thought?

"What's wrong?" he asked, keeping his voice low.

"Finn hasn't come back."

Drew looked down at them, his brow creasing. "I'll go check the fae camp on my rounds tonight," he promised. "But I'm sure he'll be back at the pub by dinnertime. If all else fails, I'll take a bowl of hot chips and leave it out. That ought to attract him."

"Drew!" Vera shrieked.

"What?" the shifter demanded. "He'd take every opportunity to rip me a new one. I'm just meeting him halfway."

"That boy's been through a lot," Wally stated. "Give him a break."

"That 'boy' is over a thousand years old," Drew argued.

"He was asleep for most of that," Eloise countered.

Vera sat up straight and stared at her. "How do you know? Did he tell you?"

"I... I don't know." She blinked as if she'd been dazed by the sun and shook her head. Finn hadn't told her, at least not in so many words, but somehow, she knew.

"Finn's life before Solace is a mystery to us all," Hardy murmured, placing a cold hand on Eloise's arm. "If he's confided in you—"

"No, it's not that," she interrupted. "I just..." Was she jumping to conclusions?

Vera leaned back in her chair and resumed sipping her Gatorade. "It's an elemental thing."

Eloise looked up at Wally and Drew, then back at Vera. "But how can I know something like that?"

Hardy chuckled and relaxed into his own chair. "Your powers are growing. That's how you know."

CHAPTER 14

Drew had never seen the night so alive with colour. He sat atop the ridge in his dingo form, his animal eyes taking in the troubling scene below.

He liked to find the high places. It made it easier to see across the whole area. From here, he could spot the dim lights of Solace and then down the highway to the south, where the faint smudge of artificial light cast by Lightning Ridge hugged the horizon. It was too far for human eyes to register, but his dingo eyes caught the edges of a lot of things.

On an ordinary night, he would've had trouble searching out the touches of magic that lived amongst the lonely landscape, but tonight it was lit up like bioluminescence floating on the surface of the ocean —a chemical reaction that made organisms like jellyfish and bacteria glow brilliant blue in the darkness. He'd seen pictures of the phenomena online, and what he was looking at seemed a lot like that.

A glowing bloom of inky blue light seeped up out of the ground and billowed in the air around Solace. It curled in places and gathered in clotting clouds in others. It even seemed to float like pollen in the wind, dusting up towards the stars.

Until now, the power being kept at bay underneath the seal was just an abstract concept. He knew it was there because he felt it in his bones, and he used it to transform his body, but it'd been invisible. Vera was the only one who could conjure the stuff into anything physical. Blue had told them Andante could as well, but Drew had never even met her, so he wouldn't know.

As he watched the iridescent magic float gently around the town, Drew was beginning to realise why Coen had taught him to 'see.' The Indigenous man wasn't coming back...or he believed the fight against the Old One would claim his life. In his absence, someone would have to keep an eye on the seal and the spirits who lived in and around Solace.

That person was Drew.

No wonder Vera felt sick, he thought. *She was breathing it in...but didn't she cast her spell already?* It hadn't worked, and he was dreading having to tell her in the morning.

Shaking his head, he watched the plumes drift lazily through the night. The blue was beautiful if he didn't think about the whole end of the world part.

Magic was strange. He often wondered what kind

turned his ancestors into dingoes, but he could never find an answer. Maybe he wasn't supposed to know. It didn't seem to matter, anyway. He was what he was and couldn't be anything else. Whatever it was, it was the right kind of stuff that allowed him to take on Coen's role as the silent protector.

Drew filled his lungs and huffed, letting all the air out in one long whoosh that ruffled the fronds of the delicate native grass in front of him. There was nothing he could do about the glowing plumes of the Old One's magic, so he turned to the night and continued on his path.

He'd promised Eloise he'd look for Finn, who hadn't been seen since that morning. Kyne said the fae had gone back to his camp to see if there was anything useful left after the storm, but he hadn't returned for dinner at the pub.

As usual, Eloise was worried about the fae, and when she'd turned those big, soulful eyes on him, Drew knew he couldn't refuse Eloise Hart.

So here he was, padding across the outback, his snout to the ground. As he approached the camp, he noticed the illusions guarding its location were gone. All traces of the fae had dissolved and even the smell of magic had blown away in the gale.

When Drew came upon the camp, he noticed that the site had dried out hours ago, but the effects of the storm were clear. It'd ripped Finn's tent to shreds and wiped away almost all signs left behind by the other

fae—it was like they'd never been there at all, save for
Finn.

Drew sniffed around the tent, poking through the
tattered fabric, nosing a book that'd been bloated and
deformed by water. Finn had clearly been here. His
scent was smeared over everything, and he'd left tracks
all around the campsite as he'd picked through the
wreckage, but there was a distinct trail that pointed to
the north-east.

It led away from Solace, and any other human
habitation. A single set of footprints that carried the
fae's signature.

Drew knew whatever choice Finn'd made to leave
the camp was of his own free will. No one else had
been here since the storm, and there were zero signs of
a struggle. He'd simply gotten up and walked.

Drew followed the fae's path across the outback,
weaving through the scrub, his eyes finding the trail
easily. Then, after a few hundred metres, it cut off
abruptly. The dingo raised his head and sniffed the
breeze, but there was nothing else for him to follow. No
scent, no magic, no footprints. *Nothing.*

Finn had disappeared into thin air.

There was nothing else he could do, so Drew went
back to Solace, where the creepy Old One glow
hovered. At least it wasn't slimy tentacles, though there
was something about this that felt worse.

Venturing past Eloise and Kyne's dugout, he was

surprised to see a light glowing by the shiny white motorhome parked underneath the carport.

The side door was open, and Eloise sat on the step, one of those cheap rechargeable camp lights Vera sold at the *Outpost* at her feet.

The elemental's eyes were focused on the sky, a troubled expression on her face that only looked more morose in the shadows cast by the lamp. If she saw the glowing cloud, he didn't know, but he hoped not.

He didn't want to frighten her by his stealthy appearance, so he dragged his paws through the gravel. The racket caused her to turn, and her expression became hopeful when she saw him slink into the ring of light.

"There was no sign of him," he said.

She stared him, bewildered. "Drew?"

"You're not the only one whose powers have levelled up."

"When did that happen?"

"A while ago." He sat beside her and looked up at the eerie glow. It hovered above them, but its light didn't touch anything around it, not like the lamp sitting by Eloise's feet.

"I found Finn's scent at the camp. I followed it into the scrub for a few hundred metres, but it ended abruptly."

"Which way?"

"North-east. Wherever he went, he went willingly. There were no signs of a struggle or that anyone else had been there since the storm."

Eloise sighed and rubbed her eyes. "Thanks for checking, Drew. I guess... Well, I guess he just has some stuff to work through." She turned her face back towards the sky, where the Old One's magic seemed to shift and billow under the weight of her gaze.

"*Can you see it?*" he asked.

"See what?"

He frowned, then decided he didn't want to worry her. "*Nothing,*" he replied. "*I better head off and you better get some sleep. It's after midnight.*"

"Yeah." She picked up the lamp and fiddled with the switch. The globe flickered and she sighed.

Drew wanted to say something to help her feel better but couldn't find the words. He didn't know if there were any.

"*Wherever he's gone, he has to go on his own,*" he told her instead.

"Yeah," she whispered. "That's what a walkabout is, I suppose."

Finn didn't know how long he'd been walking through the outback, but it was long enough that the sun should have already risen.

That's how he knew he'd left the world of the living and entered some place beyond. Was it the realm of the Dreaming that Coen always talked about? No, not exactly. He remembered the Indigenous man explaining that the Dreaming wasn't a place—it was all things, including knowing.

Memory.

The Dreaming was the sky and the stars beyond. It was the earth, air, water, and all the living things within it. It was up, down, backwards, forwards... It was the past, present, and the future. It was all those things and none at all.

The Dreaming simply *was*. That's how Finn's fae blood perceived it. For him, it meant existence.

His path had led him into the darkness of night with only the stars for company. He put one foot in front of the other, trusting that this place would show him the way.

The way to what? Redemption? Or was his destiny in the sentence the Seelie had placed upon him when he'd been thrust through the portal—in death, where his soul would be lost for eternity.

Finn was lost in the melancholy of his thoughts when he saw them in the distance.

The glowing orbs the Exiles called the Min Min hovered in the strange landscape, waiting. They undulated, rising and falling like they were bobbing on an ocean of dust, kept afloat by the unforgiving hot winds of the outback, their luminescence flaring gold and silver.

He watched the tiny specks of light—containing the spirits of the places they lingered—for a long time, their eerie presence reminding him of the spirits that roamed his home world. The deepest and wildest parts of the great forests of Lor'Iyslar were full of them. They'd retreated from towns and cities as the fae expanded into their territory, choosing the wildest places to call home.

Finn had seen them in the high mountains once. In the dead of night on the banks of Il Fir—the Pale Lake. It was mere hours later that he and Siora had left on their final quest to bring down the Seelie and end the rebellion—the final act that'd brought him here.

The Min Min were much larger, but they moved the same way—they were the spirits of the outback. If they'd appeared to him, then Finn decided he ought to follow.

The lights led him amongst the tangle of scrub, past rock formations, and through dry creek beds. The moon rose in the sky, the silver glow illuminating his path, before it fell beyond the horizon, plunging everything into darkness. Even the Min Min faded, the golden orbs shrinking until they blinked out entirely.

But Finn wasn't alone.

Ahead, a figure stood in the night, a human-shaped blob of darkness. It was a shadow in a place where there was no light to create one. A creature that was nothing short of ominous, oppressive, and terrifying.

Was it a kadaitcha—one of the vengeful spirits that'd wandered around Solace? Like most supernatural things, they'd been attracted to the magic of the seal, searching for a way to fulfil their purpose...

or escape. One of the two. But after the trouble with the Nightshade, they seemed to have abandoned their hunt around the town, retreating like the spirit orbs from his home world.

Finn knew they were still out there, watching and waiting. If the shadow figure was a kadaitcha, he was in trouble.

He looked around, feeling the otherworldliness of the outback, and knew he had to face it. Had he not done things that deserved vengeance? His walkabout had led him here for a purpose, and perhaps, this was it.

Besides, the thing had seen him and if he tried to back away, it'd only follow.

Finn took a step towards it and the shadow mirrored his movements. He moved again, and it moved, creeping closer through the night. Then, all at once, it seemed to come alive.

The shadow rippled and changed, its smoothness gaining definition as it started to run. Its hollow mouth opened, tearing a hole in its inky surface, and it shrieked at him, the sound stabbing into every part of him.

Finn was frozen in place, terror filling his heart. He couldn't move even to save himself as the creature rushed at him, lifting its arms.

The moment before it struck, Finn saw his contorted face staring back at him, his shadow eyes filled with vicious rage. Then he was flying backwards, pain tearing through the side of his head.

He landed on his back—the force knocking the wind out of his lungs—and his bag fell to the ground. The *ash'strad* rolled out, tumbling across the ground, only stopping when it hit the solid feet of the shadow creature. The silver orb spun once, righted itself, then lifted into the air.

"*No...*" Finn cried, reaching out his arm.

The *ash'strad* spun, slowly at first, then picked up speed as magic began to build inside.

"You beg for forgiveness, but you never said the one thing that mattered," the shadow spat in his own voice.

The *ash'strad* expanded, the hard silver surface rippling as it began to discharge. Electric sparks raced over Finn's body, and he felt his insides liquify.

He screamed in agony as he clawed his way towards the orb, desperately reaching for it...but it was too late. The *ash'strad* exploded, lighting up the darkness with white-hot heat that seared his eyes.

But as soon as the radiance filled the night, it was gone.

Finn lay in the dirt, tears staining his face and blood dripping down his forehead.

It wasn't real.

It was a test...one he'd failed miserably.

He lay in the ochre dust and sobbed, curling up so tight his back ached and the sheathed knife at his waist dug into his thigh.

"Rei lor'ahlei..." he rasped. "I'm sorry. *I'm sorry.*"

Sweet singing stirred him out of his despair, and Finn raised his head. His entire body ached, but the voice soothed his soul and coaxed him forwards... He sat and looked around at the desolate outback.

He knew that song. It was a lullaby. One that he knew.

She formed in the sky, stepping out from the dark places in between, gathering more stardust with each step. Her smile brought light to his heart as she held out her hand.

"Lor'anahlei," he cried, reaching towards the figure. *Mother.*

As his fingers brushed against hers, the vision broke, dissolving like grains of sand. The glittering dust caught on the breeze and billowed off into the night, returning to the stars above.

"Ahleida da..." he whispered. *Forgive me.*

Finn knew he'd done wrong and needed to atone, but he hadn't acted upon his vow. He'd helped the Exiles, in part because he cared about them, but most of his reasoning was out of his own selfish need for self-preservation.

He'd been wallowing around Solace like a spoilt child. Spending his days propping up the bar at Blue's, eating hot chips and not paying for them, drinking himself blind, and lashing out at anyone who came close.

There was a difference between remorse and redemption—one he couldn't see until now.

The Min Min had guided him to the place within himself where he could see. Now that his eyes had been opened, he could continue.

Finn stood and turned towards the darkness, but the lights were gone, leaving his path unclear. But that was the point, wasn't it?

He had to find his own way.

CHAPTER 15

Vera stood behind the counter at the *Outpost* and stared out of the windows. Another day had dawned, but she was having trouble feeling grateful for it.

Yesterday, once the water had finished draining, Vera had gone down into the cave and cast her barrier spell. A dozen shards of raw quartz crystals were currently placed around the cracked bluestone, each humming with the power of the Brinewold witches.

The moment the spell had activated, the nausea twisting her stomach in knots had disappeared. It was nice not having to worry if her breakfast was going to make a reappearance, and it also cleared her mind.

Remembering the jagged cracks that splintered the seal, Vera shook her head. It was never supposed to break, right? At least, not so easily...but maybe that's why they could feel the magic in the first place. Had it been deteriorating all this time?

The door jerked open, making her heart leap into her throat, and Drew strode in.

"Finn's gone," he declared, leaning on the counter. No hello, no how are you feeling, no nothing, but that was Drew.

"Gone?" She blinked, shoving her worries about the seal to the back burner. "What do you mean, gone?"

The shifter rolled his eyes. "Gone, as in he's somewhere else."

Vera slapped his arm. *"Be more specific."*

"I went out to the fae camp to see if he was there, *like I promised*, and found his tracks leading out into the outback. I followed, but the trail just ended." He clapped his hands together. *"Poof.* Gone."

"Gone?" she echoed. "Where?"

He shrugged. "Eloise said he's probably gone on a walkabout. If that's what he wants to do after his blue-haired girlfriend blew half the town away with her freaky storm, then let him. We've got bigger things to worry about."

Vera glanced out the window and grimaced. Despite everything she'd been through with Finn, and her traumatic past with the craglorn, she was worried about him. She and Finn had come to an understanding...and she'd even go as far as to say they were family. They were all exiles from something in their own way, which is why they all chose to live in Solace despite the trouble underground.

"Wait." Vera blinked and turned back to Drew. "What bigger problem?"

"Last night was my first night out since the storm," he told her. "When I shifted, the sky lit up like a tacky Christmas display." He wiggled his fingers in the air. "Blue bioluminescence is squirting out of the seal and coating the town."

"*Ew.*" Vera screwed up her nose. "Don't say squirt."

"I'd check the thesaurus, but it's a miracle I know what one is."

Thinking about the ramifications of the cracks in the seal, Vera felt a wave of exhaustion hit her. She leaned over, pressing her elbows on the counter. Her spell hadn't worked, but for Drew to actually *see* the Old One's magic...? She didn't know what it meant.

"No wonder you felt so sick," he told her.

"Yeah...but my spell should've contained the leak." Maybe it wasn't strong enough, or perhaps, it wasn't the right kind of barrier.

"Then why is it still sq—" Drew coughed. "Then why is it still letting out magic everywhere?"

"No," she mused. "That spell was to contain the stuff that was making us sick. I wasn't looking at it from the right angle."

"Huh?"

"If I... Yes." She clicked her fingers as a light bulb flicked on in her mind. "I could potentially slow the cracking..."

"You can do that?"

"Maybe?" She shrugged. "Right now, I have to buy us some time."

Drew scowled. "Until Coen comes back?"

She straightened, her strength returning. "You say it like you don't think he will."

"He was teaching me to take over his job," the shifter said. "He reckoned he was going to find answers, but maybe it was just his way of saying 'see you later, *losers.*'"

"He'd never leave us like that," Vera argued. "If that seal opens—"

"Yeah, yeah. The world is blown up, terrible pain, natural disasters, explosions, apocalypse, *blah blah blah.*" Suddenly, Drew wrinkled his nose and looked around the shop. "What's that smell?"

"What smell?" Vera sniffed, though she didn't have any hope of detecting what the dingo-shifter could with his senses. "I don't smell anything."

"It smells like something's rotting." The shifter prowled across the front of the aisles, his head turning in all directions as he followed his nose.

Rounding the counter, she began to search as well, getting down on her hands and knees, peering underneath shelving. Maybe it was a mouse—the native kind that was adorable and needed to be set free, not the kind that chewed through electrical wiring. Sometimes the little critters got inside and caused all kinds of strife trying to find a way out. After the storm, she wouldn't be surprised if a few had found their way in looking for shelter.

"What are you doing on the floor?" Drew asked from above.

"I hope it's not a little native mouse," she huffed. "I couldn't stand it if one came in here and got trapped. The poor little thing—"

"It's not a mouse," the dingo stated. "It's the fresh produce."

Her head flew up. "Huh?"

The fruit and veg display sat at the head of aisle two. Vera had sanded and varnished the recycled wooden crates and lined the inside with artificial grass. It was her first successful DIY after moving to Solace, and she always felt a pang of pride when she restocked them, but today they were emitting a sickly-sweet stench that made her feel sick all over again.

Standing, she moaned as she saw the wrinkled, furry mess inside. The heads of lettuce had shrivelled and wilted, and the apples had mould all over them. She couldn't even bear to survey the rest, which all seemed to rot at an accelerated pace before their eyes.

"*Oh no...*" she moaned. "That doesn't look good."

"That's not natural," Drew said, stating the obvious.

Vera turned her back on the produce. Draining the water should've helped, but it'd only seemed to make things worse. There had to be something she could do to slow the disintegration of the seal.

"Vera?" Drew asked. "What should we do?"

This wasn't a time for maybes. It was time to adopt a can-do attitude.

"I'm going to need my grimoire..." she declared, "and a can of air freshener."

<hr>

Eloise woke with a start, jerking upright. She gulped in lungfuls of air as her heart thundered in her chest.

Kyne rolled over beside her. "Eloise?" he murmured, his voice heavy with sleep.

She didn't hear him at first—her head was still full of the dream that'd plagued her during the night.

She stood in a dark outback that was neither here nor there. The black sky was coated in a thick dusting of stars, their edges silver and purple, the light colouring the earth an odd shade of plum.

Finn walked in the distance, his back to her, but no matter how loudly she shouted, he didn't turn around. He simply walked. Walked and walked towards the mountain on the horizon, his head bowed low.

The mountain.

Brilliant sapphire-blue exploded in the sky, spreading outwards like ink in water. Billowing like storm clouds full of wild magic that split the mountain open.

The Old One rose, blackness oozing out of the earth like a volcano, and still, Finn walked towards it.

Finn!

Eloise jerked again, but this time, it was only Kyne's hand on her arm. She was in bed beside him, safe and sound.

"Are you all right?" he murmured, sitting beside her. "Was it another dream?"

"Yeah..." She wiped the back of her hand across her damp brow.

Kyne frowned and pushed her tangled hair behind her ear. "You haven't had one since the stuff with Darius."

"I know, I..." She rubbed her eyes as the pieces began to lock together.

Finn had disappeared, the seal had cracked, and now her dreams had returned. None of it was a coincidence—nothing ever was around here.

Eloise began to worry the edge of the sheet with her fingers. Finn had been gone for over thirty-six hours, give or take, and there he was, in her dream.

"I think we ought to search for Finn," she said.

"With all that's going on here?" Kyne shook his head. "I'm worried about him too, but he's a grown man. He can look after himself."

"Grown fae, actually," she muttered.

He raised an eyebrow. "And?"

"I'll go myself, then." Which, she was now realising, was the point of her dream.

"You can't be serious," Kyne said, raising both his eyebrows. "You want to go into the outback and follow a non-existent trail? *Eloise...*" He sighed and ran his hand over his face.

"I wouldn't be *just wandering*," she told him. "Drew said his trail just ended. He's obviously gone someplace only I can follow."

"How do you know?"

She shrugged. "It was in my dream."

"A dream that featured the black mountain... *Eloise.*"

"*Kyne...*" She cupped his face, her palms scratching on his stubbled jaw. "The Old One can't reach me. We already know that."

"But it's trying to use others to get to you," he argued. "Could you stand against Finn if you had to?" Her expression faded. "You have to be one hundred percent sure, Eloise. Hesitation could mean not only your life, but the end of everything in our reality."

If there was one thing Eloise knew, it was that. Painfully, too.

She sighed and climbed out of bed. Gathering her clothes, she began dressing, her thoughts scattered. He had a point, but he didn't know what she did...which was just a hunch. Her magic hadn't led her astray yet, though.

"Where are you going?" Kyne asked.

"I need to take a walk," she murmured, pulling on her shorts.

The sheets rustled behind her as Kyne moved

across to her side of the bed. "Eloise, I don't want to upset you, I just—"

"You want to protect me," she interrupted. "I get it, but you can't. Not from the Old Ones." She shoved her feet into her boots and began lacing them up. "If the mountain has Finn, I'm the only one who can find him, let alone free him."

"I'm afraid that's what it wants."

Me, too.

Eloise stood, turned, bent down, and kissed Kyne on the forehead. "I love you."

Outside, she breathed in the warm air, filling her lungs to the brim.

The endless sky was mottled with bands of orange, yellow, and blue, the dawn already an hour past. A flock of budgerigars screeched overhead, flying in formation as they soared towards their usual billabong.

Free of the confines of the dugout, Eloise could think again. Kyne loved being underground, but she needed the sky. That, she supposed, was all part of their elemental affinities—earth and spirit.

Slipping her hands into her short pockets, Eloise wandered down the path towards Solace.

Circling past the boab, she was surprised to find Vera lingering underneath the twisted branches. Considering no one usually saw her this side of ten a.m., Eloise wondered if she'd had dreams of her own.

"Hey," she called.

The witch looked up and waved her over. "Hey, yourself. You're out early."

"So are you," the elemental replied, joining the witch by the tree. "What's up?"

Vera sighed. "My spell isn't working the way I want it to."

"Oh? Why not?"

"It's only blocking what's making us sick," Vera explained. "There's still magic leaking out." The witch clucked her tongue in disapproval.

"How do you know?"

"All my fresh produce rotted yesterday." The witch shuddered. "All that food went straight in the bin. Such a waste... It took two whole cans of air freshener to get rid of the smell."

"Seriously?" Eloise wrinkled her nose and wondered why the plants around them seemed to be fine, but the fruit and veg weren't. She hesitated. The fruit and veg in the *Outpost*...

"Well, let's look on the bright side," Vera went on—clearly, the connection hadn't occurred to her. "At least we won't be projectile vomiting while I try to figure it out."

"Zero vomit is always a plus."

Their conversation dipped into a lull. The heaviness of what lay beneath their feet weighed everything down around Eloise—the air, her shoulders, her thoughts—until she couldn't think of anything else but Finn. They both had a part to play in the ongoing Old One saga, she was sure of it.

"No word from Finn yet?" Vera seemed to be on the same wavelength, and it didn't seem like a coincidence.

"I don't think there will be," Eloise replied, shaking her head. "I'm worried."

"Finn can look after himself."

"I know, but..." she trailed off, her thoughts going back to her dream.

Vera's expression softened into concern. "There's something else going on, isn't there?"

Eloise scuffed her toe in the dirt, digging a little trail. "I haven't had any dreams since we stopped Darius, but I had one last night."

Vera sighed and looked up at the boab. "Well, the seal *is* cracked, so I'm not surprised."

"It's more than that." Eloise shook her head. "I'm not sure how to describe it. It's..." It was her turn to sigh. "Drew said Finn's trail just ended, right?"

Vera nodded. "Yeah..."

"We both know that doesn't mean he's vanished entirely." The more she thought about it, the more her resolve hardened. "I want to go after him."

"Go after him?" Vera's eyebrows shot up. "What did Kyne say about all this?"

"He doesn't want me to go."

"I'm not surprised. It's dangerous out there, wandering about. It's not the weather for it." The witch screwed up her nose. "It's never the weather for it, actually. The outback is a deadly place for the unprepared. You know it, more than the rest of us."

"I wouldn't be just wandering about," Eloise explained. She *did* remember, and the last thing she wanted was a repeat experience. "I'd be using my magic to follow the rivers."

"Eloise, you're having dreams about the mountain again. What if the Old One is trying to trick you into doing just that? It wants your abilities."

"I'm meant to do this. *I can feel it.*" She pressed the heel of her palm over her heart, defiant in her belief that this was her path. She was meant to find Finn and help him.

Suddenly, Vera threw her hands into the air. "*As ucht Dé,*" she exclaimed and strode off towards the *Outpost*.

Eloise had never heard Vera speak any other language before, and her eyes widened. It sounded like Irish Gaelic.

Scurrying after her, Eloise called, "Where are you going?"

"To get you something to help," Vera threw over her shoulder. "Finn left without taking anything magical to help sustain him. If you find him, he might not be the same."

Eloise caught up to her and slowed her stride. "I know, but if he's beyond this reality, he's in a magical one. Wouldn't that help?"

"Maybe, but none of us understand what that

reality is, or how the fae maintain themselves with magic." They rounded the corner of the *Outpost*. "It's better to be safe than sorry."

Inside the dugout, it was dark and cool.

Vera hurried through the beaded curtain at the bottom of the stairs, the plastic clacking as it swung out of the way. Eloise followed and almost got tangled as the witch ducked into the room she'd dedicated to her altar. The electric light flicked on, and objects began to clatter and rattle.

Eloise lingered at the door, looking at all the magical bits and pieces Vera had arranged in the room. It was all so interesting to her, the way her friend practiced her magic—with crystals, herbs, complex symbols, and talismans. Even her spell book—her grimoire—was enticing with its wrinkled pages, strange writing, and worn leather cover.

Maybe it was because witchcraft was more tangible than being an elemental. It was complex, but still a lot more straightforward than what she could do. Eloise felt like she was just making it up as she went along most of the time.

"Ah, here it is." Vera emerged with a pendant in her hand. "Just the talisman you'll need."

"What is it, exactly?"

"It's a chunk of raw citrine wrapped in threads of silver, copper, and gold, which has been soaked in a solution of salt water under a full moon...with a megadose of Brinewold magic."

"Sounds...complicated. And expensive."

"For all intents and purposes, it's a battery." Vera grimaced and held out the talisman. "Kyne's not going to be happy about this. He'll rip me a new one for not trying to talk you out of it."

Eloise grinned and closed her hand around the crystal. "You and I both know there's no talking anyone out of anything."

Vera placed her hand on the elemental's shoulder. "Don't forget what the craglorn are. If he's devolved, he won't know who he is. All he'll see is magic, and he'll do *anything* to get it."

"I know." She swallowed hard, hoping she'd find Finn in time.

"They took my entire family...an entire coven of powerful witches. Don't underestimate him, not even for a second."

Eloise's hand tightened around the talisman. "I won't."

CHAPTER 16

When Vera stepped back into the cave for a second time since the water was drained, she shivered violently, like someone had just walked across her grave.

She felt the increase in magic hit her like a wave swatting at a listless boat, and she stumbled. Her shoulder hit the wall, the rough rock scraping her bare skin.

Not walked, she thought. *Stomped on it, more like.*

"Careful," Drew said behind her. "It's still slippery."

It was more than slippery, but instead of biting back, she righted herself and continued into the cave, which reeked like something had crawled out of a dark hole and died.

Vera wrinkled her nose. "There's a certain...*air quality* down here, don't you think?"

Drew grunted. "Smells like wet tentacle monster."

"That's one way of putting it." Vera set down her

bag and looked over the crystals she'd placed. "Nothing's moved, at least." She knelt before the slab of bluestone. It may have been her imagination, but the cracks in the seal looked like they'd grown an inch overnight.

"Can you see anything?" Drew asked.

She shrugged and rose to her feet. "I don't know. It looks like the cracks are opening more, but it could be my mind playing tricks. The spell's still intact and doing what it's supposed to, but..."

"It's working, but it's not."

"No."

Drew pulled off his T-shirt and kicked off his boots. "I'm shifting," he told her. "I can see the magic better."

Vera nodded and turned her back, giving him privacy. It would be helpful to know what the Old One's magic was doing, especially when she was trying to block it. She couldn't see what Drew could, though she was kind of grateful for her blindness. It toned down her blind panic a couple of notches.

She picked up one of the quartz crystals she'd placed for her original spell. The moment the alignment was broken, the Brinewold magic in them weakened. Thankfully, the spell was still active, otherwise she'd be wearing her breakfast.

"Anything change?" she asked, looking at Drew.

"*Nothing,*" a voice echoed in her mind. "*You just pushed the cloud around a bit.*"

Vera jerked backwards, her eyes widening. She'd

been expecting a shake of his dingo head, not a full sentence.

"*Coen's lessons seem to have levelled me up,*" Drew told her with a snort. "*Don't look so shocked. It's not like I bit you on the arse.*"

"You may as well have." He'd gone and levelled up...while she'd levelled down.

Turning back to the seal, she worried her bottom lip until she tasted the metallic bite of blood on her tongue. *What was she missing?*

The Old Ones were original to the creation of the universe, while the Irish witches were born out of a single reality. It was an entire universe versus a single thread. Maybe her magic was incompatible, or simply not strong enough.

No one alive knew where the witch's magic had originated, or who was the first to understand it. The witches all made a big fuss over the bloodlines and the covens, but the waters only became murkier the farther back they went.

The truth was, for all the amazing things she could do, deep down, Vera knew she couldn't fix this problem. The best she could manage was a Band-Aid that kept losing its stick.

Maybe she'd be able to figure it out if she still had her father's Nightshade legacy. To buy them the time they needed for Eloise to find Finn, and for Coen to return with the answers they needed to banish the Old Ones for good.

Vera didn't want to be jealous of her friend, but at that moment, she was. *Big time.*

"Maybe Eloise has it right," she murmured. "She's got the guts to listen to her dreams, not that I have any of my own."

The dingo raised his head. "*What do you mean?*"

"I haven't had a vision in months," she admitted. "I used to have them all the time. I got one from Eloise's journal when we broke into her van, remember?" Her fingers traced the rough edge of the crystal. "That was one of the last times. Ever since I let go of my Nightshade legacy, I've…"

"*You've what?*"

"My spell should've worked. The only thing that's different is my magic. I'm half what I was."

"*Vera,*" Drew said, his dingo shape letting out a small growl. "*You're not any less of a witch just because you let go of that thing that was poisoning you. It's not you.*" He pointed his snout at the seal. "*It's that thing.*"

"What if I can't do anything about it?" She set the crystal in place and felt the spell reignite at full power. "Maybe I should've gone with Eloise."

"*Gone? What do you mean?*"

"She's going to look for Finn."

"*She's what?*" he barked—*literally.*

Vera raised her eyebrows. "She had another dream about the mountain, but this time Finn was in it. She thinks he might be… Well, *you know.*"

"*Corrupted? Christ, Vera! And you let her go?*" Drew

stood and began to pace, his head lowered. "*What about Kyne? Did he try to stop her?*"

Vera shrank back, her gaze lowering. "Could he stop her, though? I don't think she realises just how much power she has. If she wanted to, she could stop *him*, not the other way around." Eloise's blood had given Hardy enough juice to go up against a two-thousand-year-old vampire, so who knew what else she could do if she put her back into it.

Drew paused and looked at Vera, his dingo eyes shining eerily in the half-light of the cave. "*When is she leaving?*"

"She's waiting for nightfall, when the stars are out." That was in her dream too, though it'd taken a bit of pressuring to get the elemental to divulge it. "Apparently, it's easier to find the rivers then."

"*Rivers?*"

"The currents of space and time," Vera told him. "Remember how she sent the Dust Dogs to the Middle East? She can only manipulate what's there, and night is best."

"*The dark places between the stars...*" Drew mused. "*Coen told me about them. It isn't the stars that tell the Indigenous peoples about the Dreaming, but the places between them.*"

Vera rubbed her tired eyes. "Of course. The stars are only accents on a larger tapestry..."

"*That's why I have to go with her.*"

"What? Why?" Finn was the last person she saw Drew rushing out to help.

"*I can see, Vera,*" he told her. "*I can protect her, and we might find Coen on the way. There's a reason he was teaching me, and I don't think it was just to be a glorified guard dog.*"

Vera sighed and looked at the cracked seal. Coen always had a reason, even if the meaning wasn't clear at the onset. Sometimes his 'insights' had an annoying way of manifesting years later. Maybe this was one of them...

Still, she didn't give him her blessing either way. Vera believed both of them going was bad news, especially with the black mountain making another appearance. It had *trap* written all over it.

"Anyway, we've got hours until sunset," she said after a moment. "Will you help me with my spell?"

"*Yeah.*" Drew leapt up onto a rock, settling in for the long haul. "*Let me know what you want me to do.*"

Not go, she thought.

Pushing away her anxiety, Vera took her grimoire from her bag and opened it, the spine cracking as she flipped to the page she'd been working from.

"I'm going to attune the crystals again," she told him. "Just let me know if the glowing blue stuff stops or gets worse, okay?"

"*Sure,*" the dingo said. "*Will do.*"

Eloise slunk through the shadows behind Solace, her heart hammering in her chest. Why did it feel like she was trying to escape a maximum security prison?

Because everyone will try to stop you, that's why.

The crystal talisman hung heavily around her neck, the chain dragging against her skin. She looked around, but the night was quiet.

Kyne was down at the pub with Vera and the other Exiles. The witch had kindly agreed to keep him busy while Eloise slipped out of Solace—when she said 'kindly,' she really meant reluctantly. When she didn't show up for dinner, it wouldn't take long for him to realise where she'd gone. Then the gig would be up.

"Nice night for a jail break, huh?"

Eloise yelped as the sound of Drew's voice reverberated out of the shadows, but it was short-lived. The pang of annoyance that overcame her was far more powerful than any jump scare. "Vera cracked under pressure, didn't she?"

"I hope that's not meant to be a joke, because it's too soon." He stepped out of the shadows and into the moonlight. "Why are you running away?"

"I'm not running away."

"Sure looks like you are. Why didn't you tell us?"

"If I did, you'd all either try to stop me or want to come with." Kyne had already made his feelings crystal-clear. If he knew she intended to act on them, he'd tie her up to stop her from leaving, likely finding allies in Blue and Wally. No doubt Hardy would want to come with her, because he knew persuasion wouldn't work and he couldn't compel supernaturals with his vampire mind-tricks. Vera was the only one who'd wanted to help, and Drew... "So, which team are you on?"

"Team come with."

"Why?"

"Vera's spell isn't working," he told her. "It was fae magic that broke it, so maybe your dream was about that."

"You think Finn could fix the cracks?"

The shifter shrugged. "Maybe."

She narrowed her eyes. "We can work on that when Finn and I get back."

"Don't make this hard," he said with a sigh. "I can protect you, Eloise."

"What makes you think I need protecting?"

He took a step towards town. "I can go get Kyne, if you'd like."

"Don't you dare."

They stared at one another—Eloise glared while Drew just loitered in that arrogant 'whatever' way he had. It reminded her of the night she'd met him, when she'd found him propped up against the outside wall of Blue's pub, naked as the day he came into the world. She didn't know he was a shifter then, so it was quite the eyebrow-raising encounter.

"Looks like we're at an impasse," the shifter stated. "And yeah, I know big words."

"Stop putting yourself down," Eloise snapped.

"I will if you stop trying to be clueless tentacle monster fodder."

She scoffed as the insult hit its mark.

Drew smirked. "Truth hurt?"

"*Bloody hell*," she exclaimed. "I'm not carrying around your clothes."

"That's fine." He took off his T-shirt. "That's why I've got a backpack...but I'll need some help putting it on." He tossed his top at her.

Catching it against her chest, Eloise sighed. Looked like she wasn't going to shake him, but at least she'd get a laugh out of it. A dingo wearing a backpack...that was something she had to see.

Turning her back so Drew could shift, she folded his T-shirt into a neat square. The journey was going to be tough as it was—trying to use her scarcely used powers to find a needle in a haystack—but having someone there with her would be a comfort. Maybe it should've been Kyne, but his leg still bothered him even after a dose of Andante's magic.

"*Okay, I'm decent*," the dingo said.

Eloise peeked over her shoulder to make sure before turning back around. Seeing him in his dingo form waiting patiently for her made her smile. It was hard not to reach down and pat him on the head. That'd be a little patronising, even if he was cute.

Drew had already packed the rest of his clothes, so she slipped his shirt inside and zipped up the bag.

Kneeling beside him, she said, "Paw."

Drew lifted his left leg, letting her loop on the first strap, then his right for the next one. Then she fastened the strap around his waist, the plastic clips snapping. Finally, she tightened everything so the bag wouldn't fall off his silky dingo back.

"Your fur's really soft, you know that?"

He flicked his tail. "*That doesn't sound creepy at all.*"

"Not as creepy as giving you a belly rub." Standing, Eloise looked down at him and couldn't help but laugh. The backpack was nearly half his size. "You look ridiculous."

"*I wish the clothes shifted with me, but it ain't a perfect world,*" he drawled. "*Which way are we going?*" When she didn't reply straight away, the dingo snorted. "*Do you have a plan at all?*"

"I was going to start at the fae camp," she said. "That's where Finn was last seen."

"*You were just going to wing it, weren't you?*"

Eloise shrugged. "My powers aren't that straightforward. Neither is time and space, apparently."

"*You're following a sign left in your creepy tentacle monster dream. This isn't a time to make it up as you go along.*"

"What do you suggest?" She was starting to regret letting him come along—as if she had a choice about it. Even the backpack wasn't lifting the mood anymore.

"*We'll start at the camp,*" he told her. "*Follow the trail to where it disappeared. You should be able to find the rivers from there.*"

"How do you know? I know that's where Finn left, but they have to be there to begin with. The currents always change."

"*I can see more than you realise,*" he said with a huff. "*That's why I'm the only one who should go with you.*" He turned towards the outback and began padding across the ochre dirt, but when she didn't follow, he stopped. "*Are you coming or not? The longer we piss fart around, the longer the mountain's got to corrupt Finn.*"

"Okay, okay." She jogged to catch up with him. "When did you get so assertive?"

"*About the time I realised I was more than just a dumb dog.*"

CHAPTER 17

Eloise didn't know the moment she and Drew had stepped out of the world they knew and into the other place. One minute they were following Finn's trail, and the next, they were here.

She wasn't sure if she could call it the Dreaming, *or should*, because it didn't fit with anything Coen had told her about it. No, this place felt more like a thread of reality that resembled a world of spirits. It wasn't death—where souls went after they shed their physical forms—but a place more like consciousness.

Wherever they were, it was the perfect world for a walkabout.

"*It looks the same, but it's not,*" Drew said, his voice echoing in her mind.

"Yeah... I can feel it."

"*The sky is beautiful,*" he told her. "*It looks like the Northern Lights. Like curtains of colour are rippling in the wind.*"

"Colour?" Eloise looked up. The sky was the same star-studded bruised purple it'd been since they'd arrived.

"You can't see it?"

"No." She shook her head. "What colour is it?"

"Purple, pink, and gold. I wish you could see..."

Eloise gazed at the sky and tried to imagine what it looked like. She'd seen photos of the Northern Lights—and the southern ones too—but somehow, she thought a picture on a screen would never compare to seeing them in real life.

"I wonder why you can see it and I can't," she wondered out loud.

"Whatever magic turned my ancestors into dingoes must be linked to this place," he mused.

"The spirit of the land," Eloise echoed.

"You're an elemental. I would've thought someone like you would be able to see the same things."

"Yeah, nah..." Her true parentage was a mystery, just as it was a mystery how the first dingo-shifters came to be. "Whoever the elementals are, they mustn't come from the same place." She took a step forwards. "We better see if we can find Finn's trail."

"Eloise?"

She turned. "Yeah?"

"The cracks in the seal... There's magic leaking out of it. I can see it all over Solace."

"I thought as much."

"I told Vera, but I didn't want to frighten you."

Eloise smiled and patted the dingo on the head, knowing it'd irritate him. "I think we're past that point, don't you?"

Drew shook his head, his ears flopping from side-to-side, and padded around her. *"Let me see if I can sniff out the fae."*

As the dingo wandered off with his nose to the ground, Eloise wandered about, trying to find clues of her own. She peered at the ground, searching for footprints, and at trees and bushes looking for snapped twigs—things she'd seen people do in movies—but found nothing.

She'd been half expecting to see the Min Min or find traces of Coen. Instead, they seemed to be on their own with the strange colours and thick air.

"Over here," Drew called.

He'd made his way into a clearing ahead, moving just out of her line of sight. Passing under the bough of a low-hanging gum, she caught up with the dingo, but couldn't see what he'd picked up.

"He was definitely here," he told her.

"How can you tell?"

"If you look closely, you can see the dirt is all scuffed," he explained. *"And it helps that I can smell him. Finn has a particular ripeness about him."*

"Scuff marks?" The word brought to mind all kinds of worrying images, with a fight at the top of the list. Eloise looked but couldn't see anything. She'd have to take Drew's word for it.

"Don't worry, he's not hurt." He looked up at her, but it was impossible to read a dingo's expression. *"I can't smell any blood."*

Eloise shivered. "Can you tell what direction he went?"

"Nope. He's vanished again."

"Then he must've caught another current."

"Then we have to try to catch it. Can you find the same one?"

"Let me see..." Eloise reached out her hand and felt her fingers brush against the same coolness she'd felt when they'd stepped onto the first river. As long as she kept her intent clear in her mind, the current would carry them where they needed to go. Following the theory had seemed to work so far.

"Got it," she said. "Ready?"

"As I'll ever be."

The plum-coloured night faded to black as Finn limped across the outback.

He sang softly to himself, rambling the words of his mother's lullaby until they made no sense, but at least he was in tune.

"E'detua litua de, thadrei du'lei, an astrad du'a celest tualei..." Goodnight little one, rest your head, the stars will guide you to your bed.

Blisters rubbed on his heels, each step sending

stinging bolts of pain up his legs, but still, he walked. His face stained with tears; his soul battered and bruised. His head throbbing from where his shadow-self struck him. His back aching.

"An astrad du'a celest tualei..."

His boot crunched on rock, and he sensed a ripple in the air. A faint flutter of magic brushed against his skin, forcing an abrupt stop to his zombie-like shuffling.

Finn gazed up at the world around him. He'd left the purplish bruised dreamscape and stepped into reality once more.

He stood amongst a thick forest of stunted green gums with ghostly white trunks, the scent of eucalyptus thick around him. The night sky was the same black he remembered, the waxing three-quarter full moon hanging round and silver towards the horizon where its glow illuminated the dark peak before him.

A mountain made of piles of black magma boulders rose sharply out of the lush forest of emerald gums. Once, this spot must have been the site of an ancient lava tube, or perhaps it was the remains of an underground volcano born during the formation of the Earth. Whichever it was, the landscape was born out of the unfeeling violence of nature itself.

Even where he stood—on a rise two or more kilometres from the peak—Finn was surrounded by the signs of the forest's tumultuous past. Blackened earth dotted with piles of oddly-shaped rocks filled with shiny flecks of obsidian and ghostly trees growing at odd angles. The night, which was usually filled with the comings and goings of nocturnal creatures, was silent as a grave.

Something was wrong about this place—wrong and unnatural.

Finn felt the magic seeping from the blackness and knew it was the same. He knew it, and it knew him. This was Eloise's black mountain. The prison of the Old One.

"Finally, I see you in the flesh," he murmured.

He waited, almost expecting the mountain to reply, but the night was eerily silent, almost like a horror movie.

Finn would receive no welcome here.

Weariness had crept into his bones a long time ago, and he looked down at his hands. His body was already starting to wrinkle like an old prune left out in direct sunlight. No wonder he felt like death warmed up, because that was what he was becoming.

His walkabout had cost him more magic than he thought it would. He could neither continue nor go back.

Dropping his bag onto the ground, he gathered wood and bark from the forest floor. He arranged it all in a neat pile and struggled with lighting a fire. Rubbing his palms up and down on a stick, he cursed as threads of smoke rose, but the tinder didn't catch for some time. Not until his wrinkled hands felt raw and cracked.

As the fire grew and warmth spread into his tired bones, Finn felt the corruption from the mountain bearing down on his little camp. It was forcing him to let it in, to allow the poison to darken his soul.

Too bad, he thought. *It's already dark enough in here. Not enough room for the two of us.*

Finn would fight it, knowing it would take the last of his magic. He'd devolve, becoming the creature the witches feared most—craglorn. It was better than becoming a tool of the Old One and turning against his Exile family.

Perhaps this was the punishment the shadow had deemed appropriate for Finn's crimes. Or perhaps it was another stop on his outback walkabout tour. There was no way to know for sure, not until something happened.

So, he waited...and strange sounds found him in the dark.

Knocks echoed through the forest, three at a time. Once from the north, then an answer came from the south. *Knock, knock, knock.* Hollow clacking—stone on wood.

Then, a few minutes later, a gust of wind carried a mournful shriek towards his camp. It sent a ripple of ice through his blood, and he listened until he saw the lights in the sky. Silver orbs flew between the stars, moving in unnatural directions. Humans had created machines they'd sent up into space, but he knew they moved in straight lines, caught in the invisible tides of gravity around the planet. Were they spirits? Or were they creatures from other places?

The shriek never came again; the wind died down, and soon, the lights faded into the dark places between the stars.

Finn listened to the land and the strange noises that whispered out of the darkness, wondering what this place was and why his walkabout had led him here.

As if his mind had asked the question aloud, he was granted an answer.

The largest taipan he'd ever seen slithered out of the darkness and glided towards the fire. Its scales were a dark russet-brown colour, and its head angular and pale, marking it as a Costal Taipan—its name was a dead giveaway that it wasn't native to Solace.

As it reached the circle of firelight, Finn could see its reddish eyes watching him. He knew a lot about snakes, even the ones that didn't live in the outback. They usually liked him, especially the highly venomous ones.

A bite from the Coastal Taipan could kill a human within forty-five minutes, and its brother, the Inland Taipan, was the deadliest snake in Australia. There were a lot of the latter around Solace.

"*E'dreha*," he murmured, holding up his hand.

What little magic he had left flared and reached

out towards the snake. It continued its slithering, rounding the fire and gliding over his boots.

It was a beautiful thing, twice the size it should have been—perhaps a side effect of this strange place. The colour of its scales turned gold in the glow of the flames...but it didn't stop.

The snake ignored Finn's command and continued on its way, disappearing into the shadow of night.

I have no power here, he thought. *The air is thin, and so is the veil that separates this world from all the others.*

Looking up at the faint outline of the mountain, he understood completely. His walkabout, the shadow... It was his turn.

He took out his knife and began carving the point into a slice of bark as he began to sing softly to the night. "*E'detua litua de, thadrei du'lei, an astrad du'a celest tualei...*"

CHAPTER 18

The drone of a diesel generator echoed across Solace, disturbing the morning calm.

Kyne stood in the shade of a gum tree, his arms crossed over his chest, watching muddy water drain out of Wally's mine and dribble off into the distance.

Hardy appeared out of thin air and flicked the brim of the elemental's hat.

"Rack off," Kyne grumbled, swatting away the vampire.

"There's no use being angry about it. Eloise would've gone either way."

"I'm not angry."

Hardy raised his eyebrows. "You so are."

The miner sighed. "Yeah, so what? Eloise ran off in the middle of the night without so much as a word. How am I supposed to feel?"

"It's not like she ran off with another man," Hardy told him.

"Yeah, nah, it's worse." He turned his gaze to the mine where Wally was overseeing the water pump. "She ran off to fight that bloody mountain."

"Drew's with her. He won't let anything happen, and they didn't go to fight the mountain. They went to find Finn."

"*Sure.*"

It was cold comfort in the hard light of day. Kyne's pride was hurt, but his heart was, too. Didn't Eloise trust him? Didn't she believe in him? Letting Drew go with her only added insult to injury.

"How's the leg?" Hardy asked.

"Stop trying to distract me."

"Then stop pouting."

"I'm n—" Kyne sighed, his shoulders tense with anxiety. He *was* pouting. "My leg's a little stiff, but that's all."

"Good to hear." The vampire clapped his hand on Kyne's shoulder. "And I highly doubt Eloise left the way she did to hurt you. She knew we would've either tried to stop her or tried to go along." Kyne grunted, but Hardy still had more to say. "Whatever she saw in that dream was enough to convince her that this was the path she was supposed to take."

"What I'm afraid of," Kyne murmured, "is that the mountain has lured her onto a false trail."

"I don't think we have to worry about that."

He snorted. "What makes you say that?"

"When I tasted her blood..." Hardy hesitated and looked away.

Kyne knew the moment the vampire shared with Eloise in that tent was considered highly personal. There was a certain closeness two people in love could share, then there was a vampire drinking the blood of someone they cared deeply about. Hardy felt like he'd betrayed Kyne's relationship with her—he'd told the miner as much in the days after all the business with Darius.

"I don't resent either of you for that, mate," Kyne told him. "You know that."

"I know, I..." The vampire sighed. "The point I was trying to make is that there's more to her than meets the eye. More than any of us, or even Eloise herself, understands. I could taste it in her blood when her magic awoke."

Kyne nodded. There was a reason the mountain was desperately trying to reach her and not him, even though they were both elementals.

Over at the mine, the pump let out a stuttered chugging, then switched off. The generator kept on going, the engine chugging loudly until Wally cut the power. Silence stretched over the outback, the lack of sound almost deafening after an hour to so of the machinery running.

"Bloody hell," the old wolf exclaimed. "What in the blue blazes..."

Hardy was beside him in a flash. "Looks like tar."

Kyne jogged towards them, wondering what all the fuss was about. "What's going on?"

"There ain't no reason for it," Wally said, shaking his head. "None at all."

Kyne screeched to halt when he saw what the men were staring at. "That doesn't look good..."

The rainwater that'd flood the mine had been running free all morning, albeit full of sandy, ochre grit, but now the hose was clogged with thick black sludge. It oozed out onto the ground like slime, seeping across the red earth.

"It's got to be the fae magic from the storm," Hardy said. "We let this water sit a bit longer, maybe it...*congealed*."

Kyne took off his hat and wiped his damp brow. He'd seen something like it before in the vision he'd shared with Eloise, *and* Drew had said the seal was leaking an oil-like substance into the water.

Two and two made an Old One.

"It's not the storm," he murmured, frowning down at the goop. "It's the seal."

He felt Hardy's gaze on him, but he couldn't look away from the black tar oozing towards his boots.

Whatever this byproduct of the Old One's trapped magic was, it'd begun to leak into the earth and probably into the ground water, too. Paired with the magic that was making everyone sick and had rotted all of Vera's fresh produce, it didn't bode well.

It was in the air, the earth, and the water.

Kyne stared at the goop, his palms sweating as his anxiety rose. Half the Exiles were gone—Eloise, Drew, Coen, and Finn—and now Wally and Hardy were looking at him like he was supposed to know what to do about it.

No one understood what they were fighting, let alone how to repair the seal. Andante couldn't help, and the only other person who might know something had disappeared weeks ago.

The tar was a millimetre from touching the tips of Kyne's boots when Hardy pulled him back.

"Whatever it is, I wouldn't go around touching it," the vampire murmured.

"Maybe we should get Vera to take a look," Wally said, poking the sludge with a stick.

The men stared at the goop in silence. The pump had stopped sucking the stuff up, but the residue still seeped out of the hose and onto the ground like a bad omen.

Wally coughed. "Full moon's a couple of days away. If I can't go down there…"

"We'll figure something out," Hardy told him. "Even if we have to get Vera to spell you in the cool room out the back of the *Outpost*, then that's what we'll do."

"We won't leave you hanging, mate," Kyne added. He was grateful there was something he could do about one thing on a list that seemed never-ending.

Hardy backed away, his boots crunching on gravel.

"Let's head back into town. There's nothing we can do here for the moment."

As the two men began the short walk back to Solace, Kyne lingered a moment, taking one last look at the black tar.

He ran his hand over his face, his eyes stinging. If something happened to Eloise and he wasn't there to help her, he wasn't sure how he'd react. It didn't feel too good, being powerless.

"*Eloise...*" he whispered, his heart aching, "be safe out there."

<hr>

Finn was dreaming.

He was asleep, but he may as well have been awake for all the good it was doing him. Lucid dreaming, the humans called it. Sounded like the effects of a hallucinogenic drug.

"I just want to rest," he muttered as his mind swirled with unformed visions. "Just let me starve in peace, will you?"

He closed his eyes and turned over, his bed of leaves rustling and kicking up a waft of eucalyptus.

Finn stood in a hallway, staring at a closed door he knew should be guarded.

Looking up and down the passage, he saw nothing but black walls, plush blue carpets, and paintings that were worth more than the entire wealth of his family's castle and all its holdings combined. The mountain air sent spikes of ice across his cheeks, but his heart burned with a fire for blood that could not be quenched.

But he wasn't alone. Muffled voices ebbed through the closed door, carrying words too tempting to be ignored.

"We can't wait for the Black Sun to reemerge," a woman said. "It could take generations. The time to strike is *now*."

"It cannot be done. It's far too risky," a man replied.

"It *can*."

"Then what do you suggest?"

"A single coordinated strike across multiple targets."

"An attack on this scale..." The man sounded hesitant compared to the woman's unyielding devotion. "The *ash'strad's* will have to be planted ahead of time."

"I already have someone in mind for the task."

The man replied, but his voice was too low for Finn to make out.

"Finn," the woman called, her voice muffled by the door. "You may come in now."

Finn straightened and smoothed his palms over his jacket. Opening the door, he strode into the room and came face-to-face with Auriel de Leiran, the most powerful Unseelie in all of Lor'Iyslar.

Her straight, moss-green hair fell to her slender

waist, her silver eyes glowing against the pallor of her skin. She moved towards him, the scales of her armoured dress tinkling softly.

He paid no attention to the man standing by the table—whoever he was didn't matter, only she did.

"Finn Oreah'anza," Auriel purred. Her magic filled his senses and made his head spin. "How would you like to be a hero?"

Finn jerked his mind out of the vision, abruptly tearing away from the pain of his past.

He'd always been a pawn in their game. Deep down he knew it, but he still went ahead with their plan. He and Siora had planted the *ash'strads* inside six towns and villages full of Seelie families and countless *De'ashlide.*

The Seelie weren't fast enough to stop the orbs from detonating, but they had just enough forewarning to plan a counter-attack of their own. The attack had devastated not only Finn's home, but Siora's, and the heart of the de Leiran rebellion.

Though it wasn't a rebellion, was it? The de Leiran's had turned him and Siora into little more than terrorists. A few well-placed words, promises of power and retribution. Wealth. *Title.*

Others would argue they were seduced by the dark magic the de Leiran's welded, and they did, but Finn knew he was strong enough to resist. He'd had the power to turn his back on them, but by then, he was in too deep. Denying Auriel de Leiran would have been not only his death, but that of his entire family.

Like that was an excuse, he thought. *What a fool you are, Finn Oreah'anza. You deserve everything you get.*

Instead of planting the *ash'strads*, he should've gone home and got his family to safety. He should have...but it was far too late for that.

If there was one thing Finn could do with his last days in this reality, it would be to resist. He wouldn't let the mountain use him like Auriel had. He would not be the one who condemned an entire world to death. *Not again.*

Finn sighed and rubbed his tired eyes. By the looks of it, sleeping his way into oblivion wasn't going to be an option.

Standing, he slung his bag across his chest, the *ash'strad* laying heavy against his back, and slid his knife into his belt. Then he made sure the fire was out and the coals carried no heat before setting off into the shadows of the forest.

He walked without direction as the last threads of his magic began to fade. With enough steps, he would wither entirely. He'd become a craglorn, and the only thing he would be to the mountain was another shadow prowling its unnatural slopes, shrieking in the darkness—trapped, tormented, and serving penance for his crimes.

He supposed this was one of those near-death

moments humans talked about. The part where his life 'flashed before his eyes.'

He remembered the journey to Australia with Siora and the fae they'd met along the way. He remembered arriving in Solace and the man with the strange magic who found them in the outback—Kyne Brady. He remembered Blue and Wally welcoming him into town. He remembered Drew smashing his head in with a shovel. He remembered Vera Walsh, the witch. Vera, whose entire family was murdered by his kind.

For twelve years, Finn had lived peacefully in the remote outback with the other fae, keeping away from the world. He'd only caused pain everywhere he went, his sour Unseelie temperament a danger to everyone and everything.

Until Eloise Hart arrived. An inexplicable chain of events had been set off when her shiny white motorhome had broken down on the highway outside of Solace. A chain in which Finn had created several links of his own.

He'd made his peace with Vera and the hatred sewn between them because of what the craglorn had done to her coven. He'd helped the Exiles with Darius, choosing to risk his life to stop the *ash'strad* from detonating. He'd saved Kyne from the storm brought down on Solace by Siora. He'd stood against his own people to help the Exiles protect this world from the Old Ones. He'd lost everything to save billions of innocent lives.

Weren't those things enough?

Ever since Eloise had arrived, Finn had been trying to redeem himself, whether he knew he was or not.

But it wasn't enough. His walkabout had led him exactly where he needed to be. *Purgatory.*

So Finn kept walking.

And walking.

And walking, until...

A shadow hurled itself out of the trees and collided with his tired body, the impact pushing the air out of his lungs. They landed in a heap, then turned over and over, rolling down an embankment. Finn scrambled for the knife in his belt, grabbing hold of the hilt as they slammed into a fallen gumtree. He landed on his back, the shadow on top of him.

The blade flashed in the moonlight as it came to rest against a slender throat.

A familiar face glared down at him, silver eyes shining menacingly in the night. Eyes that twisted his heart and filled it with dread.

Siora.

CHAPTER 19

Finn dropped the knife, the blade slipping away from Siora's neck.

Her blue hair was tangled, and her pale skin was smeared with dirt. One thing she was not, was withered from lack of magic—not like he was.

"Did you follow us here?" she demanded, her hands wrapping around his neck. "*Answer me.*"

He stared at her, too exhausted to reply.

"I see..." she murmured. Her grip loosened and her fingers stroked his wrinkled skin. "*I see...*"

Finn could hardly move as he felt Siora push some of her magic into him. Warmth seeped through his chilled body and feeling returned to his weary limbs... but it also brought clarity to his muddled mind.

The music of his mother's lullaby faded as he realised the ramifications of the place of power Siora had been so adamant about. How had she found out about it? As he lay there, he regretted not asking because now they were in the line of fire, about to become collateral damage yet again.

"You've come to join us, haven't you?" Siora murmured, cupping his face in her hands. "You came all this way without magic to sustain you." A smile appeared on her face, but instead of the same beautiful fae he'd once known, he was looking into the eyes of a madwoman. "I always knew you were strong, Finn. *Always.*"

Finn was beginning to doubt the outcome of his walkabout, or if it had ended at all. Had he come here to die...or to save the Earth from yet another attempted escape by the Old One?

Either way, it was eerily similar to the choice he'd faced when he'd stood before Auriel de Leiran, and it only made him feel sick to the stomach.

Siora climbed off him and stood, her slender form backlit by the moon. Holding out her hand, she wiggled her fingers. "Come. We have a camp not too far from here."

Finn took her hand, allowing her to pull him up— there didn't seem to be much he could do about it, anyway.

As they trudged through the night, the eucalyptus forest was as silent as it had been when Finn had arrived. All sights and sounds of nature were muted— the snake remained the only creature he'd seen—and their footsteps were the only noise that suffered this strange place.

Soon, he saw the warmth ahead and wasn't sure if he was going to like what he found amongst the fae. He dreaded the same questions would come with the same answers. *Had anything changed? Anything at all?*

The other fae looked up as he stepped into the firelight. Some stood, reaching for their weapons, and others simply stared with a mixture of shock and open hatred. There were twelve now. Others had joined Siora's little band and he wasn't sure what to make of it, except for one thing.

Nothing had changed.

How disappointing.

"It's all right." Siora lifted her hand and they settled, their gazes moving to her. "Finn has made the journey without aid...and he made it. We should welcome him."

They settled, their eyes turning elsewhere. Siora's control over them made Finn uneasy as she led him to a small fire at the edge of the camp.

"Sit," she commanded. "Warm yourself."

Finn collapsed by the fire, the last of his strength giving way. He was exhausted; the magic she'd given him was already fading. His strength would return if he allowed the mountain in, but there was no way he was doing that. Not for all the hot chips and red wine in the world.

Siora sat beside him and threw more wood onto the fire. She seemed like her old self again—happy, spirited, and free of the resentment that'd fed her anger back in Solace.

"This place..." he began, looking towards the shadows.

"It is a strange place," she interrupted. "The magic here is stranger than the magic in Solace, that's for sure."

Finn shivered and edged closer to the fire. "It makes me uneasy."

"As it should. If it doesn't, you'd be a fool. This world may be lacking magic, but the places it does seep through are curious..." a soft laugh escaped her lips, "and dangerous."

Finn studied her features, watching the shadows play over the curve of her brow and across her nose and lips. Did she realise where they were? Did she know what lay inside the mountain? Finn frowned, his heart heavy. How could she when she and the others were so adamant about not mixing with the Exiles? Siora didn't know the truth about the Old Ones because she'd never wanted to listen to Eloise, Kyne, the others, or even him. Her heart and mind were forever lost to Lor'Iyslar, locked away in a past that could never change or be again.

"Siora..." Finn looked away, not trusting his expression. "Could you tell me one thing?"

Her sigh lingered in the night.

He knew she wasn't going to agree one way or the other, but he asked anyway, "I understand that you wanted to leave, but did you have to summon that storm like you did?"

Siora said nothing as she picked up a log and threw it onto the fire. The shifting coals kicked up a whirl of glowing sparks that spiralled up towards the stars.

"It almost killed Kyne," he pressed.

Her brow creased. "I'm sorry to hear it."

"Are you?"

A momentary flash of anger passed across her features. "They wouldn't have let us go."

"They would have respected your choice if you'd only acted with a calm mind."

"Like you acted?" she demanded.

"Siora—"

"If you've only come to continue with your incessant blathering, *you can leave*."

The fae around the camp stirred as her voice rose, their silver eyes turning towards them.

"No," he murmured. "That's not why I came. I didn't... When I left Solace, I didn't think I'd find you."

"So you didn't come for me?"

He shook his head, knowing it'd break her heart. "I thought I'd already lost you."

"Then why?"

How could he tell her that he regretted everything they'd fought so passionately for? How could he when she still believed with all her heart and soul? How could he after all she'd suffered in this reality? He couldn't, so he lowered his gaze and stared into the fire.

Siora edged closer and he felt her hand slide onto his leg. "Did you hear it?" Her voice was a hushed whisper, full of desperation. "Did you?"

Finn hesitated. "Hear what?"

Her shoulders tensed and she snatched her hand back as if she'd let a secret slip that came with consequences, bad ones.

"Siora," he murmured. "What happened to you? What...?" He felt the mountain bearing down on them. "Siora, *please*."

"Finn... I-I've found us a way home," she admitted, her silver eyes misting with tears. "We can finally leave this place."

"How?"

"Have you seen the lights in the dark? Heard the creatures who call to one another?"

He nodded warily. And the snakes... He'd seen the snakes.

"They guard it. The spirit living in the mountain," she told him, her smile widening. "It was trapped there long ago—long before we came—but it still has the power to open a way between worlds."

A painful coldness spread through Finn's body as he realised their journey, and his own, was no accident. He knew it the moment she'd collided with him in the dark, but he didn't want to believe it.

The mountain had corrupted them.

Just like it'd twisted the Dust Dogs, Vera's Nightshade legacy, and the vampire Darius, the Old

One had wormed its way into Siora's psyche and manipulated her for its own gain. It had lured them here all the way from Solace, knowing their magic was the next best thing to Eloise Hart.

And Finn had walked right into its trap.

He swallowed hard, trying to keep the panic from showing on his face. "What do we have to do?"

"Set it free."

Eloise and Drew stepped off the current, leaving the river behind.

She was getting better at finding the right paths and sensing the moment they returned to reality. This time, their exit caused her to gasp for breath as the air thickened like soup. Humidity settled around them as her eyes adjusted to the night.

Gum trees rose thick in all directions, the scent of eucalyptus that'd been baked in the hot sun filling her senses. Wherever they were, it was still in Australia, but it had to be someplace north due to the moisture. Queensland, maybe?

"*Uh,*" Drew said, nudging her leg with his snout. "*Eloise?*"

She looked up and her heart almost stopped.

"*Is that what I think it is?*" the dingo asked.

"Yeah," Eloise whispered. "It is." There was no denying what they were looking at.

The black mountain rose up out of the forest and stretched into the star-studded sky, the peak a blemish of unnatural nothingness on the horizon. It must only be a few kilometres away, but it felt like it wasn't there at all. Like it existed inside a bubble of negative space.

Hardened blobs of ancient magma littered the ground around them and tumbled into enormous boulders that made up the mountain itself. Glasslike obsidian shone in the moonlight, sparkling like glitter. It would have been beautiful, if it wasn't for the crushing oppression she felt emanating all around them.

They knew this was where their path might lead them, but actually seeing it was more terrifying than Eloise had expected. All they'd heard about the Old Ones seemed like a story out of an ancient book—a tale full of fictional characters that could never possibly be true. A tale too tall to see through the clouds, but now they'd parted and here they were.

Eloise's visions had come to life. All that she was and all that she was destined to do bore down on her with the weight of eight billion souls.

"*What do we do?*" Drew asked.

"I don't know, I—" The words died in her throat as she felt the Old One's gaze move onto her. A twist of nausea pulsed through her body, and she fell to her knees, her eyes wide and locked onto the mountain.

"*Eloise?*"

She barely heard Drew's frantic cries in her mind as she gasped for breath.

The mountain came alive in the night, the summit bursting open with such force it sent chunks of hardened magma flying through the air. The obsidian essence of the Old One billowed out of the fissure and reached towards them, its tentacle-like fingers raking through the sky, blotting out the stars.

"*Eloise, fight it!*" Drew cried.

It whispered to her, using words that didn't sound like words. Rasping, droning, clicking... Sounds that tore at her willpower and drew her closer. *Katu, katu, makrz izish...* Words which tasted like rotting flesh.

"No, you can't have me," she rasped, not sure if she spoke out loud or only in her vision. "*You can't have me.*"

She tore her gaze away and heaved in a desperate breath, her heart pounding. Her backside slammed onto the ground as her strength failed and tears dripped over her cheeks.

It wasn't real. *It wasn't real.*

"*Eloise?*" Drew was before her, nudging her with his snout. "*Are you okay?*"

She nodded and buried her fingers into the sandy blond fur around his neck, taking comfort in his warmth.

The mountain sat silently before them, its peak unbroken. The stars shone down on them as brightly as ever, but she still felt the Old One's parasitic magic.

It bled into everything it touched—the air, the earth, the pants, the animals. It twisted it all, plunging the bush into a half-life dream-state.

"*It feels like the river here,*" Drew said, sitting beside her.

She nodded as her breathing evened out. "But it's different."

The shifter nodded his dingo head. "*Do you hear that?*"

Eloise listened, but all she could detect was the whoosh of blood in her ears. "I can't hear anything."

"*Exactly,*" he told her. "*There's no sound here. No animals, no birds, no insects.*" He sniffed the air. "*They know to stay away.*"

They sat together in the dark as Eloise caught her breath. The bush smelt like warm eucalyptus and earth, which was a far-cry from the acrid stench the mountain had sent up her nose a moment before.

Just as the silence reached a crescendo, a knock echoed in the distance. Like stone bashing against wood.

Knock, knock, knock.

Eloise looked frantically into the shadows, straining to hear.

Then an answer came from somewhere far away, faint but clear.

Knock, knock, knock.

Drew nestled against her, his pointed ears flicking

in all directions. He could hear things she couldn't, but she was too afraid to ask what.

Something did live here, something dark.

Eloise's imagination ran wild with shadows, spirits, and creatures so twisted, they could only live in the darkest corners of her nightmares. What kind of poison had the Old One leeched out into this place? What had it done to those poor animals? What had it done to Finn?

"*It's not as empty as we thought,*" Drew said after a tense moment.

"Whatever it is, it must guard the mountain," she whispered, her gaze darting about the shadows. Suddenly, Eloise was glad Drew had come with her.

"*What do you think they are?*"

"Other souls the Old One has tried to manipulate into freeing it." Her fingers tightened in his fur. "It couldn't be anything else."

He must have sensed her fear because he edged closer. His sharp gaze never left the ring of shadows around them as he waited for her to gather her strength.

"Drew, it... It spoke to me."

His head turned towards her. "*What did it say?*"

"I didn't understand. I'm not sure they were even words... I—" She took a deep breath and forced herself to look up at the mountain where the Old One was imprisoned. "It was so dark. It tasted foul, like it filled everything with rot."

"*It wants to overpower you*," he said, resting a paw on her leg. "*But you're stronger than anything it can throw at you.*"

Her hands trembled, and she tightened her fingers into fists. There was no choice. She had to keep moving. She had to keep fighting.

"We have to keep searching for Finn," she managed to say. "I can't bear the thought of him being at the mercy of that thing."

"*Are you sure he came here?*"

"Yes. The river wouldn't have let us go anywhere else." She narrowed her eyes at the mountain. "Not even for *it*."

"*All right*," Drew said, standing as she did. "*Keep your eyeballs peeled. We don't know what's out there, and Finn...*"

"I know," Eloise murmured, dusting off her backside. "It might not be him anymore."

CHAPTER 20

Finn's one saving grace was that he didn't seem to be corrupted by the Old One's magic...*yet.*

"Set it...free?" He stared at Siora's hopeful face beside him, the sharp edges of her angled features lit by the shifting firelight.

"Yes. Once the spirit's power is unbound, it can open a way between our worlds...and grant us the power we need."

Finn's brow creased. "Power for what?"

"The Tuatha line still rules, but it is no longer laced with pure Unseelie blood," Siora told him, her voice filling with disdain. "We have to help them. *We have to go back.*"

"What are you talking about?" He didn't like where this was going. It felt like history was repeating itself, and not in a good way.

"You know as well as I do that they stole our birthright, Finn."

Of course he did. A thousand years before he was born, the Tuatha de Dannan fae ruled Lor'Iyslar. They were of Unseelie blood and were ruthless and powerful because of it. They invaded other worlds, collecting power and territory, until they'd met their match in a small band of magical beings who called themselves the Celestines.

To prevent a war that would only end in mutual destruction, they formed an alliance that was to be sealed with the marriage between the daughter of the Celestine leader and the first son of the Tuatha.

Strife and decimation had followed in the wake of that union, but one child remained—one child to create the ruling family of Lor'Iyslar. The bloodline had existed for a thousand years, but over the centuries, it'd become mixed with Seelie blood until little of the Tuatha remained.

That was why they rebelled. That was why Auriel de Leiran called the Unseelie to fight. To take back what the Seelie destroyed. To repay the oppression forced upon them.

"We're forced to live on the edges of their world, hated and trodden upon," Siora went on. "You and I both grew up in the north, in the forgotten ice."

"You speak like we were treated like the *De'ashlide,*" Finn said, edging back. "We had plenty, Siora. We had magic, homes, and places of worth amongst the Seelie. We both had *families.*"

His words seemed to glide right past her. "*Finn,*"

she grasped his hands, "you must come with us. I can't do this without you."

As Finn sat there, he realised the mountain had twisted Siora's memory so much, that she'd forgotten the last thousand years spent trapped on Earth. To her, the civil war still raged on Lor'Iyslar.

It all seemed so pointless to him now. The fighting, the death, the destruction. It was all wrong.

"Are you listening to yourself, Siora?" he demanded. "Can you hear what you're saying?" She blinked as his hands slipped out of hers. "Aurel has been dead for a thousand years. She was executed, and we were exiled to Ireland for the rest of our lives. We became craglorn, Siora. The rebellion was lost."

She blinked and her silver eyes seemed to clear. "I know that. That's why we must return. Lor'Iyslar is our home, and while we still breathe, there is hope."

"Hope for what? Another rebellion?" Finn shook his head. "Auriel de Leiran used us. She used her magic to blind us to the truth of what we were doing. She manipulated us. All she wanted was power."

"No, Finn." Siora narrowed her eyes. "She may have manipulated you, but she never had to with me."

Finn hesitated, his surety that they'd both been lured in by the maniacal wiles of Auriel de Leiran, fading. "What are you saying?"

"I knew you'd never go along with it," she murmured. "You were only going to go so far...but not far enough."

For a thousand years he'd believed she'd been bewitched into that final attack like he'd had. For the twelve years they'd been living in Solace, he'd loved her. She'd loved...

She'd loved Auriel.

Siora had known exactly what she was doing from the very beginning. She knew how many lives would be lost by setting off the *ash'strads* and was still willing to go through with it.

He looked up at her as he realised just how far she'd gone. "It was your idea."

"The rebellion had to end," Siora said, jutting out her chin. "We'd fought for so long and nothing had changed."

Finn shook his head in disbelief. "All this time... All this time I believed you were like me."

"Like you?" she scoffed. "I look at what you've become and feel nothing but *pity*."

Her words cut deep, and he felt tears well in his eyes. "When we stood on the shores of Il Fir and you told me... When you said you loved me...was it a lie?"

"I could never love you the way I love her."

The words sliced into his heart and all he thought he knew about Siora—their past, the rebellion, and Auriel de Leiran—came crashing down around him. Finn had been nothing more than a pawn in a game he never had any chance of understanding...and look what he'd wrought because of it.

"You wanted to put your queen on the throne, no

matter the cost," he hissed. "Do you think once Auriel had her crown, she would have allowed you to stand beside her as her equal? Ruled with her as her lover?" He shook his head, his heart broken. "Auriel used you, just like she used everyone around her. Just like the mountain is using you now."

"You played your part in it, Finn. Not all of it was because of Auriel. You joined the rebellion of your own free will!"

"Yes," he murmured. "Yes, I did. And it's a choice I've spent the last thousand years regretting." Siora jerked back like he's slapped her. "Do you want to know why I help the Exiles? Because I want to atone for all the suffering I caused back in Lor'Iyslar. I can help save this world, and so can you."

Siora stood, her face twisting into a mask of pure rage.

Finn rose, ignoring the other fae who'd now awoken, their magic humming in warning. He'd never be a pawn again, and he would never let Siora lead those fae into another pointless war...if the Old One intended to let them pass at all.

"If you lead the others into that mountain, you will only be repeating the past," he said loud enough for everyone to hear. "It won't let you go home, and if you free the mountain, it won't be a few towns, it will be an *entire world*. Are you willing to sacrifice billions of innocent lives for your own selfishness?"

For a moment, Finn almost believed he'd reached

her through the dark power twisting her mind, but her expression hardened and her eyes turned cold.

"*If that's what it takes.*" Siora lashed out, her magic slicing across his chest with enough force to knock him off his feet. He landed on his back, but he didn't raise a hand to protect himself.

Finn focused his gaze on the stars above, and just beyond his awareness, he felt the mountain looming, its gaze shifting.

Siora stood over him, her entire body shaking with unrestrained rage. "Why won't you fight back?" she cried as the fae circled them, prowling like wild animals.

"Why won't *you?*" he rasped.

Her magic flared again as she struck him on the side of his face. "*Fight back!*"

"No." Finn coughed, the taste of blood on his tongue. "I'm done hurting others. I've... I've made my peace."

"Then so be it!" Siora shrieked, her eyes wild with blind anger as magic exploded around her, twisting the world into shards of exploding ice crystals.

Then the world fell away, piece by piece like a shattering mirror until there was nothing left.

The last thing Finn heard was his mother's voice in the dark. "*E'detua litua de, thadrei du'lei, an astrad du'a celest tualei...*"

Goodnight little one, rest your head, the stars will guide you to your bed...

Drew watched the lights dance in the darkness and decided not to tell Eloise. Especially not after the Old One had tried to get in her head.

The forest at the foot of the black mountain was more alive than she realised, though he suspected she felt more than the presence of a distant shadow knocking a bit of rock against a tree.

His magic seemed to act like one of those fancy purple blacklights scientists waved over bacteria to make it glow fluorescent. Or the bulbs that hung in nightclubs to make everything shine neon. Except he wasn't at a laboratory or a rave party.

Drew's eyes showed him a world of luminous poison. That's the only way he could describe what he was seeing. Mostly, the forest was a darkness so black, it seemed to suck all light into it like a plughole in a bathtub, but there were plenty of traces of glowing gangrenous tendrils that carried a corrosiveness that felt a lot like acid to him. They didn't smell nice, either.

As Drew sniffed the air, searching for a trace of Finn, he wondered if this was what Eloise saw when the mountain appeared in her dreams. They'd all joked about the Old One looking like a tentacle monster, but now that he saw what it was doing to the bush around it, it wasn't such a hilarious concept anymore.

He carefully picked his way through the clearing

where they'd landed. Eloise lingered behind him, her magic a point of warmth at his back.

A waft of sour grapes and greasy canola oil filled his nostrils. It was faint, but it was Finn.

"*This way*," he said.

Drew padded through the forest, his nose to the ground. Eloise brought up the rear, her anxiety so potent, even he felt it.

Finn's trail was clear, even though he hadn't left behind any footprints. He and Eloise hadn't seemed to leave any either, not that they were trying to hide. It felt as if the mountain was erasing their presence as much as it was sucking all the light and magic into itself, but it couldn't erase everything.

"*He made a camp here*," Drew said, circling a patch of coals that'd appeared out of the gloom like magic.

Eloise knelt beside him and poked the blackened earth with a stick. "There's no glow." She pressed her palm over them and shook her head. "There's a little warmth, but not much."

"*He left here a few hours ago at least*," the dingo mused. "*But we're on the right track.*"

Drew resumed his search for the trail and found a faint whiff of snake as Eloise poked about the campsite. She studied the ground, turned over a log for some unknown reason, and picked up a strip of bark.

She let out an abrupt gasp. "There's carvings on here." She flipped it over so Drew could see.

It reeked like Finn. He'd carved a detailed scene

into the bark with the tip of a heavy knife, the gouges rough but accurate. A group of people surrounded a ball that had lines coming out of it to represent light. In the background was a forest with a castle on the slopes of a jagged mountain. It wasn't half bad considering the fae had done it in the darkness cast by this creepy place.

"*I never knew he was so good at that,*" Drew mused.

Eloise raised her eyebrows.

"*I've seen him carve things before,*" he explained. "*He carved a totem thing for Vera, but I never looked that closely at it.*"

"A totem?" Eloise murmured, her gaze moving back to the bark.

"*It was some sort of memorial, I guess. For her coven.*"

Her expression turned thoughtful, and she set down the bark. "Let's see which way he went. He can't be that far ahead of us."

"*There was a snake here,*" he told her, knowing how the fae liked to charm the things. "*It went west, but I think Finn went east.*"

"Towards the mountain..."

Sensing the panic in her voice, Drew picked up the pace, weaving a path through the poisonous tendrils cast out from the mountain. Finn's scent was easy enough to follow now that he'd found traces, but the farther they went, the more it seemed to change.

Drew knew Finn had risked losing his magic by leaving Solace, and if that happened, the fae would turn into a twisted creature that would kill people like him and Eloise on sight. He hoped that wasn't what he was smelling—the slow starvation Finn was going through—but it also gave Drew faith that he was fighting back against the mountain.

He came to a sudden halt and looked down an embankment. *He fell here.* He skidded down the decline, his paws scratching in the dirt, and sniffed the fallen gum tree at the bottom. A new scent joined Finn's and he looked up at Eloise.

"What is it?" she called.

"*Siora*," he replied.

"*Siora?*"

"*I guess we know where the fae went.*" He circled the patch of earth. "*They fell down the embankment here.*"

Eloise rubbed her palms up and down her arms. "I've got a bad feeling about this..."

He did too, but he'd already caught the beginnings of a new trail moving into the bush. It wasn't just Finn they had to worry about now; it was six fae and a conclusion even Drew wasn't ready to jump to just yet.

"*This way,*" he called up to her. "*She might still be with him, so be ready.*"

It wasn't long before the trail merged with an explosion of scents—flowers, the sharp tang of magic, cooking smells, and eucalyptus-tinged woodsmoke.

"*There was a camp here,*" Drew said. "*A big one.*" He dropped his snout to the ground and sniffed a path through the churned-up earth. "*Fae were here. About twelve of them. Four fires…*"

"*Twelve?*" Eloise asked, aghast. There'd only been six living in Solace.

"*They've multiplied.*"

"Where have they gone?" Her gaze darted around the silent clearing.

Drew raised his head. "*You really have to ask?*"

"No, he can't have gone to the mountain." She strode across the camp, searching. "He couldn't have." She thrust her hands into her hair and called to the dark, "Finn? *Finn?*"

"*Shh,*" Drew yipped, snapping his jaws at her. "*You'll bring down all those creepy shadows on us. Not to mention that blue-haired fae chick.*"

That was one fight he didn't mind running from. He'd seen what she could do with a storm, and he didn't want to find out what other tricks she had up her sleeve, especially since she had a mountain behind her this time. Drew was ninety-nine-point-nine percent sure the fae were all corrupted.

So much for their 'place of power.'

"*Hardy should never have let them go,*" he said. "*We should've fought them in Solace.*"

"You want to argue about that now?" Eloise asked, scowling. "We thought we were doing the right thing."

Drew snorted and helped her search the abandoned campsite. He covered the whole area, finding traces of the fae, then signs of Finn by a cold fire at the edge of the clearing. Breathing deeply, he turned his gaze to the shadows, his eyes *seeing* the magic left behind.

That's when he saw a lumpy mass lying in a ditch —a mass that looked familiar... Silver threads clung to the body, faintly shimmering like gossamer spiderwebs, and Drew knew.

"*Eloise!*" He leapt towards Finn as she sprinted across the clearing. "*He's here!*"

"Finn!" She lunged towards the fae and fell to her knees beside him. "*Finn!*"

"*Careful,*" Drew said beside her, but Eloise ignored him as she pressed her hands on his withered cheeks. He was starting to look like an unwrapped Egyptian mummy.

She pulled Vera's talisman from around her neck and pressed it into Finn's withered hand.

"Vera sent it for you," she murmured. "Take it. *Please, take it.*"

Drew watched closely, looking for the moment Finn's skin began to smooth out, but nothing seemed to change.

"*Shouldn't he be doing something?*" he asked.

"Vera said... He should take the magic. He's..." Eloise let out a faint whimper and grasped Finn's hands in hers. "He's not here."

"*What do you mean?*" Drew looked at the fae. "*He's right...*" he trailed off as he realised Siora must have done something to him.

Those threads must have something to do with it.

Finn had always been a pain in both his arse cheeks, but Drew was beginning to realise exactly where the fae's allegiances laid, and it wasn't with his own people anymore. Looked like it had cost him, too.

"There's something on him," Drew said. *"Silver threads. It must be Siora's magic."*

Eloise's brow furrowed. "Threads?"

"It must be why he's not taking the magic."

Her breath caught and she looked down at Finn. "I'm going to try something. Keep watch in case they come back."

Drew let out a soft bark and circled them, his gaze flicking back and forth from the darkness then to her... and what he saw took his breath away.

Golden light poured from within Eloise, the warmth glowing with swirls of shining silver. Her magic bled into Finn, the threads binding him falling away. They floated into the air, burning gold, then dissolved like ash until there was nothing left.

Drew's gaze followed the last of the flakes into the sky, the stars shimmering as if they were answering a familiar call. Now he understood why she was Coen's favourite...and why the mountain desperately wanted her.

And she didn't even know. She couldn't see how her magic came alive and cut through everything around her. She didn't have the sight Drew did, but she could wield her magic, nonetheless.

Where had she come from? Who were the elementals? The only thing he was sure of, was that they weren't from around here.

"It's working," Eloise whispered, pressing the crystal into Finn's palm as the light dimmed inside her.

Drew watched as the fae's silver eyes opened, his golden fur crackling with the last sigh of the elemental's magic.

"Finn?" she whispered, her eyes full of tears.

"There she is..." the fae rasped, closing his hand around the talisman. "I thought I smelt you, desert pea."

CHAPTER 21

Eloise helped Finn sit, the fae coughing as air returned to his starved lungs.

He clutched the crystal talisman in his hand as he trembled, his eyes slowly regaining their usual silver spark.

Drew prowled around them, sniffing and watching the dark for signs of Siora, but they seemed to be alone for the moment. Eloise didn't even feel they eye of the mountain on them and chose to see it as a bit of good luck—no matter how brief it might last.

"You shouldn't be here," Finn managed to say. "It's you the mountain wants."

"If you thought we were just going to let you leave without so much as a goodbye, then you were deluding yourself," she told him. "Besides, the mountain's already tried it on."

"Eloise—"

"Finn, we all know that it can't corrupt me."

"But it *will* use Siora and the others to get to you," he argued. "You've made it easy for them by coming here."

Eloise sighed, wondering when Finn would accept that there were people in this reality who truly cared for him, despite his past. Perhaps that's what this entire journey was for him. She and Drew were just passengers on his walkabout.

"She's my problem to solve," the fae went on. "So far, I've been able to resist—"

"*And look where that got you,*" Drew drawled.

Finn's eyes narrowed. "*Great.* Now the dingo can speak in my mind. And here I was thinking I might have some peace and quiet."

"You can't help yourself, can you?" Eloise said, glaring at Drew.

"*It's our thing,*" the dingo huffed.

"Yeah, well, it isn't such a great 'thing' anymore." She looked up at the outline of the mountain. Siora was on her way up there right now. "How much time do you think we have?"

"Siora's magic is strong," Finn told them, "but it'll take a while, even with the mountain helping her."

"*But she has another twelve fae,*" Drew said.

"Yeah…" Eloise murmured.

They had to go up the mountain and stop Siora, that much was certain, but Finn was in no condition to walk, let alone use his magic to fight. He needed more time with the talisman, and Eloise needed more time to work out a plan. This was one battle they couldn't wing.

"Do you think the fae will come back here?" she asked, looking away from the mountain.

"To the camp?" Finn shrugged. "If the Old One commands them to search for you, then yes. But I think she'll try to break it free herself first. If she has one weakness, it's her pride."

"Good," Eloise declared. "Then we've got a little time to rest before we go after them."

"Eloise—"

"Drew?" she called, ignoring Finn's protests. "Are you able to keep an eye out for trouble?"

The dingo lifted his head. "*Nah, yeah. I'll have a sniff around.*"

Once Drew had slunk off into the inky shadows, Eloise turned to Finn, who was scowling something fierce. At least his skin looked healthier; his wrinkles were evening out, and there was a pink flush to his cheeks that looked much better than the blue they were before.

"Is the talisman helping?"

Finn's hand tightened around Vera's crystal. "Yes."

"Finn... When we found you, you were... Well, you were *gone*." She glanced at the bag by Finn's feet. "I had to use my magic to wake you up."

"I know." His voice was a whisper she could barely discern, even in the silence.

"What did she do to you?"

Space opened between them for a long minute. Whatever it was, it must have been awful.

"She used her magic to shatter me," Finn managed to say, "but it didn't work... I guess a part of me wanted to live after all."

"Shatter? What does that mean?"

"All *Shri'danann* fae can use magic," he murmured. "We can all do small things, but we each have one skill that defines us. A skill passed through blood, through curses, through blessings... Siora's *gift*... She can shatter a spirit like glass. Take what makes a person and break it beyond repair. Unable to transcend, unable to be reborn." He lowered his chin, hiding his face from her. "That's why Auriel wanted her. A jewel in her twisted crown..."

Eloise knew that by being sentenced to exile on Earth, the fae had already faced their final deaths—no transcendence, no rebirth—as punishment for their crimes on their home world. The same fate they forced upon all the souls that were taken with the *ash'strad* that he told her he'd used during the rebellion.

But what Siora did by trying to 'shatter' Finn was install a fail-safe. Not only would it take him out of commission where the mountain was concerned, but by some off-chance he survived and made it home to Lor'Iyslar, she wanted to make sure that this life would be his last. *No matter what.*

"Oh, Finn..." she whispered, her heart breaking.

"It's no more than I deserve."

The pieces he'd left out of his story were beginning to click into place—the rebellion, the bombs, his punishment—though she wasn't sure she had them in the right order. She did know that Finn felt remorse for what'd happened and was trying to atone. He'd sacrificed himself over and over again for Solace, even losing his place amongst his people...and maybe even his family. To her, his soul was worth saving ten times over.

"We found the carving you did," she said. "On that bit of bark."

Finn said nothing.

"That's what happened to your family, isn't it?"

The fae thrust his hands into his hair, his fingers twisting in his dusty dreadlocks.

"I knew it was going to be hard," he rasped. "But the pain... I did it to them. *It was my fault.*"

"Finn..." She lay her hand on his arm, unsure of what to say.

"I haven't told you all of it," he sniffed and let go of his hair, "and still, you came anyway." It sounded as if he was speaking more to himself than her.

"I'm here regardless," she told him. "If it makes you feel better, tell me now. But it won't change how I feel about you."

He lifted his head, and she saw his silver eyes swim with unshed tears. "How do you know?"

Eloise smiled and pressed her hand over his heart.

Her magic pulsed and he heaved in a deep breath, his lungs filling to the brim.

"You have that much faith in me?" he whispered.

"One hundred percent."

Once his heart was steady—her magic doing its work—he told her the twisted story of the rebellion and how Auriel de Leiran had led them all down a path of darkness. How he'd gladly followed until the final attack.

He told her about his life in Ireland until the day the portals closed. About Siora finding him in his cave and how they journeyed to Australia.

He told her of his remorse and regret, his pain and suffering. The attempts at redemption he felt would never be enough to make up for the lives he took.

Then how his walkabout had led him to the mountain and the truth about his relationship with Siora...and the lie he'd believed until that very night.

"And now she climbs those slopes with the fae to set the Old One free," he murmured. "She will destroy this world so she can plunge Lor'Iyslar into another war. That's if it lets her pass at all..."

A war that ended a thousand years ago, Eloise thought.

"There's still time for you and Drew to turn back," he told her. "You don't have to do this, Eloise."

She smiled up at him and wound her arm around his waist. "We're right where we're supposed to be."

Laying her head on his shoulder, she looked

towards the horizon. Past the mountain, the first signs of the rising sun coloured the sky and the stars began to fade.

And then, out of the lengthening shadows, hopped *Marlu*.

The kangaroo bounced towards them, and in her wake came a little joey. Its limbs were long and gangly, but it sprang with the wide-eyed awe of a life newly emerged from its mother's pouch.

Eloise lifted her head as the kangaroos joined them in the dawn and knew Coen had returned.

Coen sat by the fire and held out his hands, allowing the warmth to spread through his body.

After such a long walk on the trails, he'd almost forgotten what it felt like to be comfortable. He'd flown amongst the dark places and listed to the songs, and they'd brought him here. To the mountain and to Eloise, Finn, and Drew. *Marlu* had come too, finding her way across the currents that flowed around her country.

When Coen had found Drew prowling in the shadows, he'd laughed at the dingo's backpack. The shifter hadn't liked that, snapping out a frustrated growl—a sound Coen had become familiar with—but the dingo had learned and would *see* long before the end.

Now they all gathered together, huddling in the circle of light cast by the fire. The dawn approached, but the sun would not reach this land...not fully.

"How did you find us?" Eloise asked.

"You showed me the way," he told her. "A bright light in the dark."

Drew sighed. "*You really know when to show up, don't you?*"

"Yes, I do!" Coen clapped his hands together. "You are all here where you're supposed to be. I have a story to tell...and a song to sing."

"*A corroboree?*" Drew asked, flopping down in the dirt. "*At this hour?*"

Finn frowned. "A what?"

"A corroboree," Eloise said. "It's a ceremony where Indigenous peoples tell stories from the Dreaming. I saw one once at Uluru. It was a welcome to country ceremony. The singing and dancing...the sound of the didgeridoo... It was something special."

"It *is* special," Coen told them. "It is an honour, but it is not just telling. They become one with the Dreaming."

"A ritual," Finn murmured. "I understand."

"We have no time for that," Coen said, sweeping his hand across the sky. "Darkness comes quickly in this place. The sun will not linger. Time rushes forward like a river. I must tell you, so you can follow the current."

"*What's he saying?*" Drew wondered.

"He's saying time doesn't work here the way it's supposed to," Finn replied.

"So, did you find the answers you were looking for?" Eloise asked. "Do you know how we can stop the Old Ones?"

Coen had learned much on his walkabout and heard many things from within the dark places. He remembered things he'd long since forgotten and pieced together others that were broken. And he remembered his part in the song that led all of them here to this moment—the great walkabout that was his life.

"First, we must acknowledge country," he stated. "For country is life. It is memory. It is spirit. If you understand this, you will be safe. To know country, we tell stories. We see, we smell, we *hear*."

Finn nodded. "We have a similar way of knowing in my homeland. *Ashlar an lor, shride lei an val'ash*. Honour the dead, for they give us life. We honour those who have passed and the spirits who guard them."

"Your mob sees their country," the Indigenous man said. "Your country of magic." He wrapped his arms around himself. "Your story will always keep you."

"And your story?" the fae asked. "I hope it has an ambiguous moral that'll help us with the mountain. We could do with some hope."

Coen pressed a finger to his lips. "The land reflects the sky, and the sky reflects the land," he told them. "People fell from the Milky Way and made mobs of their own." He gestured with his hands, making the shapes of meteors rocketing through the air and colliding with the earth. "*Boom, boom, boom.*"

"*What's this got to do with anything?*" Drew wondered.

"By telling a story, a place lives on. If you respect the country on which you sit," he told the dingo, "you take care of its spirit."

"*So, the things I see...it's the spirit of the land?*"

Coen smiled, glad that Drew was seeing, and returned to his story. "The people who fell from the sky made mobs all over. From the north to south, from east to west. Many mobs came to be. Many mobs came to be in other ways, for there is more than one way to create life. Spirits came with them from the sky and made their home, too." He looked to Eloise, then to Drew. "The land, the sky, the water, and the wind... All together, they were a paradise and all were happy—the people, the animals, and the spirits—but a shadow grew... From the heart and the mind, it spread across all that was made."

"The Old Ones," Eloise whispered.

Coen nodded. "The great emu flew with the eagle, the serpent, the kangaroo, the dingo, and with the greatest warriors from the ancient countries. Mobs from far and wide answered the call, for they knew the songs the land spoke, and the animals knew all the paths. They fought to drive the shadow back before all was lost...but they could not face it. The shadow withered all it touched and turned their hearts against one another."

The darkness edged towards the light cast out from the fire, the flames shrinking under the power bearing down from the mountain. Coen reached his hand towards the coals and swept his palm through the air. The flames rose again, and the shadows crept back.

"The eagle called to the great emu for help, and from the spaces within its feathers, came the spirits of memory. They fell to the ground as others did before them, but as they found their feet, they discovered their light was broken. They were not who they once were, and their memory had been put together all wrong. But they had no choice if they were to send the shadow away." Coen lowered his gaze and felt the magic of the old places above stir within him. "They joined with the eagle, the serpent, the kangaroo, and the dingo. Together, they sealed away the shadows under rock gifted to them by the serpent that created all."

"And so, this reality flourished..." Finn murmured, holding Vera's talisman against his heart, "until now."

"We create paths by walking," Coen told them. "And sometimes we must walk old paths to find new ones."

Eloise looked at him, her eyes full of understanding. She felt it, too.

"Coen..." she began but couldn't find the words.

Drew and Finn didn't have the same look in their

eyes, but he knew she would. She was more like them than she was human. The closest thing to unbroken that walked the land.

"The time is almost here," he told her.

She glanced at the mountain, and he heard the question in her heart. The one she was too afraid to ask.

"*Almost*, but not just yet." Coen smiled as *Marlu's* joey folded itself into his lap. "First, we repair what was broken."

CHAPTER 22

As the Exiles sat around the campfire, they watched the sun fast-forward across the sky. The dawn gave way to morning, then noon, and began to lower all in the space of an hour.

Finn traced the delicate threads of gold and silver on Vera's crystal talisman with his fingertips. There wasn't much to say about Coen's story, the moral was pretty clear.

"Well, I guess we know why Kyne, Hardy, and Vera weren't invited," he said. "I'm supposed to fill the role of the serpent, huh?"

"Sometimes stories are exactly what they seem," Coen stated. He was probably the kangaroo, considering the company he kept. The dingo was obvious, and the eagle was Eloise. Coen had called her that before, and Finn had even given her a feather back when she'd first arrived in Solace.

The elemental was silent, her expression tense.

There was something she'd gleaned from Coen's story that the rest of them were missing. Her role in this would always be greater, but what had her so worried?

"The mountain was never going to let them go home," Finn said, "but they still might set it free. Between them, they might just have enough magic to crack open the seal on that thing."

"It's already broken," Eloise murmured. "That's why this place is like it is." And it was a glimpse at what Solace would become if they didn't learn how to fix it. Maybe that's what had her so rattled.

"*So what do we do?*" Drew asked. "*We can't just charge up the mountain and hope for the best.*"

"We divide and conquer." Finn narrowed his eyes and knew his walkabout hadn't ended and wouldn't until he faced Siora. For better or worse, his soul and his redemption lay at her feet.

Eloise looked up, her eyes wide. "You want to split up?"

"My walkabout led me here for a reason," he told her. "And now I understand why."

"*Siora,*" Drew murmured.

"She is my destruction...or my salvation." Finn grimaced and shook his head. "A dozen corrupted fae stand between us and the Old One. I can't help you seal the mountain, but I can help you get there."

"The mountain will have taken them by now," Coen said. "They will roam as shadows." He looked to Drew.

"And now I can see them," the dingo replied. *"That's why I should go with Finn."*

Eloise turned pale, her flushed skin fading into a ghostly white. "What... How... I don't even know what to do."

"I will guide you," Coen told her. "We will climb the mountain together."

Finn took her hand. "If anyone can face the Old One and prevail, it's you."

"But it won't be gone," she argued. "It'll still be here like the one in Solace. Hidden underneath a bit of rock that could crack again."

"If it's trapped under a seal, it won't be able to corrupt anyone anymore, right?" Drew asked.

Coen nodded. "It will be silenced, but not banished."

"By sealing away the Old One, we're buying ourselves time," Finn reassured her. "Then you'll be able to find a solution."

Eloise's bottom lip trembled. "You say that like you think you're not coming back with us."

Finn didn't want to upset her, but they all knew how dangerous their quest was, so he simply said, "I don't know what's going to happen."

His thoughts went to the fae, hoping there was some way he could free them from the corruption of the mountain. They may not be able to go home to Lor'Iyslar, but their life was good in Solace. The Exiles would welcome them once more, and this time, they would not be apart.

But Siora… It wouldn't be easy to convince her. Finn wouldn't know what to do, or how deep the corruption had taken her until he found her on the slopes of the black mountain. Though he feared it might already be too late.

"When the sun sets, we will follow our own paths," he said, draping the silver chain that carried the crystal talisman around his neck. He sensed the warmth of Vera's magic—the salty tang of the ocean and the wildness of the waves colliding with the rugged Irish cliffs—and felt his old strength return….and his deeper power awaken. "And we will remember why we have come."

They waited until full dark before putting out the fire and setting off into the shadow of the black mountain.

Drew took the lead, using his eyes and nose to guide the way through the poisonous tendrils cast out by the Old One. Coen had wisely left *Marlu* and her joey behind—this was no journey she should undertake, especially with a little one barely out of her pouch.

Drew had also left his backpack hidden in some bushes and could move freely again—he was glad to be rid of the extra weight, which wasn't a bad thing considering they were expecting a fight. Last thing he wanted was to get a strap caught.

It was just the four of them, just like in Coen's story. The eagle, the serpent, the dingo, and the kangaroo. All they were missing were the spirits the great emu sent down, but Drew knew Coen wouldn't guide them here if they didn't have a chance...not that they had much of one with Siora and her backup shadows blocking their way.

The silence seemed to thicken around them, and Drew focused his sights on the dark places between the ghostly gumtrees. Even the creatures that'd knocked to one another the night before had gone still. Maybe they didn't venture this far...or they knew something was about to happen. Either way, it made his skin crawl.

They followed a winding path through the forest as it began to thin, and the rocks of the mountain took over. The closer they came to the mountain, the blacker the ground became.

Coen said it was hardened lava that'd spilled out of the Earth's core millions upon millions of years ago, and that the boulders were where the stuff had bubbled up out of the vent. Over time, it'd formed slices of glossy obsidian which now sparkled in the dark as it caught the moonlight.

The volcano was long gone, likely flattened by a mega colossal eruption during the formation of the planet. What remained was an echo of a volatile past.

No wonder the Old One chose this place to break through the fabric of reality—it was like fragile scar tissue.

Drew stopped as he felt a change in the air. It sent a tingle down his spine and his hackles rose.

"Drew?" Eloise asked, her voice hushed.

"*There's a change here,*" he told the others. "*It's... darker. The magic in the ground is thicker, too. Less spread out.*"

Coen joined him, his eyes on the peak. "This is where we must part."

Eloise glanced at Finn. "Already?"

"You will find the fae here," Coen explained. "The mountain has seen us and will send them. They are coming."

"*That's what that creepy feeling is?*" Drew wondered. "*We tripped the Old One's trail cam?*"

"We would never have passed unseen," Finn said. "No illusions can trick a creature born out of the fabric of the universe itself."

"So this is it." Eloise threw her arms around the fae's neck. "Be careful."

"You better take your own advice up there, desert pea."

She let him go and knelt before Drew. "That goes for you, too."

"*I'm stubborn and reckless. Of course, I won't.*" Drew licked her cheek, and she ruffled the fur on his head—they were on the same wavelength.

"Luckily, I know you're pulling my leg." She smiled and rose to her feet.

Coen gestured to Eloise. "Come."

"What? No hug?" Finn asked, holding out his arms.

"He does things like that when he expects he'll see us again," Drew told the fae. *"But in what capacity...who knows?"*

Coen chuckled and backed into the shadows. Eloise followed, throwing one last glance over her shoulder, then they were gone. The darkness had swallowed them up, even taking the sounds of their footsteps to another place.

Suddenly, Drew felt cold without the elemental's light to warm him.

"It's just you and me now," Finn said, wrapping his hand around the strap of his bag.

Drew looked up at the odd sound in his voice and frowned. It was almost like the fae was glad he was there. They'd once hated each other, clashing at every opportunity, but now they were here as... As what? Sometimes it was difficult to tell where they stood with one another.

"Remember when you hit me with that shovel?" Finn asked, the fae's silver eyes shining eerily in the moonlight.

"Yes, of course I do. It felt real *good at the time."*

The fae chuckled. "Not to me. You left me out in direct sunlight."

"Don't tell me fae get sunburn?"

"No," he replied with a smirk. "We don't, but we do dehydrate...in more ways than one."

"You're making a joke at a time like this?"

"If there's a better time, I don't know it." His gaze turned to the boulders rising out of the thinning forest.

Drew sniffed the air, but the lack of trees hadn't lifted a shred of heaviness off them. *"So, do you have a way of finding Siora or do we follow my nose?"*

"I think they'll find us first."

"Better us than Eloise and Coen."

"Drew..." Finn hesitated. "Thank you for being here with me."

Drew didn't know when things had changed between them, but as he looked up at the fae, he saw the colours of his magic shift around him. Finn had gone through something life-changing, but they all had. Drew was no longer the man he was a year ago, and neither was Finn. Now he could *see*—it was clear in his magic.

Drew nodded, wondering if Finn could sense it, but decided it didn't matter. Eloise, Solace, or even the mountain weren't the only reasons they'd come. They all had battles of their own to fight, and right now, Drew was glad to stand beside Finn as friends and as *brothers.*

"I'll use my magic to call to them," Finn said, answering his earlier question. "It will flush them out and lead them away from the mountain."

Drew tensed, readying himself for whatever came

next. *"Are you prepared? You might have to..."* He didn't want to say the word 'kill,' but it might come down to it.

"I have to be."

"Then do it." He tensed, readying himself to leap. *"Let's lead them on the chase of a lifetime."*

Finn took a deep breath and held out his hands, palms facing up. When he let go of his magic, Drew felt the pulse vibrate through the air. His entire body reverberated like a gong, shaking him from the tips of his ears, down to the point of his tail and back again.

"Are you sure they'll come?"

Finn nodded towards the darkness ahead. "I am."

Drew tensed as he saw the first signs of the fae flicker through the gaps in the rugged terrain. They were black shapes that glowed with the same sickly-green corruption that ebbed from the mountain.

He knew this was what they'd face, but courage wasn't feeling like it was enough as the figures moved towards them with silent footsteps.

The fae whispered in the dark, speaking a flowery, foreign language. *"Ah'ila lei, ah'ila lei... Ash..."* Whatever they were saying, it didn't sound good.

"They're not craglorn," Finn said as they revealed themselves. "They're—"

"Shadows."

Drew edged backwards, his claws scratching in the dirt as the shadow fae prowled between the blackened volcanic boulders. He counted, his gaze darting from one featureless face to the next.

Ten, eleven...

Siora wasn't with them.

His head turned towards the mountain, and he knew she'd gone ahead to try to free the Old One. There was nowhere else for her to go.

Eloise and Coen. If Siora caught up with them, she'd kill them both or worse...deliver Eloise straight to the mountain.

"*Finn!*" he shouted, leaping up onto the closest boulder. "*She's gone after them! We have to stop her!*"

The sound of his voice triggered the shadow fae, and all at once, they swarmed, darting out from between the boulders.

Finn drew the knife at his belt and called on his magic. Drew felt it pulse through the fae and into the blade as he collided with what had once been his kin. The knife slashed and the shifter smelt the flowery tang of fae blood.

A pang of hope twisted his heart. They weren't full shadows yet, which meant they could be stopped. They had a chance.

The dingo leapt over Finn and the shadows, his paws pushing off sharp obsidian, and he flew at the nearest shadow fae. The force of the collision knocked it to the ground, and he closed his jaws around the shadow's neck.

"Drew!" Finn cried. "*Don't—*"

But it was too late. The shifter tore out the throat of the fae, his mouth filling with rancid blood. Gagging, he spat the foul stuff onto the ground and turned to his friend.

Drew saw the look in Finn's eyes and knew he'd hoped to save them, but it was too late. The dingo could see the light had long left their bodies and what made them fae, or even craglorn, was gone. They were now servants of the mountain—their souls had been corrupted to the core.

"*They're lost,*" Drew said. "*They're not your friends anymore. They're gone.*"

"You killed... You—" Finn cried out as another blackened body flung itself on top of him. Black fingers clawed at the fae's face as the shadow shrieked like a wild animal, its attack relentless.

Drew lunged, his paws pushing off the ground with such force, it felt like he was flying through the soupy air. He smashed into the shadow fae, knocking it off Finn, and they tumbled across the clearing.

He collided with a rough boulder, his back screaming as it scraped over rock. The shadow fae loomed over him and just as it was about to strike, Finn grabbed hold of it with a roar and pushed it away with a shock of magic.

"Get up!" the fae shouted at him. "Run!"

Drew scrambled to his feet, his scraped back stinging. He leapt up onto a boulder, his heart beating wildly and looked down at his friend. "*Finn!*"

"Stay back," the fae shouted, a strange light growing around him. "*Stay away…*"

The shadows circled Finn, closing in as Drew looked on, helpless to do anything. There were too many; they were too close.

"*Ahleida da*," Finn said, his voice wavering as he held out his knife. "*Ore di ah'anith an.*"

Drew's eyes widened as he watched the scene below. *Forgive me*, he realised. That's what Finn had said. *Forgive me. This is the only way.*

"*Rir de'ash zalde. Rir de'ash zalde…*" *I set you free.*

Finn's head fell backwards and the knife clattered to the ground as his magic exploded. Pulses of midnight-blue vapour pushed outwards and engulfed the shadows. They shrieked as the vapour twisted around them, coiling around their arms and legs. It snaked around their necks and poured down their dark throats, choking them as they tried to break free.

The shadow fae groaned and gagged, falling to their knees and writhing, their torment causing Drew to take a step backwards. As they choked, the shadows began to break apart. Their limbs crumbled to ash and fell away like sand in an hourglass, dissolving into nothing.

It was in that moment, as the shadows evaporated, that Drew realised what Finn's 'gift' was. Siora could 'shatter' someone's soul, but Finn… Finn could erase someone entirely—he was a living *ash'strad*. Perhaps he was the very person the bombs were designed to emulate.

No wonder... Drew thought, thinking of the way Finn was. It wasn't because he was Unseelie, not at all.

As Finn let go of his power and the vapour disappeared, he fell to his knees with a strangled gasp, his palms colliding with the rocky ground. Drew smelt the blood as the obsidian cut into the fae's palms, and he leapt off the boulder.

"Mercy..." the fae whispered, tears streaming from his eyes. "Is this mercy?"

Drew sat beside his friend and nudged his arm with his snout. *"The mountain can't use them anymore. It's the best end they could've had..."* Considering their other options.

"I vowed to never use my power..." he mumbled. *"I vowed..."*

"Finn, you did it to save Eloise and Coen. To save this world," the shifter reminded him. *"But now you have to get up. They still need us."*

"Siora."

"Yes." He nudged Finn with his nose again. *"We need to keep moving."*

Finn looked up at the night sky, his silver eyes shining. *"Ashlar an lor, shride lei an val'ash,"* he whispered, his voice so mournful, it brought a tear to Drew's dingo eyes. *"E'shrilae... Ahleida da."*

CHAPTER 23

The darkness swallowed Finn and Drew the moment Eloise stepped away from them.

"Come," Coen said. "The mountain is tall, and we must find the heart."

"The heart?" she asked, climbing up the rise behind him.

"It lives deep inside the blackness. We must find it there."

"Fair enough. Lead the way."

They set off up the mountain and the forest gave way to a maze of black boulders made of hardened magma. They climbed amongst them, their path becoming more treacherous the steeper the grade became.

It truly felt like the entire mountain was made from a pile of rocks, and that if she slipped and fell, she'd disappear down a crack and tumble all the way to the centre of the Earth.

The starry sky stretched overhead, and the whispers of the forest below were silenced by the thick magic ebbing from the Old One above. Wherever Finn and Drew had gone, they were lost inside the strangeness of the bush below.

Soon, any semblance of a path was gone entirely, so they began to climb, scrambling up over boulders and slippery obsidian. Coen seemed to know where he was going, but Eloise was beginning to worry they would have to go right to the top. She wasn't that fit, to be honest. Her lungs were already screaming at her, the thick air burning her chest as she drew in shallow breaths.

"Coen?" she wheezed. "Are you sure this is the right way?"

"Yes," his voice echoed down to her.

"Are you sure there isn't a river...or an elevator?"

The Indigenous man's head appeared above, and seeing how much she was struggling with the climb, he chuckled. "The waters are muddy in this place. No river flows."

"*Great.*"

"It's not far. I remember this path...a little."

"Wait." She leaned against a boulder and massaged the heel of her palm over her sternum. "You've been here before?"

Coen shrugged and darted up the next rock. "Keep climbing, Eloise Hart," he called over his shoulder. "We are not alone."

Eloise let out a little yelp and glanced about, her nerves almost failing her as she scurried up the rugged slope.

She clambered over boulder after boulder, her hands rubbing raw and her legs turning to jelly. She followed Coen, pushing past the ache in her muscles. Her hands and feet mirrored his path until they found what they were searching for.

A large opening gaped before them, and Eloise let out a sigh of relief. At least there'd be no more climbing involved...but now she began to worry about what they'd find inside. Finn had told her about the overgrown snake he'd met in the forest, and she hoped they preferred trees to holes in the mountain.

Coen led her into the tunnel, his footsteps unafraid. The darkness was broken up by shards of moonlight streaming between boulders, the smooth rock slippery underfoot.

It felt stranger in here than it had outside, the magic colliding with her chest like a blow from a heavy sledgehammer. Her fingers trailed across the rough wall, her head swimming.

They were travelling down into the depths of the ancient lava where the forces of nature had blown the Earth apart. Eloise felt it, and she felt the presence that'd haunted her dreams.

"We are here," Coen said, waving her forwards.

They emerged to a cave made of solid magma. When the volcanos here had been alive, a bubble had hardened inside the liquid rock, forming a rough, flat-bottomed dome. Holes dotted the ceiling, letting in shards of steely-blue light that reminded her of glow-in-the-dark stickers. And at the centre lay a large lump of shattered blueish-grey stone, the surface flecked with tiny grains of glittering quartz.

Eloise recognised it immediately.

"It's the same as the stone in Solace," she murmured, her breath finally catching up with her. "It's the mountain's seal." But it was broken enough so the Old One could emerge and poison everything it touched.

"Yes," Coen said. "The rock the serpent gave."

"Where did it come from?" she wondered, walking around it. A fissure splintered through the centre of it so deep, it'd almost cracked in two.

"This is a special stone," Coen told her. "It came from the sky, from the places where life came to our country."

Eloise peered at the seal, and missing piece of a puzzle she didn't even know she was trying to solve clicked into place. It wasn't bluestone or quartz, or even any stone found on Earth. "It's a meteor."

Coen looked down on the place where the Old One had broken through from a reality far away from their own, his expression unreadable. "It is broken, though the final seal holds. It will eventually open. Perhaps today, perhaps in a million years...but it will open one way or another."

Unless she did something about it.

Eloise took a deep breath and pushed away everything around her. The oppressive weight of the mountain bearing down on them, the thick darkness, the billions of human lives depending on her, the Exiles in Solace, Kyne whom she loved with all her heart, and the fabric of their entire reality. Everything depended on what she did here and now. There was no room for failure.

"What do I have to do?"

"Bring your magic and give it to the stone," Coen told her. "Place your hands upon the rock gifted by the serpent and follow the path."

She blinked and glanced at the broken seal. "That's it?"

"A path can have many turns...and many bumps." He nudged her towards the seal. "Repair what was broken, Eloise Hart."

Her hands trembled and she wiped her damp palms against her jeans. "What will you do?"

"I will guard your spirit. Like *Marlu*, I will watch." He smiled, his white teeth flashing in the strange light of the cave. "Go... Fly like the eagle."

Eloise stood before the broken meteorite. It was double the size of the one in Solace and stood as tall as she did. Chunks of it had tumbled across the cave floor, but the bulk remained wedged into the mountain.

Taking a deep breath, she placed her hands on either side of the jagged fissure and felt the now-familiar warmth inside her. Her elemental magic answered her call and she reached out for the path.

Light flared and she was plunged into a bright summer morning. Her Doc Martin boots clattered down a set of stairs, the laces trailing dangerously behind her. Dumping her school bag by the front door, she skulked into the kitchen, looking for a snack to take with her on the bus, but someone else was already in there.

Eloise jerked to a stop, her eyes widening. It was her adoptive parents—her mother and father, who she hadn't seen in a decade.

It was like nothing had changed, like no time had passed at all.

Eloise sucked in a shaky breath. Was it all a dream? An awful nightmare she could push to the back of her mind and forget about?

Her parents bustled around in the kitchen like they did every morning—her father getting ready for work, the end of his tie almost dipping into his coffee cup, and her mother trying to force a slice of toast spread with Vegemite into his hands before he hurried out the door.

"Mum? Dad?" Eloise lingered in the doorway, her heart beating so fiercely she thought it would burst out of her chest.

"Oh, El," her mother said, setting down a Vegemite-smeared knife. "What are you still doing here? You'll be late for the bus." She clucked her tongue and reached for Eloise's tie. "Fix that tie or you'll get another note."

"Yeah, I'm going," she heard herself say as she ducked out of her mother's reach. "Give me a break. And the uniform thing was just one time."

Her dad raised his eyebrows. "Second," he reminded her, his words muffled by a mouthful of toast. "Third time won't be lucky, El."

She rolled her eyes in the way only a teenage girl with a chip on her shoulder could. "Yeah, I'll fix it before I get there."

Eloise's blood ran cold as he reached out and touched her mum's arm. She remembered this morning...it was the morning where everything changed.

Her mother's expression twisted into pure hatred, her eyes turning dark as she stared at her adopted daughter like she'd crawled out of the pits of hell to destroy their perfect, suburban lives.

She was a moody fifteen-year-old, struggling to figure out who she was as an adopted teen—all while her elemental power manifested in the worst possible way. She'd made the only people she loved more than herself despise her, her touch turning everything into hateful darkness.

Eloise stood frozen in her childhood kitchen, her parents glaring with pure hatred, and realised what Coen had meant.

She had to fix what was broken.

But before she could reach out, a hand wrapped around her arm and pulled, forcing her out of the vision.

Eloise gasped as the cave jerked back into view. A pair of silver eyes bore into hers and dread filled her heart, the light cast by her magic almost going out.

"*Siora*."

The fae smirked, her grin malicious in the half-light. "Expecting someone else, Exile?"

"*Coen!*" She struggled against the hold on her arm, feeling the corruption of the mountain bleed into her skin.

"The sprite can't help you," Siora rasped. "You're all on your own."

Eloise looked around the cave, her heart thrumming a wild beat, and let out a strangled sob as she saw Coen laying on the cave floor, his vacant eyes staring upwards into nothing.

"*No*," she wailed. "*Coen...*"

"Don't worry," Siora's other hand shot out and wrapped around Eloise's neck, "you'll join him soon enough. But you've got to unlock a little door for me first, *Lor'astra*."

A dark shape flew through the air behind the fae and collided with her, tearing her hold on Eloise. The elemental jerked and fell, hitting the ground hard enough to draw blood.

The sounds of growling and snapping filled the cave, the echoes booming like a drum.

She saw the creamy outline of a dingo and her heart skipped a beat or ten. "*Drew?*"

Warm hands grasped her arms. "*E'dreha*, desert pea."

Eloise looked up into Finn's silver eyes and let out a strangled sob of relief. "Finn?" Her gaze flickered to Coen. "He's—"

"Going to wake up in a few hours, annoyed he missed your big moment."

"He's not... He's not dead?"

"No. Not today." Finn helped her to her feet. "*Ak'ande lei, Shr'lei de astrad.*" He nodded towards the seal. "Whatever happens, do not stop."

As Drew let out a yelp, Finn turned and leapt towards Siora, leaving Eloise behind. With tears streaming from her eyes, she turned to the seal and called on her magic.

Finn turned to Siora as she hurled Drew off her. The dingo flew through the air and collided into the wall, then tumbled to the ground...and was still.

She rose, her throat and face covered in blood, and turned her gaze to Finn. He was the last one standing. If she got through him, Eloise would fail.

"You cannot stop the mountain," Siora said. "It's too late for that."

"You will not lay a hand on her," Finn rasped. "I won't allow you."

"Move aside." Her lip curled as her gaze fell onto Eloise, who had fallen back into the vision cast down by the mountain. "The *Lor'astra* is *mine*." She lunged, her body propelled by her magic, and Finn leapt out to meet her.

"I said, *no!*" he roared, letting go of his power—the deeper magic inherited through blood that had plagued his entire life. The same curse that'd taken the lives of his people on the mountainside.

They collided, the force sending a shockwave through the cave, and they sailed into the tunnel, buffeting against the obsidian walls. Pain tore through his body with every collision, but he didn't let go of her, not even when they emerged into the night and fell down the mountainside, smashing into boulder after boulder.

Finally, when they came to rest on a plateau, Siora tore from Finn's grasp and scrambled to her feet. She limped a few steps away, clutching her side.

A boom echoed deep within the Earth and the whole mountain shook, the volcanic rock wobbling like jelly underfoot. Finn held out his arms to steady himself, but was flung backwards as the plateau cracked, a fissure opening behind Siora.

Magic poured out of the rift and shot up into the sky, pulsing green and black as another appeared farther up the slope...then another and another until the whole mountain was on the verge of blowing its top.

Finn stood as the thick pool of magical vapour enveloped him, the potent swirls of muddy-green hiding Siora from view, through she'd only stood a few paces away from him moments ago.

"Siora!" he shouted, his heart thrumming and his battered body stinging. "*Siora!*"

She emerged from the haze, dirt and blood smeared across her face, her turquoise hair floating in all directions. Gravity fell away as the mountain struggled against Eloise, and another tremor rocked the ground beneath their feet.

"It's too late, Finn," Siora said, her magic pooling around her body. "The mountain is breaking free." She swept her arms wide and laughed, her eyes flashing manically. "Can't you feel it? Lor'Iyslar is within reach!"

"Eloise will prevail and there's nothing you can do about it," he told her.

"The *Lor'astra?*" Siora scoffed. "She's just as broken as the rest of them. Your little elemental is already losing."

Finn took a step towards her. "Siora, you need to stop before it's too late."

The fae smirked, wiping the back of her hand across her bloodied nose. "That was always the problem with you, Finn. You were never willing to do what it took to win."

As Finn looked into the eyes of his one-time friend and lover, he knew Drew was right. The dingo could see the corruption in the fae as surely as he'd see it in Siora now if he were here to witness it.

The woman Finn knew was gone. He knew it in his heart, and he knew it in the broken pieces of his soul.

She was beyond saving.

He looked down into the fissure, his magic parting the poison oozing out of the Old One. Whatever the being was, it didn't have a physical body. It was pure energy that existed on a plane of life far removed from their own. To think they had the power to stop it was foolish.

But they would fight anyway.

"No," he murmured. "I never did have enough conviction, did I?"

She smirked and took a step towards him.

"Now I understand why," he added. "I was wrong... but this? This is right."

"And so it is done." Siora grinned, her eyes turning black as she moved towards him. "*Rir de'ash zalde,* Finn Oreah'anza.*"

Her power rose as she lifted her hand, but Finn had been anticipating it. He knew Siora too well, it seemed. They'd fought many battles together, and he knew every move she favoured...including how she liked to kill.

He lunged, his shoulder colliding with her chest, and she shrieked as they tumbled towards the fissure.

She lost hold of her magic as they fell into the torn Earth, the mountain's poison enveloping them both.

Finn lost his grip on Siora and she fell away from him, tumbling into the pulsing energy that made the Old One.

He was glad to join her in death, to have his soul destroyed as a final payment for his sins. He'd go, knowing he'd helped Eloise defeat the mountain. Perhaps now, he'd finally atoned.

As Siora was swept away, he caught her gaze one last time. Her silver eyes opened wide in shock—

A hand clamped around Finn's wrist, and he felt his body jerk to a stop, his shoulder jarring. As the poison cleared above, his gaze met a pair of human eyes and he choked back a sob.

"You're not kicking the bucket today," Drew said. "Not on my watch, mate."

CHAPTER 24

Eloise stood in the kitchen of her childhood home, her hands shaking.

Everything was on the line. *Everything.*

"How about showing us a little bloody respect, Eloise?" Her mother dropped the butter knife, the stainless-steel clattering on the benchtop. Butter and Vegemite smeared across the usually pristine cream quartz. "Maybe we should just ground you now because we both know you'll be coming home with another note, this time with a suspension attached."

"Marg!" her father exclaimed. "What's gotten into you? It's just a *tie*."

As he began to move, Eloise cried out. "Dad, no!"

He pushed between them, his hand settling on his daughter's shoulder...and she felt her magic take hold of his mind like an industrial-strength magnet.

"*No...*" she moaned. She couldn't stop it.

Her father's angry eyes turned on her. "After all we sacrificed for you, this is how you treat us?"

"You're not even our real daughter," her mother spat. "Our real child would never be as ungrateful as you are."

"Thousands of dollars, Eloise," her dad went on. "That's how much we spend on that fancy private school, and all you do is flout the rules."

Eloise stumbled backwards, her heart thrumming painfully as her entire body shook. Her back hit the wall as her parents advanced on her.

The bright summer sunlight streaming through the windows flickered, then the entire room darkened as s cloud settled over the sun.

Katu, katu, makrz izish…the dark words boomed around them, echoing off the walls and making the whole house rattle. *You spread discord wherever you go, Eloise Hart. Your power is a curse. Set me free, and I can make it all go away. I can give them back to you…*

Eloise gasped, her fingers curling around the doorjamb behind her. Her parents glared, their eyes full of twisted, poisoned evil.

The shadows grew outside the windows, pooling like ink in water. Tendrils snaked on the other side of the glass, tapping against the panes, trying to get in.

Sliding down the wall, Eloise cowered in terror as the mountain bore down on her. The weight was too much, her resolve was crumbling like ash underneath its dark touch. How could she ever think she had enough power to stand against it?

Her heart was fragile. *Human.*

She was nothing compared to a being made of the very fabric of the universe, nothing at all.

"You are nothing but a disappointment," her father said, a cruel sneer twisting his mouth.

The ground started to quake, wobbling like jelly under her feet. A picture fell off the wall and crashed to the floor, glasses jerked off the kitchen counter and smashed, and the jar of Vegemite followed, sending the potent brownish-black spread across the white tiles.

"Your own parents never wanted you," her mother snapped. "They dumped you outside a hospital like rubbish. Now we see why."

"You will never amount to anything."

"You don't even know who you are, so how could anyone love you?"

"This world has nothing for you. All you'll ever be is a drain on society. I don't pay taxes to keep pathetic trash like you alive."

Eloise thrust her hands into her hair and sobbed. "Liars! You're lying! *You're lying!*"

"Deep down, you know we're telling the truth," her father drawled. "The sooner you accept it, the sooner you can do what's right."

"What's right?" she managed to squeak.

He knelt before her and pressed a kitchen knife into her trembling hands.

The Old One whispered again, the sound dripping into her ear like acid, *Katu, katu, makrz izish…*

"No!" Eloise screamed, flinging the knife away. It clattered across the tiled floor and skidded out into the hall. As her father jerked back, his black eyes widening in shock, she lunged towards him and grabbed his face in her hands.

Her magic rose like a flood, filling the kitchen with a blaze of golden light. The darkness retreated, the whispers of the Old One fading as the quaking slowed.

"Eloise, what are you doing?" her mother shrieked.

She let one hand fall away from her dad's face and snatched her mother's wrist. "Fixing what I broke."

Her voice sounded strange, like it wasn't her own. It echoed from someplace far away, the sound wrapping her parents in golden light, cradling them in a cocoon of warmth that kept them safe from the mountain.

Eloise had always assumed she'd mistakenly pressed her own self-loathing onto others. How they acted towards her after her magic touched their minds was how she saw herself. Her struggle with her identity as an adopted teenager—who felt like she never fit anywhere, who was manifesting a strange power that was the stuff of fiction, *of nightmares*. Fumbling in the dark for some kind of meaning and finding nothing… until her van broke down outside of Solace.

Eloise knew who she was now. She understood her heart, her power, and she knew how to fix what she broke.

She gave it all to them—her memories, her love, her hope, her dreams for the future...and her promise.

She felt the mountain rage beyond the glow of her magic, but she didn't care. Its anger was nothing now, its dark words meaningless compared to the love she felt for the people who'd taken her in as an infant, no questions asked. They'd loved her, cared for her, raised her, and had never asked for anything.

She fixed what she broke, filling the cracks with all that she was.

They blinked down at her, the shadows fading from their eyes, and outside, the sun began to shine. It was an ordinary summer morning, and Eloise was going to be late for the school bus.

Her eyes filled with tears. "Mum? Dad?"

"El?" Her father looked dazed as he scratched his head. "I don't... What just happened?"

She let out a sob and threw her arms around his neck, holding him tight. "I'm sorry. I'm sorry. *I'm sorry.*"

"Sweetheart, it's just a tie," her mother said, placing a hand on her back. "It's not the end of the world."

The vision began to dissolve around her, taking her parents with it. The puzzle had been solved, the battle was won...but she didn't feel like celebrating.

"It wasn't real," she whispered as the cave began to show through the remains of the kitchen. Her parents were still out there...and they still hated her.

Her legs turned to jelly the moment she felt her parents' touch disappear. A wave of exhaustion caught up with her all at once, and her knees gave away.

"Eloise!" A pair of arms caught her, and she was lowered to the ground.

She caught a glint of silver above her as hands smoothed her hair away from her face. "Finn?"

"You did it, desert pea," the fae murmured. "You filled the crack. Look." He nodded towards the shattered meteor, where the fissure that'd split it almost in two was now filled with shimmering gold.

Drew stood beside the stone in his human form, his dirt-stained nakedness hidden strategically behind the meteor as he studied the seal.

Then Coen appeared beside her, grinning from ear to ear.

"You flew!" he declared. "You flew like the great eagle!"

Finn sat beside the campfire, his heart heavy as the dawn approached.

Eloise nestled beside him, resting her exhausted head on his shoulder. Drew had reclaimed his backpack and had dressed, busying himself with keeping up the fire. And Coen lounged with *Marlu* and her joey, waiting and watching as Finn did.

The poison that'd plagued the mountain and the surrounding bush was fading, releasing its twisted hold on the spirits of the land. Noise was returning as the shadows dimmed, and the life that'd long since fled came flooding back.

The lightening sky brought iridescent colour—midnight-blue that held the yellow tint of the coming sun. Birdsong and the rustle of native animals erupted in a triumphant cacophony as they came back to claim their home from the Old One.

Finn knew his walkabout was over, but the conflict in his heart still tugged at him.

He regretted having to use his magic on the fae up on the mountainside, but Drew was right. They were lost long before they'd found them in the boulder field. Finn had felt what little was left of their souls the moment his power took hold of them, and there was nothing there that he'd recognised.

But knowing it didn't make his choice any easier.

Then there was Siora. Despite their past, and the things he'd learned on his walkabout, there would always be a part of him that regretted her end and his part in it. She'd made her choice over and over again, always putting her belief in the flawed doctrine of Auriel de Leiran's so-called rebellion. Had it always been about love for her? He supposed he'd never know.

But despite all of that, Finn couldn't shake the image of the moment Siora had been taken by the Old One. He'd thought he'd caught a glimpse of her old self just before she was swept away. A flash of recognition had passed across her face...or was it regret? But she was gone before he could be sure.

All he could do now was come to terms with his part in all of it...and hope he'd done the right thing.

"It's beautiful, isn't it?"

Finn looked up at Eloise's question and saw the dawn glowing behind the black mountain. The sky was alive with a strange curtain of colour—purple, pink, blue, yellow, and even the fiery orange of the rising sun—that reminded him of the magical rainbows on Lor'Iyslar. They always appeared after a potent burst of magic, the echo of which was a coloured sky that hung in the air for days.

"Yes," he murmured. "It is."

He couldn't sense any trace of the Old One's poison at all, though the nature of what he was would always try to connect with the magic it emanated, even through the seal that bound it. And it was still there, simmering below the renewed seal, just like it did in Solace.

Eloise hadn't mentioned a single thing about what she'd been through during her battle with the mountain, but whatever she'd done, her magic had cleansed the land and brought back the spirit of the country.

"What you said to me in the cave..." she asked, lifting her head. "What did it mean?"

"*Ak'ande lei, Shr'lei de astrad,*" Finn murmured.

"Yeah, that's it."

"*Ak'ande lei* means 'save them.' *Shr'lei de astrad* means, 'Blade of the stars.'"

"Blade of the stars..." she murmured, smiling dreamily as she watched the sunrise. "Cool."

Finn felt Coen's gaze on him from across the fire. He looked up and the Indigenous man grinned.

"You've made peace," Coen told him. "You can rest easy now."

"Perhaps," Finn replied. "I can't help but feel it's a bittersweet ending."

"It can't have been easy," Eloise murmured. "I'm sorry you had to... Well, I'm sorry."

His choice had cost him the last link he had with Lor'Iyslar and his people, but as he looked around the fire, and thought of the other Exiles waiting for them in Solace, Finn knew he wasn't alone.

"The mountain cannot hurt anyone anymore," he told her. "Now we have time to find a way to lock the Old Ones out of this world forever."

Eloise sat up, her gaze searching his. "But if we win, you won't—"

"I know," he whispered. "Let's not think about that until it's time."

"The currents are returning," Coen declared, interrupting at the right moment for once. "It is time to return home."

"Sweet," Drew said. "I need a shower." He sniffed his shirt and wrinkled his nose. "*Bad.*" He stood and began to dump dirt on the fire.

Eloise rose, dusted off her jeans, and ran her fingers through her tangled hair.

But as the others made their preparations for the journey back to Solace, Finn wandered towards the edge of the eucalyptus forest. No matter what they said, his heart was still restless.

"Finn?" Drew called.

"Give him a moment," he heard Eloise say.

He picked his way across the hardened magma to a jagged fissure the quake had opened and stared down into the dark hole. Opening his bag, he took out the spent *ash'strad* and held it in his hands, the cool metal burning his palms with the memory of all the pain of his former life.

Coen was right. It was time to let it go.

"You brought that with you all the way from Solace?" Drew asked, appearing beside him.

Finn nodded. "It was a reminder of my past."

"Your magic..." the dingo began.

"The *ash'strad* was created in the image of the curse that plagued my family. Our magic was weaponised and enhanced." He held up the silver orb and narrowed his eyes. "*Rir de'ash zalde.*" He tossed the *ash'strad* into the fissure and they watched it clatter into the darkness.

They listened to the last of the metallic clangs as it tumbled to the bottom, and when it finally lay silent, Finn raised his hand and cast an illusion over the spent relic.

And there it would lie forever, hidden for all time, forgotten until the long ages of their world—the world Eloise Hart would save—had turned its poison to dust.

"Come, brother," the serpent said to the dingo, "it's time to go home."

CHAPTER 25

T he morning sun shone over Solace, the light dimming every so often as a fluffy white cloud sailed past. A light breeze fluttered, carrying the warm scents of the outback—eucalyptus, pollen, and the bold tang of red earth.

It wasn't too hot or too cold, the temperature was just right. All in all, it was a perfectly mild autumn day.

Kyne stood in the shade of the boab, the brim of his hat pulled low, all the natural splendour lost on him. His heart was heavy with worry and his stomach had been twisting into knots for days.

It'd been three days since Eloise and Drew had left in search of Finn, and for three days, there'd been no word...except for the earthquake that'd rattled him awake the night before.

No part of Australia sat on a fault line, so they were rare—a once-in-fifty-years type event—but there was no mistaking the rolling waves that shuddered through the ground. He was an elemental and knew all about the comings and goings of the Earth, and there wasn't anything else it could've been.

His first thought had been of Eloise. Anyone else would've dove underneath a table, but he knew Solace was only feeling the outer edge of the quake. The epicentre was hundreds of kilometres away to the east.

"Still brooding?"

Kyne looked up as Vera joined him in the chunk of shade cast down by the boab. "It's been three days…"

"I'd say that you shouldn't worry, that Eloise is tough as nails, and she's got Drew with her, but you won't listen," the witch told him. "You haven't listened the thousands of other times I've told you, either."

He grunted and looked up at the tree. The bloated trunk of the boab was the largest he'd ever seen anywhere in the outback, the size of it rivalling some of the bigger specimens across the world. Sometimes he wondered if there was magic inside it, and that's why it grew so large here. Its proximity to the seal accelerating its biology, or something like it.

Coen certainly liked it…wherever he might be.

"Do you think the boab's changed at all?"

Vera trailed her fingers over the bark. "It looks…*bruised.*"

Kyne frowned. He'd hoped it was all in his head.

"It could just be storm damage," she told him.

"Maybe, but too much is happening all at once to rule any one thing out." The seal was cracked and leaking poisonous magic everywhere, the black mountain was always out and about, trying to corrupt supernaturals... It was all linked. Of course, it was. "I don't think we can wait anymore."

Vera raised her eyebrows. "It's only been three days. That's no time at all."

"Vera, the seal is damaged." He pointed to the boab. "I know you're trying to look on the bright side of things, but we have to be realistic. It's *dying*. The boab is *dying*."

She swallowed hard, her gaze lowering. "I've tried everything I can think of. Barrier spells, cleansing rituals... Nothing works. My magic can't fix it."

"We still have the coral key."

After Drew had stolen the odd circle of coral from the Dust Dogs, Kyne had used his elemental magic to hide it in the outback. Word was, it was the key to unlocking the seal underneath Solace, but there was no proof that it did anything. As far as he was concerned, it was the only thing they hadn't tried.

Maybe they ought to consider it.

"Uh," Vera said, looking uncomfortable about the notion. "I think that thing should stay hidden. It caused enough trouble with the Dust Dogs as it was."

"We don't even know what it does," he said with a shake of his head.

"If it does anything at all," Vera added. "It might just be another red herring, like Darius and that bloody iron ore. At the worst, it might set the Old One free."

Kyne ran his hand over his face, his palm scratching against three days' worth of stubble. "I can't just sit here on my arse and do *nothing*."

"I know—"

"She went out there to face the black mountain on her own!" he exclaimed. "If anything's happened to her, how would we know? She'd just never come back, and I've just been here doing nothing!"

"Kyne... Eloise went to find Finn."

"Who was sucked in by the mountain with all the other fae!"

"We don't know that," she murmured. "Not for sure."

"It's crystal bloody clear to me," he seethed.

"Kyne, don't be angry with her... Eloise... She knows what has to be done and besides, the mountain can't get to her."

"I'm not angry with her," Kyne said, rubbing his tired eyes. "I'm afraid, Vera. I..." He sighed and threw his hands into the air. "I love her."

Vera's expression softened and she placed a hand on his arm. "We all do."

"I have no power... I just..." He took a deep breath. "I have to know one way or the other."

"Know what?" a familiar voice said behind them.

"*Drew?*" Vera spun around and let out a squeal.

Kyne's heart leapt into his throat, and he turned.

Coen, Eloise, Drew, Finn, and *Marlu* and her joey stood behind them, looking like they'd all been dragged through a hedge backwards.

He blinked in astonishment at the Exiles, wondering where on Earth they'd come from. It must have been one of Eloise's 'rivers.' Drew was covered in dirt, Finn looked a little green, Coen beamed, and Eloise...

They rushed towards one another at the same moment, colliding in a puff of dirt and dust. They were like two dusters clapping together, but he didn't care. She was back. *She was safe.*

"We did it," Eloise murmured into his ear. "We sealed the mountain."

"Don't be so modest," Drew said. "*You* sealed the mountain."

Eloise drew back and looked up into Kyne's eyes. "It won't hurt anyone anymore. Its power is locked away."

"And you're okay?" He ran his hands over her face, cupping her flushed cheeks in his palms. "You're not hurt?"

"No," she said. "I'm okay. Tired, but okay."

"Thank bloody hell."

Kyne kissed her, not caring that the others were looking on or that they still had one hell of a battle before them. All that mattered was that they were all safe. They'd come back...and Eloise had come home to him.

"I love you," he said between kisses. "I'm never letting you out of my sight again."

"Even when she's on the dunny?" Drew called out, triggering a chorus of laughter. "That's a bit much, don't you reckon?"

Eloise awoke, bleary-eyed and muddy-headed.

She didn't know how long she'd slept, but it must've been a good long while. Her entire body felt as if it'd become one with the mattress. Rolling over was an effort, but she managed to turn to Kyne's side of the bed.

He wasn't there, but a slip of paper sat on his pillow. *Gone into town. Back soon. - Kyne*

She found her way to the shower, shuffling through the hall like a zombie. The water eased her sleepy muscles, though it had the added effect of stirring her memories. Why were showers so thought-inducing? It was rather inconvenient.

The last thing Eloise wanted to think about was what'd happened in the vision inside the mountain. She knew it was just her subconscious struggling against the Old One—she hadn't truly fixed what she'd broken—but it'd stirred feelings in her that she'd tried her hardest to forget. Which was mainly guilt over not returning to see her parents now that she understood who she was and what she'd done.

Shutting off the water, Eloise climbed out of the shower and dried off, the closed air in bathroom weighing down on her. Heading out for a walk, even though she was well and truly aware of the cracked seal, sounded like a good idea.

Maybe she'd find Kyne. They needed to talk about a lot of things.

Dressing in some fresh clothes, which felt as good against her tired skin as the water did, she ventured out into a brilliant autumn outback day. The sun shone, the sapphire sky was dotted with puffy white clouds, and a lukewarm breeze tickled her cheeks. It was a day far removed from the storm that'd torn through only a week ago.

Her first stop on the search for Kyne was the *Outpost*.

"Eloise!" Vera exclaimed from her regular perch behind the front counter. "How are you?"

"Okay," she replied with a shrug. "I feel a little hungover."

"I wouldn't doubt it. You made front page news," the witch said, holding up the newspaper she'd been reading. "And registered as a 7.2 on the Richter scale."

"Oh no," Eloise moaned, taking the paper. "No one was hurt, were they?"

"Nope. Just some reports of minor building damage. People felt it all the way down in Melbourne!" She chuckled and shook her head. "You really know how to make a bang, don't you? I bet if we checked online, it'd be international news, too." She reached for her phone. "Wanna look?"

Eloise shook her head as she scanned the article. "I think I'll pass."

An earthquake this far from a fault line was rare, but they did happen. At least the supernatural reason would remain a secret, and something other than war and strife would dominate the news for a day or two.

She sighed and handed Vera back the newspaper. The world would never know how close it came to complete and total destruction.

Vera smiled. "It's a thankless job, isn't it?"

"Yeah," she murmured, "but that's not why we do it."

"Nope." The witch grinned and handed the elemental a lollypop. "It's on the house. Cola-flavoured, too. Total classic."

"Thanks." Eloise twirled the stick in her fingers, spinning the dark blue wrapper, and smiled. "Have you seen Kyne this morning? He'd already headed out by the time I woke up."

"Nope, not this morning." Vera frowned as she caught a spark of something in the elemental's expression. "Is something up?"

"Not really, I guess." She sighed. "Well... He was a little tense yesterday, I suppose. I think I hurt him pretty bad when I left to find Finn."

"I don't think it was that," Vera told her. "He was worried about you. Kyne's always been the guy who protects everyone, whether he wants the job or not. With you, he wants to." She chuckled and flipped her curly hair over her shoulder. "That's true love."

Eloise flushed.

"Oh, Finn's set up a new camp not far from Drew's dugout. I thought you'd like to know."

"He doesn't want to stay in town?"

"Nah," Vera said. "The fae have always felt boxed in by houses in this world. It's got something to do with the lack of magic, I think."

She nodded, knowing it was a little more than that, but close enough. "I'll go see him after I find Kyne."

Vera chuckled. "I think you might find Drew there, too. Whatever happened out there, I think it sparked a bro-mance."

Eloise laughed, feeling lighter than she had in days. "Miracles *do* happen. That gives me hope."

"You and I, both." The witch began unwrapping a lollypop, struggling with the plastic shrink-wrap. "Unlike this packaging."

Eloise backed towards the door. "I'll see you at Blue's tonight?"

"Wouldn't miss it for the world."

Outside, Eloise stood on the verandah and scanned the highway. When she saw Coen standing by the boab tree, she hesitated. He rarely appeared for no reason, only choosing to reveal himself when he had something to say.

Eloise headed towards him, wondering what was on his mind. "Coen?"

The Indigenous man turned and smiled. "Hello!" he said cheerily.

"You sound much better than I feel," she said as she stood beside him in the shade cast by the bloated trunk of the old tree.

Coen chuckled. "It will take some time to feel better again. You need to charge up like a battery."

"I guess so." Eloise glanced at the boab. "What are you doing out here?"

"Listening."

She frowned and tried the same, but whatever he was hearing seemed to be only for him. Instead, her thoughts rose from inside, coming loose from where she'd pushed them earlier.

She thought of Kyne and the elementals rejection. Wally and his transformations. Vera and the Nightshade. Drew and the Dust Dogs. Hardy and Darius. Finn and Siora. If only she could've faced the mountain earlier, maybe she could've saved them all from their heartaches.

No, she thought. *I wouldn't have been strong enough.*

She was supposed to grow and understand her powers first, otherwise the Old Ones would have been able to control her like they did Siora, Darius, and the others. Her path was a journey she needed to follow without a map, for none existed for the things she could do anyway.

"Coen?" she asked, turning to face him. "You made my van break down, didn't you?"

Coen grinned and clapped his hands together. "Boom! *Just like that.*"

She laughed, shaking her head in disbelief. He'd stopped her travels before she reached the mountain, knowing who she was all this time—and cost Wally over three thousand dollars in repairs. She couldn't believe it, *but then again...*

"Did you lead me here?" she asked.

"No," he replied. "Your path came here all on its own."

A warmth bloomed in her heart. There was still hope for her, then.

"What now?" she wondered. "Where does my path lead next?"

"You woke when you helped Hardy," Coen said, poking her between the eyes.

Eloise jerked back, blinking. "My third eye?"

"You see what you are, though you don't know your song. Not yet."

"Oh..." She felt the faint stirrings of the seal under Solace. "What about the seal? Should I try repairing this one, too?"

"The mountain was broken a long time ago. Long before much of the memory in this country became known."

Eloise wondered how and when the mountain's seal had cracked, but she supposed it didn't really matter. "So, we have time before it becomes a problem?"

Coen nodded. "The mountain is squashed back down, but it will return. The waves crash against the walls binding it, but the wall will not break. Not in your lifetime, Eloise Hart."

Even so, if they left the seal in its current state, it'd cause all kinds of problems. The same poison that'd twisted the bush around the mountain would taint the beautiful, pure opalised heart of Solace and corrupt everything good about their home.

Looking up at the boab, she saw it was already manifesting. Bruise-like lesions had appeared on the bloated trunk, dimming the magic she usually felt emanating from the tree. They were faint, but soon they'd darken and spread.

"We need to find a way to plug both holes permanently," she said. "That's the only solution."

Coen sighed. "The Old Ones seek to erase this reality. It's too beautiful to let them."

"Despite all the ugly?" Eloise asked, thinking about all the awful things humanity was capable of—war, consumption, pollution, hate.

"Good and bad. Light and dark. Night and day. All these things cannot exist without the other."

"Perception is in the eye of the beholder." Eloise pressed her hand against the boab. She felt its magic and the stirrings of the Old One, and she wondered why it was her. Out of all the elementals that must exist in the wider world, why was her power so special?

"Our story is a song of broken things," Coen told her as if he'd been listening to her thoughts.

Her hand slipped away from the tree. "*Our* story?"

"There is a reason the Old Ones seek you out, Eloise Hart." Coen pointed a finger to the sky and smiled, his eyes sparkling mischievously. "The answer is there, waiting for those with the courage to find it."

Her expression faded as she realised where she must go. She saw her path as clear as day, the trail winding before her. All that was left to do was find the strength to take the first step.

Eloise had to find the elementals—the people the great emu had sent down to help the eagle, the serpent, the kangaroo, and the dingo. *Our story is a song of broken things*. She understood now. Eloise was the key to banishing the Old Ones forever, but only the elementals could show her the lock.

Kyne had told her where he'd found them—at a hidden billabong deep in the Pilbara. It was beautiful country, but it was remote, dangerous, rugged, and a place she couldn't find with her magic. It looked like she'd have to do things the old-fashioned way.

"I have to find Kyne," she told Coen. "I feel like this path should be walked by him, too." The elementals had turned him away, but they would not refuse her. They'd both get answers this time.

"Yes," the Indigenous man replied, grinning like a

proud parent. "But first, *recharge*. Drew and I will watch." He looked over her shoulder.

Sensing she was dismissed, Eloise nodded. "I suppose I'll know when it's time to head out, huh?"

Coen simply chuckled and looked back at the boab.

That was the end of that, then.

She left him to his musings and returned to the highway, her mind heavy with what she must do. It was exciting in a way, to know she might finally meet the magical beings who'd birthed her, but it was also a little scary. It seemed old fears were still difficult to let go of, even now.

Eloise felt Kyne's presence long before she saw him standing out the front of Wally's garage. He'd pulled his black Akubra hat low over his eyes, but she felt his gaze on her as surely as she loved him...and knew wherever he was, she would always find him.

Smiling, Eloise ran to meet him, and as they came together, he flung his arms around her in a tight embrace.

Their next adventure wouldn't be easy, but with Kyne by her side, she knew they would make it. That was the true power of love.

ABOUT NICOLE

Nicole R. Taylor is an Australian Urban Fantasy author.

She lives in the western suburbs of Melbourne dreaming up nail biting stories featuring sassy witches, duplicitous vampires, hunky shapeshifters, and devious monsters.

She likes chocolate, cat memes, and video games.

When she's not writing, she likes to think of what she's writing next.

Follow Nicole Online:

Website: www.nicolertaylorwrites.com
Facebook: facebook.com/nrtaylorwrites
Newsletter: www.nicolertaylorwrites.com/newsletter
Email: nicole.this.is@gmail.com